BEVERLEY NICHOLS

The
Moonflower

THE POPULAR BOOK CLUB
LONDON

MADE AND PRINTED IN GREAT BRITAIN FOR
THE POPULAR BOOK CLUB (ODHAMS PRESS LTD.)
BY ODHAMS (WATFORD) LIMITED
WATFORD, HERTS
S.356.TL.

1

IT WAS a bitter night. From Land's End to John o' Groat's Britain was being buffeted and sleeted and hailed upon; her coasts were a roar of angry waters; and the weather chart on the television screens was so menacing that sensible citizens turned off their sets and sighed themselves to bed.

In no part of these islands was the night more dark and dreadful than on Dartmoor, and over no part of Dartmoor did it strike with greater fury than against the granite walls of Princetown prison. For such a night, indeed, the prison might well have been constructed; its cold grey stones matched force with force; and to the tempest that screamed through its turrets it threw back an exultant echo, as though it were defying the storm to rescue the wretched men who mouldered within. "Free them if you can! Free them if you can!" So rang the cry of the turrets through the uproar of the elements . . . and it rang so clearly that it struck a chill to the heart of many a man inside, sitting on a grey blanket, leaning against a white wall, staring at a row of black iron bars.

But there was one man to whom the wind was not a chill but a challenge. For he had escaped from the world of grey blankets, white walls, and black bars . . . at the cost, admittedly, of a little patch of crimson, which trickled from the skull of the warder he had murdered. He balanced himself on the parapet drinking in the wind in great draughts, as though it were a potent, icy wine, as indeed it was—the wine of freedom. He must have his fill of it; it must swell his powerful lungs; it must run through his veins in all its sweetness. A man could do anything, with the wind as his friend . . . the wind and the darkness. He could fight the world, he could defy the heavens, he could even fly.

The man took a last, shuddering breath. He closed his

7

eyes. For a brief second a pale, distracted moon escaped from the torment of the clouds, to throw a glance towards the earth. A white light gleamed on a square, brutal face, framed in lurid red, for even the prison shears could not rob Copper Jack of all his colour.

A gigantic gust swept up the valley. It told him . . . now or never. "With the wind for a friend. . . ."

He jumped.

Five minutes later, the sirens sounded.

II

"Dear me," murmured Mr. Green to himself. "One never seems to have a moment's peace."

He was sitting in the saloon bar of The Greyhound, a little inn in the hamlet of Moreton Fallow, some fifteen miles distant. It was nearly eleven; the last few customers had long since taken themselves away; he had looked forward to a pleasant half-hour by the fire, sipping his ale, and reading an essay in the *Journal of the Royal Horticultural Society* on some new aspects of the tropical convolvulus. Then the telephone had rung, and after a few moments' breathless conversation, Ivy, the barmaid, had hurried in with the news.

"I call it shocking," she exclaimed. "Reely shocking. That's the third one got away in six months. A girl can't sleep at night, not with that sort of thing going on." She helped herself to a tot of whisky. "I don't often indulge, not at this time of night, but reely. . . ." She swallowed her drink, patted her peroxide hair, and waited for Mr. Green to speak. He wasn't much company for a girl, to be sure—just a funny little man, on the plump side, with a bald head and horn-rimmed glasses. And ever since he'd arrived, that afternoon, he'd had his nose bent over that old gardening book. Wouldn't say boo to a goose, not by the look of him. Still he was better than nobody at all.

Mr. Green sighed and put away his book. "Did they give the name of the man who escaped?"

"They did. Jack Borley, they said it was. And they said he was called Copper Jack on account of his being a redhead." She shuddered. "That somehow makes it seem worse. Ever heard of him?"

Mr. Green gave the shadow of a smile. "Yes," he said. "I have heard of him."

Copper Jack! The ring-leader in the case of the Bessingham diamonds, some seven years ago. Yes, Mr. Green had certainly heard of him; indeed, it was largely through his own brilliant deductions that the man had been apprehended . . . though even then, the police had not been able to prove the murder of which he was undoubtedly guilty. Not a pleasant customer to meet on a night like this . . . particularly as Copper Jack had a long memory, and had sworn to "do" Mr. Green, as soon as he got outside.

"D'you think he'll come here?" demanded Ivy.

"I trust not."

"He *might*. It's only fifteen miles, as the crow flies. He might be on his way at this very minute. Oh lor . . . it's not civilized, living like this, it's just not *civilized*."

Mr. Green detected a note of hysteria.

"I do not think that we need be too concerned," he observed, gently. "A man on the run is hardly likely to make for this village. He would certainly keep to the open till he'd put the moors behind him."

"That's right," she admitted. "All the same, you never know. Mind you, it's not so much for myself I'm thinking. It's for Mrs. Keswick, upstairs." She pointed to the ceiling.

"Is that the landlord's wife?"

"That's right. She's expecting. Her first."

"Dear me!" (Never a moment's peace!)

"Any time it may be, now. They've sent for the doctor once already, but it was a false alarm. If she was to hear about *this*, anything might happen."

As though to answer her suggestion, a young man pushed through the parlour door. He was tall and well built, with the ruddy Devonshire complexion that tells of perfect health. He was in a state of considerable agitation.

9

"Thank God you're still up, Ivy," he began. . . .

"Is it . . . has she . . . ?"

"No. She's just the same. But I came down to tell you not to let her have any idea of what's going on outside."

"As if I should!"

"I know you wouldn't do it on purpose. But you might let something slip out when you took up her tea."

She tossed her head. "I'm not one that lets things slip out, Mr. Keswick, as well you ought to know by now."

"Sorry, Ivy. Bit upset, that's all." He ran his hands through his tousled hair. Then he noticed Mr. Green sitting in the corner.

"Beg pardon, sir. Thought you'd gone to bed." He turned back to the barmaid. "Better go up and sit with her, Ivy, while I lock up."

She departed with another toss of the head.

The locking up was soon accomplished, and the young man came back to the fire. "Not much of a welcome to Dartmoor, I'm afraid, sir. Storms, convicts . . . and now the missus. Maybe it'll all be cleared up by to-morrow night. Will you be staying with us for long?" He saw Mr. Green's eyebrows rise, ever so slightly. "Excuse me, sir. None of my business. Afraid I'm not making much sense to-night."

Mr. Green's eyebrows descended. He was a kindly little person, and he suddenly realized that he was not being very co-operative.

"But of course it is your business," he replied. "And I quite understand that you should be feeling overwrought. No, I do not think I shall be staying very long. It depends on. . . ." He paused. He had no great wish to discuss his private affairs, but they might perhaps distract the young man's attention from the drama in the room above. So he continued, with a twinkle. . . . "It depends on the behaviour of a certain flower."

To Mr. Green's surprise, the young man did not look mystified. He merely nodded. "That'll be the moonflower, I suppose. Up at Candle Court."

10

"Yes. I have come down specially to see it. So you have heard of it, too?"

"Oh, everybody's heard of it in this part of the world. There's been quite a lot about it in the local press." He leant across the bar and handed a newspaper to Mr. Green. "That was in this morning's *Devon Gazette*."

Mr. Green read:

MYSTERY FLOWER AT CANDLE COURT
£1,000 per seed
Will the Moonflower Bloom?

"The great conservatory at Candle Court, residence of wealthy Mrs. Faversham, is a scene of mounting drama. In the next few days she will know whether her greatest gamble is to be crowned with triumph or with failure.

As readers of the *Devon Gazette* are aware, it was Mrs. Faversham, nearly a year ago, who financed the expedition to the Uruguay river, in search of the 'magic moonflower' ... a form of giant tropical convolvulus. The expedition, which is reputed to have cost over £12,000, was headed by the famous botanist, the Hon. Hilary Scole.

Six weeks ago, on Christmas Eve, Mr. Scole returned to England, bearing with him thirteen seeds of this exotic plant ... at £1,000 a seed! The seeds had travelled in a specially designed electric cabinet, in which the temperature was thermostatically controlled. They were planted on Christmas Day, in the great conservatory which has already seen so many spectacular horticultural experiments.

The *Devon Gazette* has exclusive information that several, at least, of the seeds have germinated, producing long, trailing plants with leaves of a green so dark that they are nearly black. None of the plants, however, has yet flowered. Unless the flowers appear within the next week, the experiment will have failed.

The fact that the Hon. Hilary Scole is expected to arrive at Candle Court to-morrow gives foundation to

11

the rumour that the 'magic moonflower' will indeed blossom."

"Dear me!" murmured Mr. Green. "I hope the *Devon Gazette* is right."

The young man nodded. "A thousand quid a seed—I wouldn't mind a packet of them. You know the old lady, sir?"

"Yes, I know her. But only slightly."

He drew nearer to the fire. He wondered if anybody knew the fabulous Mrs. Faversham more than "only slightly". Twenty years ago—or was it twenty-five?—when she was a brilliant hostess in London, he had done her some service. Another jewel robbery, and not a very pretty one, for there had been more than a suspicion that her own schoolboy son had been involved. A sulky, good-looking boy, he remembered, who had later been expelled from Eton. At any rate, she had paid Mr. Green very handsomely for his services. Shortly afterwards, on the death of her husband, she had left London and bought Candle Court, where she proceeded to rescue its enchanting gardens, and to restore its famous conservatories, after the neglect of many years. It was a curious departure for a selfish, worldly woman, late in life —an arresting example of the way in which a mania for collecting can assume psychopathic proportions. She now collected rare plants as avidly as, in the past, she had collected diamonds . . . and men.

The moonflower was her crowning triumph . . . or rather, it would be, if it flowered. It was all very well for the Royal Horticultural Society to disparage it, as it had done, in the learned article he had been reading; it was all very well for the botanical bigwigs to suggest that it would probably turn out to be not a new genus but a mere species. They could not alter the fact that the entry of this dominating old lady into the botanical world had been salutary, because of the very passion with which she had swept through the door. It was as though a roll of kettle-drums had scattered the dust on the library shelves.

12

"It's sort of exciting, when you come to think of it."

The young man interrupted his reverie. He might have been echoing his own thoughts.

Mr. Green nodded. He was warm and sleepy by the fireside, half in bed, as it were, and half out. He felt a pleasant kinship with his host. It was good that so very normal and virile a young man should feel the thrill of these delicate things.

"A flower like that—out of the jungle—blooming up there on the hillside, on a night like this. Sort of romantic."

The words were simple, the setting was crude, but for a moment poetry was born. Yes, thought Mr. Green, it was romantic. Up there, on the hillside, in a fragrant cage of crystal, the silver petals of a flower might be sleeping, waiting to open on to a strange world.

Then the telephone rang.

"Hell!" said the young man.

He walked across to the alcove, and lifted the receiver. "Hullo—hullo!" Then he smiled and his voice softened. "Oh it's you, miss? No, she's much the same. Doctor seems to think another twenty-four hours. Well, miss, if this storm keeps up I shouldn't have thought you'd have felt like coming, but it'd make a world of difference. Yes, miss, I'll tell her we can rely on you, and I do thank you, miss, indeed I do. Yes, miss, I'll ring the moment the doctor says. Sometime to-morrow, I expect. Good-night, miss."

He came back to the fire.

"Well—there's a young lady in a thousand, sir," he said. "Miss Sandra Wells, up at the Court."

Mr. Green tried to appear interested, but he was really very sleepy. It was only through a haze of fatigue that he heard his host extol the virtues of the unknown Miss Wells, who had come to stay at Candle Court six months ago, as nurse-companion to Mrs. Faversham . . . how beloved she was by all the family, how patient, how kind, how tireless in her good works in the village, of which this offer to come and help his wife was typical.

Mr. Green stifled a yawn and rose to his feet. "I shall look

13

forward to meeting this young lady," he murmured insincerely. "And now, I must not keep you talking any longer. Good-night."

He went up the little staircase to his room. It was clean and white and airy; it had the tang of the moors in it. Somebody had given him a hot-water bottle, which was very agreeable.

And so to bed.

III

"Never a moment's peace!"

Superintendent Waller woke up in his little house in the suburb of Putney Hill, raised himself on his pillow, and listened to the insistent clamour of the telephone in the hall below. A glance at the luminous dial of his wrist-watch told him that it was past midnight. For once in a way he had been able to get to bed early, and now. . . .

He had a darned good mind to let the damned thing go on ringing. If he got out of bed he'd wake the missus, and she was just as fed up with all these late nights as he was himself.

"Better answer it, dear," came a soft voice from the other pillow.

"Thought you were asleep," he grunted.

"I was, but it woke me up. It must have been ringing quite a while. Better answer it. It may be important."

"It'd better be, at this time of night."

He switched on the light, and heaved himself out of bed with a groan of protest. Even in his fifties, clad in a pair of pink woollen pyjamas, the superintendent was a figure to command respect—six foot two, without an ounce of surplus flesh on him, and only a trace of grey on his temples. As he looked down at the smiling figure in the bed, he reflected that Mrs. Waller had worn pretty well, too. A bit plumper perhaps, but not so very different from the girl he had married, twenty years ago. Still, this was no time for connubialities.

14

"Who'd be a policeman on a night like this?" he growled. "That's a slate just blown off the roof. If this wind keeps up there won't be any roof at all by the morning."

He slipped on an old cashmere dressing-gown and went out.

"Yes, yes. Waller speaking. Who is it?"

"Sanders here."

Waller straightened himself. Sanders was the Deputy Commissioner at the Yard, and a person before whom one automatically straightened oneself, even at the other end of the telephone.

"You've heard about the Princetown outbreak?"

"Can't say I have, sir."

"Copper Jack's killed a warder and made a break-away."

"Phew! That's certainly news, sir. But I went to bed early to-night."

"Of course. I remember. The smuggling case. You've had a pretty tough forty-eight hours. I expect you feel you've earned a rest."

"Well, sir. . . ."

"You *have* earned it. However, I'm afraid I've got another job for you."

Waller heaved a deep sigh, which was not lost at the other end.

"Sorry, Superintendent, but you bring these things on yourself. You shouldn't be so efficient."

Waller closed his eyes, and sighed again. Sanders was "putting on the charm," the old devil.

"If you'd sometimes fall down on a few jobs, we wouldn't need you so urgently, and you'd sleep sounder of nights."

He'd talk the hind leg off a donkey, thought Waller to himself. All the same, he felt a sort of inner glow.

"What was it you wanted me to do, sir?"

"I want you to go down to Princetown, first thing in the morning. That'll mean catching the seven-thirty from Paddington."

"But sir. . . ."

"Just a moment. I want you to understand the importance

of this business. This is the third escape in six months. What's more, it's come right on top of a very ugly riot, three weeks ago. The public are getting worried, but not as worried as the Home Secretary. He's got this new Prison Reform Bill to steer through Parliament, and even in the best of conditions it's not going to be too easy; it's a pretty revolutionary document. If he tries to do it in this sort of atmosphere, the press'll be down on him like a ton of bricks. Mollycoddling murderers, and all that sort of thing. The public have got to be reassured. There must be no more escapes. That's where you come in."

"I still don't see what I can *do*, sir."

"To be quite frank, neither do I. Nor—in confidence—does the Home Secretary. All the same, he wants you to go, if only for the look of the thing. He told me so himself, only an hour ago."

The glow inside Waller's massive chest grew perceptibly warmer. "Did he mention me personally?"

"He did." An ironic chuckle came from the other end. "He must have read about you in one of those whodunnits."

Waller ignored this sally.

The note of authority came back to Sanders' voice. "So that is the assignment. It's a difficult one, but I trust you. You will make a full check of all security measures, report on any possible leakages, and make any suggestions you think fit. Naturally, if you can assist in the apprehension of our Copper friend, that would be a considerable feather in your cap. However, that's not your main job. Your principal function is to act as a figure-head for the Yard, to let the public know that everything that can be done is being done."

Waller had one last comment. "I'm not accustomed to being just a figure-head, sir."

"I'm well aware of that, old friend. I don't expect you to be. I expect results, and with you I know I shall get them. My apologies to Mrs. Waller for this intrusion. Good-night. And good luck."

He hung up. So that was that. Off again in the morning. He'd have to set the alarm for six. Same old routine . . . day

16

after day, month after month. He'd better go out to the kitchen and lay the breakfast. However tired he might be, he wasn't going to have *her* getting out of bed and coming down. Though of course, she would. She always did, bless her heart.

He turned on the gas fire . . . might as well come down to a bit of warmth . . . and stepped out into the corridor. As he did so, he paused. Lord, what a night! The storm seemed to be assaulting his little house with a personal fury; blow after blustering blow—tearing at the roof, rattling at the door, stinging at the windows, roaring and cursing, and threatening.

He shivered, and for a moment his mind sped west, to the naked hills of Dartmoor, where in some deserted gully a desperate man was groping his way through the dark fury of the storm.

Who would be a policeman on a night like this? If it came to that, who would be a convict?

IV

"Never a moment's peace!"

"Is that my fault?"

The man, by the mantelpiece, did not reply. He merely stared into the fire.

"Is that *my* fault?" she demanded, even more shrilly.

He turned his head, scowling. "For the Lord's sake, don't shout. You'll wake the whole house."

"On a night like this?" She walked across to the window. "One could commit a murder without anybody hearing." She pushed aside the heavy curtains, and stared out into the darkness.

"That's an idea," muttered the man by the mantelpiece.

She turned swiftly. "Yes," she said. "It is an idea."

In the split second in which these two stared at one another—the moment in which their eyes met, and wondered, and exchanged secrets and shared fears—let us introduce them, and sketch their background.

17

They were standing in the yellow bedroom at Candle Court. A long, narrow room, with tall windows, giving on to the valley below. It was dominated by three flower-like chandeliers, in Venetian glass, of pale crusted gold. Underfoot there were three long Aubusson rugs, in faded primrose; they had once been trodden by the Empress Josephine; Napoleonic bees were woven against a background of meadows brimming with delicately stitched daffodils. The curtains, of ivory and gold, had come from a *château* near Chartres, whose owner had once annexed them from the Cathedral. Like many other rooms in the great houses of England, it owed its beauty partly to money, partly to taste, and largely to loot—but most of all to Time, the Ultimate Interior Decorator.

Candle Court stood on rising ground, above the valley of the River Fallow, in which nestled the hamlet of Moreton Fallow. If you had looked out of the window you could still have seen, far below, through the driving rain and sleet, a tiny speck of light from the porch of the Greyhound Inn, where Mr. Green was staying. Had the night been clear, you could have traced the graceful Queen Anne façade of the house itself, with its lofty Palladian portico. And you would have been delighted or distressed—according to your taste —by the Regency wing, with its domed conservatory, that shone on moonlit nights like a silver bubble against the dark tapestry of the woods beyond.

"Yes," she whispered again. "It is an idea."

She turned and walked back to the fire.

Beryl Faversham was thirty. She had distinction rather than beauty. Slim, tall, with fine grey eyes and a high forehead, framed in dark straight hair, which she dressed in the style of a Florentine madonna. Already a few streaks of grey were showing. She had much breeding but little assurance; she gave a curious sense of spiritual malnutrition, suggesting an inner hunger. When she spoke, although her voice was an agreeable contralto, there were disturbing echoes in it, as though she were speaking in an empty room, from which she could not escape because she had lost the key.

Those echoes were very clear to-night.

"The whole thing is monstrous." Her fists were clenched in anger. "Turning us out of this room at a moment's notice! For Pusey—of all people!"

"Perhaps Mother didn't really mean what she said."

"Really, darling . . ." and the word of endearment was charged with scorn . . . "in the eighteen months of our married life, I've got to know your sainted mother very well, and I've come to realize that she *always* means what she says. She means it to the last syllable, even if she only says it in a whisper, with one of those little smiles of hers that all the old gentlemen find so enchanting."

"Was that how she said it to-night?"

"As it happens, no. She said it quite casually, as though she were talking about the weather. It was after dinner. We were sitting by the fire and Ackworth had just brought in the drinks. . . ."

"Was Sandra there?"

"Of course Sandra was there! Have you ever known an occasion in the last few months when Sandra *wasn't* there? I wish you wouldn't interrupt. Your mother had just switched off the television; I think she must have realized I was enjoying the play. And she turned and said to me: 'By the way, darling, you know that Mr. Pusey will be staying with us to-morrow. I should *so* like him to have the yellow room, if you wouldn't mind.' I was so completely taken aback that I couldn't speak. Then she went on to say how happy we should be in the Chinese room, and how Mrs. Ackworth would help me to move my clothes."

"What did you say to that?"

"Nothing. I couldn't. Anyway, there was hardly time to say anything, because she got up, with *such* a pretty smile, and said 'That's settled then', and went up to bed."

Kenneth Faversham sank heavily into a chair. Everything was heavy about him, his limbs, his hands, his jaw, his eyelids. Yet he gave an impression not of strength but of weakness.

"The Chinese room's quite a decent room . . ." he began.

19

"Darling!" And this time the word was like a blow. "If you're going to play the part of the loyal son. . . ."

"That's hardly the point!"

"Quite. It isn't." She controlled herself with an effort. "The point is that this is *my* room. It always has been my room. I was born in it, brought up in it. I had my first lessons in it. Long before your family were ever heard of, *my* family had lived here for two hundred years. . . ."

"Need we go into all that again?"

"When I married you, the thought of coming home. . . . I can't tell you what it meant to me."

"More than *I* meant, apparently."

She turned on him. "Well, what if it did?"

He shrugged his shoulders. "Nothing. You're not telling me anything I hadn't guessed before."

"That, at least, is a consolation."

There was a moment's silence. "What are we going to do?"

"What she wants, I imagine. What else?"

"It mayn't be for long."

"What makes you think that? It wasn't going to be for long when she took away the Rolls and asked us if we would mind using the Morris. It wasn't going to be for long when she shut up the London flat and asked us if we would mind using an hotel. It wasn't going to be for long when she cut down your allowance to rather less than the wages she pays Ackworth. . . ."

"For God's sake, shut up!" He rose abruptly, and walked towards the dressing-room, from which a dim light was shining. "All this hatred's getting us nowhere. Hatred never does."

"Never?" she echoed.

"What do you mean?"

"It might, you know. It might."

Once again their eyes met, wondered, exchanged secrets and shared fears.

Then he went out, leaving her staring into the dying fire. The dialogue which had stopped so abruptly was taken

20

up by the storm outside, in a wild argument of wind and weather. It was as though the storm were enveloping the house in a hatred of its own. There was, indeed, a surfeit of hatred in Candle Court that night; it crept down every corridor and lingered in every shadow.

The only person who seemed quite unaware of any inner or outer disturbance was the old lady who was the centre of this animosity. Mrs. Faversham, at the other end of the house, slept peacefully in a great bed whose crimson hangings rustled and whispered in the draught from the window which, even on nights like this, was always kept open for a few inches. A long tranquil sleep which must have been coloured by pleasant dreams, for a faint smile hovered on her lips . . . as it always hovered, when she had managed to do something particularly unpleasant.

2

ON THE following morning, shortly before noon, Mr. Green set out for Candle Court. The wind was still high, but the dark curtains of cloud had been wrenched from their celestial hangings, and were streaming northwards in rags and tatters. There was already enough blue in the sky to make a sailor's jacket, and that—as his old governess used to say—was a sign of a fine afternoon.

It was only a short walk up the hill, with the sound of the falls growing clearer every moment. When he reached the great iron gates he paused, partly to regain his breath, partly to enjoy the prospect before him. The house was pleasing enough in itself, with its elegant façade of faded brick, and its long, Regency conservatory stretching away from the south wing; but it was to the site that it owed its special charms. It stood on a narrow plateau, with wide views of the valley, and the hill rising steeply behind—a tangled mass of silver birch and wild rhododendron, that gradually thinned into the moorland. Down this hill leaped the little Fallow river, flashing through the woods, making sport over the granite boulders, laughing and singing in the shallows. When it reached the ground on which the Court was built it flowed silently for a brief space, alongside the low wall which bounded the cherry orchard, only to plunge, with a roar of triumph and a sting of spray, over a sheer drop of fifty feet, into the dark mystery of the woods below.

This water-music was a perpetual accompaniment to the lives of all who dwelt at Candle Court; they came to accept it as naturally as the air they breathed. It lapped its walls, whispering through every window and echoing down every corridor. In midsummer, when the moors were brown and parched, and the river had dwindled to a trickle, the music was faint indeed; in the front rooms of the house one heard

22

it only as a ghostly echo, like a muted violin played in the far distance. But as the autumn came, and the leaves yellowed and fell, and the high storm clouds swept in from Hay Tor, the little river found its voice again, and a lusty voice it was, through all the winter months.

Mr. Green walked up the short drive as the stable clock struck twelve. Ackworth, the butler, was at the door to meet him—a little wizened man with a face like a pear that had been stored on the shelf and forgotten, and gone dry.

"Always on time, sir," he wheezed, helping off Mr. Green with his coat. "Quite like the old days."

"And how is Mrs. Ackworth?"

"Frail, sir. Very frail. Still, it's only to be expected. We're none of us as young as we were." He gave Mr. Green a shrewd glance. "Though I must say, sir, that *you* seem to be bearing up."

"Thank you. I hope so." Mr. Green was used to Ackworth's melancholy. He was not nearly so old as he looked —a mere sixty. But his hypochondriacal wife had decided that he should put one foot in the grave, nearly twenty years ago, and he had never had the courage to draw it out again.

"Mrs. Faversham is expecting you, sir."

He led the way across the great hall, hung with the famous Beauvais tapestries of the four seasons, and opened the door of the drawing-room. Mr. Green had forgotten how beautiful a room it was—pale and bleached, a symphony in half-tones and quarter-tones, in which any strong colour would have struck a discordant note. The panelled walls had faded to a silver grey; the curtains were a dim ivory brocade; even the lacquer cabinets, which had been daffodil-yellow in the days of Queen Anne, had acquired a pale patina. It was because of this subtle and suggestive background that the little figure of Mrs. Faversham stood out so vividly. She was a plump five foot; she was in black; she looked like a sharp, modern full-stop on a page of illuminated parchment.

"Horatio!" she exclaimed, advancing towards him with outstretched arms.

Mr. Green winced. He had always been sensitive about

his flamboyant Christian name, and he fancied that it was because Mrs. Faversham was aware of this that she used it so frequently.

"How many years is it? Fifteen?"

"Fourteen and a half," murmured Mr. Green.

"As accurate as ever, and just as plump and sweet! And far, far more famous! Horatio, my dear man, I've missed you." She linked her arm in his. "But I must introduce you." She turned to a pretty girl who was standing by the fireplace. "Sandra, darling, this is Mr. Horatio Green. I should tell Mr. Green that your name is Miss Wells, but I am sure that he will soon be calling you Sandra, like everyone else."

The girl came forward with a shy smile, and shook his hand. "I have often heard your name, Mr. Green."

He smiled. "And I have been hearing a great deal about you, too."

"About me? But how? Where?"

"I am staying at The Greyhound. Your ears must have been burning last night."

"Oh . . . I see—the Keswicks!" She laughed and flushed prettily. "Yes, I promised to help with Mrs. Keswick's baby."

"She promises to help everybody and everything," said Mrs. Faversham. "Babies, kittens, sick dogs . . . it's a wonder she has any time left for *me*. Which reminds me, my dear, that my tonic hasn't come. Will you run along and telephone to that wretched chemist?"

"Of course."

She hurried out.

"What I should do without that girl I simply don't know."

"Has she been with you long?"

"Only six months. It was like a gift from the gods. It happened at the garden fête last July. It was terribly hot, and I'd been doing too much, walking about and talking to all the local people; and suddenly I collapsed—practically into her arms."

"How did she happen to be there?"

"She was taking a holiday in the district; she'd seen the

24

posters in the village, and she'd come along and paid her shilling with all the rest."

"I gather she is a trained nurse?"

"Brilliantly trained, yes. She nursed in India during the war. Old Doctor Reesdale says that if it hadn't been for her, I shouldn't be here at all. She took charge of everything, and when I got better I simply couldn't let her go. She really is an angel—an angel!" She turned abruptly. "Which is more, Hilary, than one can say about *you*."

The man to whom she addressed this remark, paused in the doorway. Mr. Green, as he glanced towards him, felt a profound shock. The famous Hilary Scole looked years older than his photographs . . . a pale shadow of his former self. The tropics had certainly taken their toll of this gallant adventurer, who had hunted flowers—and women—with the same relentless zest, all over the world. Not many women in these days, thought Mr. Green, would surrender to his charm, nor indeed, many flowers to his pursuit. And yet, this was the man who only a few months before had tracked down the most elusive flower of all.

"For heaven's sake come in!" snapped Mrs. Faversham. "And shut the door; there's a draught." Mr. Green raised his eyebrows; she spoke as if she were addressing a servant. "I needn't tell you who *this* is, Horatio; he's had enough advertisement as it is."

Mr. Green bowed. "I am honoured, sir," he said.

"Thank you." Scole's voice was very soft and gentle. "I should like to think of some new way of saying that 'the honour is mine', but the old one will have to do."

"Which will be quite enough compliments for this morning," retorted the old lady. "And anyway, Hilary, he didn't come here to feast his eyes on you; he came for something much prettier. Let's go and look at it."

She led the way to the great bay window at the end of the room. To the left of it was a door which she pushed open with her stick. They found themselves in a long, vaulted corridor, whose walls were hung with flower prints of the early eighteenth century. At the end of the corridor was a

25

door of frosted glass opening into the main conservatory.

A tall dark man, with a baize apron over his working clothes, stood by the door, cap in hand.

"You remember Wilburfoss?"

Mr. Green extended his hand. "Indeed yes."

"Good morning, sir. It is good to see you again," said the man. His voice was deep and dark. It was a Devonshire voice, but it had an undertone of breeding. So indeed had his whole bearing.

"Wilburfoss has been faithful to me for nearly thirty years," said Mrs. Faversham. "Haven't you, Wilburfoss?"

He appeared not to hear her. Instead, he turned and led the way to the further end of the conservatory, which gave on to the Holy of Holies, the smaller tropical house, in which the moonflower was waiting for them.

Mr. Green, as he walked along with the little procession, was only too conscious that he was breaking the tenth commandment. How could any man of his temperament fail to covet a place like this? It was the quintessence of romance, a perfumed crystal cage set against a background of wild moorland, a frail bubble defying the elements, holding in its core the fiery colours of the tropics, even though its roofs were rimmed with ice. It was a place in which nature was set at naught, a place in which time stood still . . . most of all, it was a place in which all his senses were made enchantingly alert. The scent of the gardenias was like the scent of a sweetmeat in a fairy-tale, haunting and honeyed with his first memories of the *Arabian Nights*. It played its part against a background of a thousand other scents, from the ghostly tang of the golden ferns to the opulent odour of the Temple lilies, lolling on the surface of the baroque fountain that dominated the centre of the house. And always, from outside, came the sound of the falls . . . singing, bubbling, arguing, fighting . . . out there in the cold air, a multi-coloured orchestra of water-music that seemed, by a curious paradox of nature, to enhance the stillness within.

Wilburfoss was opening the door of the Holy of Holies.

Mrs. Faversham was beckoning to him.

He saw before him another little cage of crystal. Six pots stood on the floor. From them came a wreath of leaves, twining and curling up a trellis of delicately tangled wire. The leaves were dark and glossy, almost black; they had a wild fierce energy of their own, as though they were racing against time. But there was a hot mist over them—a mist that made them waver and tremble. . . .

"Here we are." It was Mrs. Faversham's voice. It came from the most distant stars.

"I think," said Mr. Green, "that I am going to faint." And he did.

It was only a matter of seconds . . . a sudden stumble into the arms of Wilburfoss, a swift blackness, as though a curtain were drawn across his brain. And then the curtain swung back again and he found himself sitting on a wheelbarrow in the cool house next door, blinking into a pair of dark, pretty eyes.

"That's better," said Miss Wells in a gentle voice. "Lean back while I loosen your collar."

"I must apologize . . ." he began.

"Don't be so foolish, Horatio," interrupted Mrs. Faversham. "And don't dare to talk. Sandra, dear, give him my smelling-salts."

The keen tang of the ammonia brought back the colour to his cheeks.

"I cannot imagine . . ." he began again.

"Then don't try. Wilburfoss, run round to Ackworth and ask him for a glass of brandy." He heard the sound of hurrying footsteps. He closed his eyes again. Then the footsteps returned and he was sipping the brandy, and he felt restored.

He handed back the glass to Miss Wells. "See!" he said. "My hand is quite firm."

"I should sit down for another few moments." She gave

him an appraising glance. "Did you ever have sun-stroke?"

"Yes. In India."

"I thought so. You should be careful of such sudden changes of temperature."

"What did I tell you?" It was Mrs. Faversham who spoke. "Sandra knows everything."

"So I see. What *is* the temperature next door?"

Hilary Scole stepped forward. "Seventy. And that's five degrees too low."

"Too low?" Mrs. Faversham's voice was very sharp. "How's that, Wilburfoss?"

"Well, madam, it's a big house. It's not always possible. . . ."

"Really! From the fuel bills you send me I should have thought you could have had it like a furnace."

"That would be worse still," said Scole, in a dry voice. "It's a very delicate business."

"You needn't remind me of *that*. Only six seeds germinating out of thirteen! And now, letting the temperature drop so that heaven knows what will happen to the others. It's enough to try the patience of a saint. Wilburfoss!" Her voice rose shrilly. "Wilburfoss . . . where are you going?"

The only answer was the slamming of a door as the gardener strode out of the house.

She stared after him, beating on the stone floor with her stick. "One day I shall sack that man."

"You would be very ill-advised."

"Nobody is indispensable, Hilary. You should know that, of all people. You don't seem to realize. . . ." She paused, checking herself with an obvious effort. "But we are forgetting our invalid."

"You need call me that no longer." Mr. Green rose to his feet, a little unsteadily.

"Let me help you," said Miss Wells.

"You are very kind." He took her arm. Then he turned towards the door of the hot-house. It looked infinitely alluring, in its tropical richness, with the dark leaves of the moonflower gleaming in the shadows. "Might we not have one more look? Just for a moment?"

"I never heard such nonsense, Horatio. You've caused quite enough trouble for one morning."

He sighed heavily. "I'm afraid I have."

"Perhaps after luncheon," suggested Miss Wells.

With which he had to be content.

III

But there seemed to be a conspiracy to keep him from the moonflower.

Luncheon dragged on till nearly three o'clock, owing to a long-drawn-out discussion about the various cars in which the members of the party were going to a dance that night.

"I can't imagine why Pusey shouldn't take all of you," said Mrs. Faversham. She turned to Mr. Green. "Pusey is my lawyer. He eats too much and is usually drenched in lavender-water, but he knows his business."

"He mayn't even want to go," sniffed Beryl.

"Pusey? Not want to go to a ball given by a countess?" Kenneth Faversham leant forward scowling. "If we all go with Pusey, we shall all have to come back with Pusey, and he'll probably want to stay till the crack of dawn."

"Then one of you can take the Morris."

"Oh dear!" It was Sandra who spoke now. "I'd hoped I might have the Morris in case I'm wanted at The Greyhound in a hurry."

"Hasn't that woman had her baby *yet*?"

"I'm afraid not. It'll probably happen to-night." She hesitated. "Of course, I could walk. . . ."

"That's out of the question," interrupted Hilary, "with an escaped convict in the neighbourhood."

"Nobody asked for your opinion," snapped Mrs. Faversham. She turned to Sandra. "I had forgotten the convict. Of course you must have the Morris."

"In which case we shall be obliged to take the Rolls," observed Beryl.

"You are not obliged to go at all," retorted the old lady. "Perhaps you would prefer us to use the station-wagon?"

And so they bickered, on and on, in mean and narrow circles. Mr. Green had a sense of deep hostilities, secret feuds; it was a thwarted, unhappy atmosphere. He was glad when at last they rose from the table. Perhaps he could slip out to the greenhouse unobserved?

But just as he thought his opportunity had come, there was the sound of a car drawing up outside, and a moment later Mr. Bernard Pusey was announced. He strode into the room as though he were walking a stage; indeed, his whole make-up suggested an old-fashioned actor-manager. He was a fine figure of a man, in his early fifties, tall, florid, with an abundance of silvery hair. Like many other city men who find themselves suddenly transported to the country, he had overdressed the part; his tweeds were a shade too loud, his plus-fours a shade too baggy. He was not quite a gentleman and he was an appalling snob, but he was one of the shrewdest lawyers in the country.

"Lavinia!" he cried, advancing towards Mrs. Faversham with both hands outstretched.

"You've put on weight," was her only greeting.

He laughed heartily, as though she had paid him the greatest compliment. With his hands still outstretched he turned on his heels. "And Kenneth . . . and dear Beryl!" They offered him mechanical smiles. His eyes rested on Mr. Green. "And surely . . . surely I see another old friend?"

"How do you do?" murmured Mr. Green. It was not a very passionate greeting, but somehow it seemed warmer than the others.

Mr. Pusey walked stagily across the room and planted both hands firmly on Mr. Green's shoulders. "Horatio Green!" he exclaimed, as though he had made a great discovery.

"Don't maul him about," snapped Mrs. Faversham. "He's in a very delicate condition."

"*That* I refuse to believe. He looks as young as when I saw him ten . . . twelve years ago . . . ?"

30

"Thirteen years and five days, to be precise."

"Still the same miraculous memory! It was at Lady Bessingham's, was it not?"

"It was."

"Dear Lady B! How *is* she nowadays?"

"I have no idea."

"But surely you keep in touch?"

"We move in different circles." Mr. Green's tone was polite, but terse. "She employed me in a purely professional capacity."

"Good for you, Horatio!" chortled Mrs. Faversham. She turned an ironic smile on Mr. Pusey. "Really, Bernard, you are the most appalling snob."

He was unabashed. "If you say so, Lavinia. Though I should prefer to call it a romantic. And the case of the Bessingham diamonds was pure romance."

Oh dear, thought Mr. Green . . . here it comes again! The case of the Bessingham diamonds. Why would people always remind him of that hoary old affair? Of course, he had to admit that it was a classic in its way, and it had caught the public fancy because it was the first occasion on which a detective had literally smelled his way to the heart of a crime. If it had not been for the scent of the lemon verbena, on the door of the safe, he might never have solved the mystery. However, that was ancient history, and he resented the suggestion that he owed his successes to the delicacy of his nose; the delicacy of his brain was more important.

The memory of the lemon verbena reminded him all too poignantly of the many fragrances that were waiting for him in the great conservatory; the desire to return to it became overwhelming.

Suddenly the opportunity presented itself. With a brusque gesture Mrs. Faversham summoned Pusey to her chair, and began to speak to him in a low whisper. He caught Hilary Scole's eye. A moment later they were both outside, smiling at each other like two schoolboy conspirators.

31

"You're sure you feel up to it?" said Scole, as he opened the door of the first house.

Mr. Green blinked, sniffed and pondered. "Perhaps I might take it by degrees?" he suggested. "We might rest here for five minutes and then go to the hot-house."

"As though we were going through a Turkish bath," laughed Scole. "A very good idea."

"And while we are waiting, perhaps you would be able to tell me some of the peculiarities of this celebrated flower?"

Scole hesitated. "I do not think they would be of much interest except to a botanist."

"I have a fondness for flowers."

Scole became suddenly brusque. He was a courteous man, but amateurs annoyed him. "A fondness for flowers is hardly enough to qualify one for a botanical degree."

A faint flush lit Mr. Green's cheeks, but he checked the retort that occurred to him. Scole was so obviously a sick man.

As though he were speaking to a child, Scole continued. "There are a dozen peculiarities which I should find it difficult to explain to you. But one of them, at least, you can understand. The moonflower is the only form of plant life which has never been found in a wild condition. Invariably, when it has cropped up, there have been traces of human influences, human cultivation . . . even if they were centuries ago."

"Did you say the *only* form of plant life?" interposed Mr. Green.

"I did."

"Surely we are forgetting the *ginkgo biloba*?"

It was Scole's turn to flush.

"That has never been found in a wild condition, either," continued Mr. Green. "Such a charming tree, I always think. I never could understand why some of the experts used to class it with the *taxaceae*. However, I am interrupting you."

Scole gulped, and appeared to be on the point of saying something very sharp. Then he relaxed and smiled.

"*Touché*," he chuckled. "I *had* forgotten the *ginkgo*. Perhaps I should not have been so careless if I had realized you knew what you were talking about."

"I am a very humble amateur."

"If so, you're putting up a good show." He became, once more, his amiable self. "As a matter of fact, this peculiarity *is* rather interesting. And from the point of view of an adventurer . . . that's all I really am, a botanical adventurer. . . ."

Mr. Green made a gesture of dissent.

"There is no need to be more polite to me than I have been to you . . . a botanical adventurer . . . from that angle it was fascinating. It gave one's searches a purpose and a shape. One wasn't faced with the prospect of merely plunging into the jungle, marching blindfold through the undergrowth. One had to set one's course towards a civilization, even if it was only the ghost of a civilization."

"I see."

"To put it more plainly, I was searching for a flower that would only be found by the side of a path that had been trodden by men. Or in the shadow of a temple where men had worshipped. Even if it was only climbing over a broken pillar that was sinking into the mud." He paused abruptly and cleared his throat. "Forgive me. I am talking like one of my own books. And you want facts. Anything in particular?"

"There is one small thing, though it may not be of any great importance. I seem to remember our hostess saying that only six out of the thirteen seeds had germinated. Can you account for that?"

"No, I can't." There was a deep frown on Scole's face. "It's an unsolved mystery. And I don't like unsolved mysteries, in botany."

Any more, thought Mr. Green, than he himself liked them in life. "Were they all given the same treatment?"

"Precisely. The same compost. The same temperature.

33

The same degree of light. At one time I had thought of varying the treatment, but as their natural conditions were perfectly reproduced, it seemed unnecessary."

"Could it have been due to any omission on the part of Wilburfoss?"

"It seems most unlikely. He's a highly skilled man—conscientious to a fault. All the same. . . ."

"Yes?"

He paused, as though he were debating with himself. "There *is* one thing that puzzles me. When I came down, and asked to see the seeds which hadn't germinated, he told me that he had thrown them away!"

Mr. Green blinked, very rapidly.

"Incredible, isn't it? Even an amateur would have known that I should have wanted to examine them. There might have been disease in the seed itself, or some bacteria in the compost . . . some unusual thickening in the husk of the pod, some variation in the moisture content. There might have been a hundred things which would have given me invaluable information. But he merely said they'd 'gone rotten', or words to that effect. I could hardly believe my ears."

"And yet he is normally very particular in such matters?"

"Ultra-particular. Tiresomely so, in fact, all the years I've known him."

"How long is that?"

"Nearly thirty. He began as a groom, you know. He used to take Mrs. Faversham riding, when he was a young man. One day, she called at his cottage and noticed how beautifully he kept his own little garden. It was then that she suggested he should change his vocation. Within five years he was her head gardener. And has been so ever since."

"He might have sat for Praxiteles," murmured Mr. Green to himself.

Scole stared at him. "What was that?"

"I beg your pardon. I was merely thinking that he must

34

have been a very striking young man. And now, may we go inside?"

They rose to their feet and walked slowly to the hot-house.

v

"There she is!"

Scole had to raise his voice almost to a shout, for as soon as the double doors of the hot-house were opened, the full roar of the falls assailed them. Had Mr. Green been less intent on the moonflower he might have reflected once again on the strange whim that had prompted the designer of this architectural conceit to place his crystal cage in so unlikely a position. But the moonflower called him; and this time he looked on it with eyes that were clear and unfatigued.

There were six plants, varying in height from three feet to nearly five. They sprang from deep pots that had been set in a bed of thick, moist moss; alongside ran a hot pipe surmounted by a shallow trough of water from which a faint steam was rising.

The first impression was one of fierce, exultant life. One felt that the swirl of dark, glossy leaves had a purpose . . . it was as though they were swarming up the wires hand over fist, against time . . . they were racing to fulfil themselves. And already their fulfilment was near. At the summit of each dark, glossy pinnacle was a pointed bud, still green but flecked with ivory, exquisitely folded but trembling on the verge of opening.

Mr. Green sighed and stepped backward.

Scole gave him an anxious look. "It's not too hot for you?"

He made a gesture of dissent. "I shall not disgrace myself again." Not physically, at least, he thought—though he felt a mist gathering over his eyes, and an unmanly inclination to weep.

For everything he loved in life—everything that raised life from the jungle rut to the high paths of the spirit—

35

seemed to be concentrated in this moment. He stretched out his hand, and very gently his podgy fingers stroked the smooth, dark leaves of the moonflowers. He could have sworn that he felt the tingle of the cold green blood that raced within.

So he stood, his little fingers straying, his little eyes blinking, his little nose sniffing . . . in a warm, ecstatic trance, against a background of triumphant water-music. It was indeed a moment to remember . . . but a moment that must not be unduly prolonged, for once more he felt the sweat gathering on his forehead.

He gave a final pat to the leaves, and then he turned and went out.

He was too *émotioné* to seek out his hostess, and requested Scole to make his excuses. "You will keep in touch with me?" he asked eagerly.

"About the moonflower? Of course."

"How long will it be now, before it flowers?"

"It cannot be much more than forty-eight hours."

"There is no chance of them opening to-night?"

Scole laughed. "Not unless you break into the house and force them open, out of sheer impatience."

What a great deal of excitement we shall have in the next forty-eight hours, he thought, as he walked back to The Greyhound. The moonflower, opening its magic petals. Mrs. Keswick, giving birth to a child. And Copper Jack . . . whom he had almost forgotten. The thought of this gentleman caused him to quicken his footsteps. Though they were old acquaintances he was not the type of person whom he would care to meet in a lonely lane.

VI

When Mr. Green stepped into the bar parlour, a burly figure rose to greet him.

"Waller, my old friend!" He stretched out both his hands. "This is a pleasant surprise. What brings you to these parts?"

Waller gave him a grip that made him wince. "You, of course." He had a very genuine affection for this little man, half paternal, half filial.

"But seriously?"

Waller explained his business. "It's a hell of an assignment," he said. "The governor's a good chap, and from what I saw of the staff this afternoon, he's got a first-rate crew. But Princetown's an ugly place."

"Prisons usually are."

"I wasn't talking of bricks and mortar. I meant the soul of it. You wouldn't call me a mollycoddler, would you?"

"Hardly."

"All the same, when I came away, and looked back at those grey walls, with the lights just coming on in the windows, I felt I'd like to blow up the whole darned institution."

Mr. Green pursed his lips. "Do you propose to suggest such a course to the Deputy Commissioner?"

"I do not. I'm a working man with a job to do. I shall do it. I came down here to stop the leaks, and I shall stop them. But I don't pretend to enjoy the job. I know that most of the men in Princetown deserve to be in Princetown. They're rats, and I don't like rats. But I'm not too partial to traps, either. If I see a rat in a trap I've got an illogical urge to let it out. Come and have a drink."

He turned abruptly and led the way to the bar. Mr. Green followed, rejoicing in the dual personality of his old friend. It was a personality that had something in common with his own. He too disliked traps even more than he disliked rats, for he could never bring himself to forget that even the least endearing of God's creatures were . . . well, God's creatures. The curving spine of the viper had been sketched with a divine pen; the poisons in the mouth of the adder had been compounded in a heavenly pharmacy. "Dear me," thought Mr. Green, as he sipped his mild-and-bitter, "I am mixing my ales, and soon I shall be mixing my metaphors."

So the evening passed, and the night swept over the moorland, and the two old friends exchanged their stories of the past and their hopes for the future.

37

And so our story begins. It is unfashionable, in these days, for an author to step out of the frame of his picture, to take the reader by the arm, to draw his attention to this character or to that. Yet it is a risk that I shall dare to take, for this is the last chance we shall have of seeing our picture as a whole.

Here, then, is the setting of the drama. A wind-swept moor, with a desperate criminal skulking in the shadows. A great house, with a rich old woman and her young companion. A fabulous cage of crystal, warm and dark, with a rare flower unfolding its tropical tendrils. Various minor characters, moving in the wings . . . an old butler and his wife, a sullen gardener. And over the hill, the lights of two cars speeding away to a great ball. In the first car, a lawyer, a botanist, and a woman; in the second car, the son of the house.

Down below, in the valley, a pleasant inn, where a woman lies in child-birth. In the bar parlour, a police superintendent swopping yarns with our hero, who has yet to prove his quality. In case Mr. Green is not physically alive for you, let us ask you to regard him once more. He is five foot three, plump, inclined to baldness. He wears horn-rimmed spectacles to correct a slight astigmatism. At first sight you might take him for a commercial traveller, but he is evidently a gentleman, and when he speaks it is with the leisurely precision of a Cambridge don. (In *Who's Who* he is listed as an honorary fellow of Peterhouse.) He has no features which would distinguish him in a crowd, and only his intimate friends are aware of two slight peculiarities which manifest themselves when his interest is aroused. The first is a rapid blinking of his mild grey eyes; the second, a curious quivering of the nostrils of his stubby nose, which is an organ of exceptional sensitivity.

This, then, is our scene and these are our *dramatis personae*. But we have forgotten one essential element . . . the sound of the falls. Night and day, through the lives of the actors in this strange tragedy, there is the echo of these turbulent waters. Not only in the shadow of the great house does this angry music proclaim itself, but all through the valley, for the Fallow river splits and forks in many narrow channels, arguing, wrangling, protesting, accusing, as it sweeps with all its secrets to the sea.

Mr. Green was not the only person, in the next few weeks, who wished that he might read the language of those waters.

3

MR. GREEN awoke on the following morning with no trace of his recent indisposition; he felt rested both in body and in mind. This was the more gratifying because his night had been far from tranquil; from midnight onwards there had been a constant coming and going on the staircase outside his room, the corridor had creaked with hurrying footsteps, and through his dreams had drifted a low murmur of voices —the voice of Sandra, of the landlord, of the doctor. And just before dawn, the shrill treble of a new-born child.

He lay there, in his warm bed, indulging in the sort of sentimental reverie which was fitting to an elderly bachelor on such an occasion. Only a few yards away a tiny bundle was breathing the air of its first morning in this world— gasping, gurgling, throbbing, expanding, moment by moment, breaking through the surface of the dark waters from which it had emerged, making its first strokes into the sea of life. For sixty, seventy years or more, it would swim over that sea, long after he himself had sailed beyond the horizon. . . .

He pushed the thought—and the bed-clothes—aside. His horizon, he hoped, was still some distance away. That is a consoling feature of the geography of the human spirit; the ultimate horizon is always retreating—or so we can flatter ourselves.

When he entered the breakfast-room, Waller was just coming out. "Care to drive over to Princetown with me this morning?" he said.

"Very much indeed," replied Mr. Green. "Though I do not know if I can be of much assistance."

"Oh, I don't suppose they'd let you into the prison," chaffed Waller. "Even with *my* influence. They don't like amateurs prowling round the place. But the drive would do you good." He gave Mr. Green one of those slaps on the back which he so much disliked. "See you in the hall. Nine sharp."

Mr. Green sniffed indignantly. Really, Waller's humour grew heavier every day. "Amateur" indeed! However, the savoury aromas of breakfast were too alluring to allow of any pause for argument. He went inside, and joined Miss Wells at a table by the window.

"So the population has been successfully augmented?" he said, sipping the coffee which was almost immediately set before him.

"Very successfully," she answered. "A boy. Seven pounds, two ounces. Mrs. Keswick is doing very well." She gave a tired smile. "And there is a chance that even Mr. Keswick may eventually recover. I hope that we didn't keep you awake?"

"Really . . . as if that would have mattered. You must be exhausted yourself."

She nodded frankly. "I am. I've been here since eleven o'clock last night. I don't think I've been able to sit down for the last eight hours."

She covered her eyes with her hands. Mr. Green did not disturb her, but devoted himself to his breakfast. By the time he had finished she had recovered, and was asking him to give her a light for her cigarette.

As she did so, Ivy the barmaid poked her head through the door. "Wanted on the telephone, miss," she snapped. Ivy was never at her best in the morning.

"Who is it, Ivy?"

"Somebody at Candle Court. Says it's urgent."

Miss Wells rose to her feet with a gesture of impatience. "I do think I might *sometimes* have a moment . . ." she began. Then she checked herself and forced a smile. "You will excuse me?" she murmured.

She hurried out, followed a moment later by Mr. Green. He was in search of the morning edition of the *Devon Gazette* which would be laid out on the centre table of the bar parlour. In order to reach this agreeable chamber he

41

had to pass by the alcove where Miss Wells was telephoning. Having the instinct, as well as the breeding, of a gentleman, he quickened his footsteps as he passed her; he confined his eavesdropping to strictly professional occasions. But as he opened the door, he stopped in his tracks, arrested by an exclamation from behind him. It was so shrill, so dramatic, that he would have been inhuman to ignore it.

"Strangled!"

He turned his head swiftly. It was from Miss Wells that the word had come. She had stepped back from the telephone, and was staring at its black face as though it were some evil thing that might assault her.

"Strangled!" she cried again. She took another step backward, and as she did so, the light from the open doorway fell on her face. Mr. Green, of an instant, ceased to be a gentleman, and became a professional, for he sensed that this had suddenly become, in the grimmest sense, a professional occasion. He focused her face with eyes as keen and sharp as the lens of a high-speed camera, registering every nuance of expression. There were many, but one of them predominated—an expression of sheer incredulity. This was emphasized by the words that followed.

"Are you sure . . . are you *sure*?" She was shaking her head as though to deny it. And then, she seemed to pull herself together. "Of course," she said, "I am being foolish. But it is so terrible . . . I hardly know what I am saying. Yes, yes—I will come at once."

She hung up, and stayed there for a moment, quite still, keeping her hand on the receiver. Then she stepped outside. She came straight up to him.

"Mr. Green, thank God you are here!" She put her hand on his arm. "The most terrible thing has happened. Mrs. Faversham has been. . . ."

She closed her eyes, and gripped more tightly. For a moment he thought that she was about to faint. Then she shook her head, and took a deep breath, like a diver coming to the surface.

"Strangled," she said.

"Mrs. Faversham? Murdered?"

Her eyes met his. "Yes. Sometime during the night."

Her fingers gripped tighter and tighter.

"Do you know any details?"

She shook her head. "No. They seem to think it must be that man—the convict. The jewels have gone . . . and the safe." She swayed slightly. "I think I would like to sit down."

A dark shape loomed behind them. It was Waller. He put a strong arm round her waist. "Better come over here, miss. You look all in." He led her to a settee by the wall. "Afraid I overheard what you were saying. Old Mrs. Faversham, is it?"

"Yes."

He turned to Mr. Green. "That's good-bye to our little trip to Princetown this morning. I'd better get through to the Yard at once. They'll want me to deal with this." He paused, and even at this sombre moment a fleeting twinkle came to his eye. "I might persuade them to let you come as my assistant."

"You are very kind," snapped Mr. Green, who thought his remark in poor taste.

Waller was gone for nearly a quarter of an hour. When he returned, there was no trace of a twinkle. He was his old, keen, sober self, with no nonsense about him.

"That's that," he said. "We're to get going at once. By the way, the Deputy Commissioner sent you his kind regards. And if it's of any interest, he told me I was damned lucky to have you with me."

Mr. Green's heart was lit by a glow of pleasure. That was generous of the Deputy Commissioner—and even more generous of Waller to pass it on.

They struggled into their coats. When Waller said he would fetch the car, Miss Wells stopped him. She would rather walk; it was only ten minutes, and the cold air would do her good.

As they stepped outside, the cry of a child echoed from

an open window above. Mr. Green stopped and looked up. There it was, the plaintive, puzzled cry of the little swimmer, breasting the first waves of the great dark sea. But this was no time for sentimental reflections.

II

They were all gathered in the hall, waiting for them.

Kenneth was the first to step forward. He looked white and half-stunned.

"Where is Miss Wells?" he demanded.

"She is walking; she will be here in a few minutes."

Beryl came up. "Didn't you tell her?"

"Yes. But she has been up all night at the inn, and I think she wanted to pull herself together." Mr. Green turned. "This is Superintendent Waller of Scotland Yard."

"Good morning."

Waller went up to Beryl and took her hand with a gesture of natural dignity and kindness. "I am deeply sorry, madam."

"Thank you." She was trembling violently. "It is all too terrible. Will you tell us what to do, please?"

Waller glanced over at two policemen who were standing by the fireplace. "Are these two gentlemen . . ." he began.

The taller of the policemen stepped forward. "Sergeant Fisher, sir, Exeter Division." He motioned to his companion, who clicked his heels. "Sergeant Cobb, Moreton Fallow."

"Glad to meet you both."

"We've made a preliminary investigation, sir."

"Good work. I'll have a word with you in a moment. In the meantime. . . ." Waller faced Kenneth, but he spoke in tones loud enough to be heard by the others—Beryl, Scole, Ackworth, and Wilburfoss . . . "in the meantime, I hope that nobody will leave this house. There are certain formalities which will have to be observed."

"Such as?" There was an echo of truculence in Kenneth's voice.

"I shall need a record of fingerprints."

"But Good Lord . . . if it was that convict chap. . . ."

44

"Whoever it may have been," interrupted Waller, "I shall need a record of fingerprints." He ignored Kenneth's snort of indignation and returned to the tall policeman. "May I have a word with you, before we go upstairs?"

Sergeant Fisher proved a man of exceptional competence. He had not wasted a moment of his hour's start. He had a detailed description of Mrs. Faversham's bedroom and the disposition of the body. He had made his own notes on the condition of *rigor mortis,* not trusting to the evidence of Doctor Rudyard, who was still upstairs. He had taken statements from all and sundry—rough and ready, but none the less valuable. And he had come equipped with all the apparatus that Waller most needed.

"You seem to have left me very little to do," observed Waller drily.

Sergeant Fisher flushed with pleasure. "Thank you, sir. Though I dare say you'll find a lot I never thought of. Excuse me, sir, I think that's our photographer."

He beckoned towards the doorway, where a breathless young man had just arrived, loaded with photographic apparatus. Waller nodded curtly, and led the way upstairs.

As he reached the top step he paused. For the moment he had forgotten Mr. Green. Where was he, and what was he up to? He seemed to have disappeared. An affectionate grin transformed the superintendent's face. He had a suspicion that Mr. Green was sulking. For all his modesty, his apparent self-effacement, the little man liked being in the centre of the picture. But nobody, so far, had even asked for his opinion.

Well, thought Waller, he would ask for it, when the time came. Not that he seemed likely to need it . . . the case was obvious enough. A blunt, brutal, unimaginative business. Which reminded him that he must phone to the Yard for Copper Jack's fingerprints.

With which he turned, and allowed Sergeant Fisher to conduct him to the door behind which death was waiting. Where for the moment we will leave them.

III

Superintendent Waller had done Mr. Green an injustice. He was not sulking; he was thinking.

He was thinking, not of murder and sudden death, but of the moonflower. Mr. Green had a very individual sense of values; he did not think that the world was much the poorer for the loss of Mrs. Faversham—though, being a kindly soul, he regretted the manner of her decease. But he was quite certain that the world would be very much poorer for the loss of the moonflower. Who would care for it now? He had no knowledge of the terms of the old lady's will, but even if Candle Court passed to Kenneth it seemed highly improbable that he would be able to maintain the great house in its former splendour. The hot-houses, almost certainly, would be closed. The best one could hope would be that Kenneth might dispose of the plants to some public body like the Royal Horticultural Society . . . but it was doubtful whether even the richest organization would care to undertake the responsibility of maintaining so frail an exotic, even if it were to survive the dangers of transportation. For a moment he toyed with the idea of bidding for one of the plants himself—taking it away with him to his little Surrey greenhouse; but he quickly dismissed the notion as grotesque. It would have been as impractical as adopting a tiger cub.

He was seized with an urge to see the flower once more; it might be his last chance. True, there was no hope that it would yet be in bloom . . . how long was it that Scole had said it needed? Forty-eight hours. That would mean to-morrow night, at the earliest. Even so, he *must* see it again, and see it alone.

He had no difficulty in making his exit unobserved, for they were all standing round like waxworks, staring at the staircase, waiting for Waller's return.

Here he was at the door of the cool-house. He opened it and stepped inside. His sense of urgency was so great that he repressed his natural longing to linger among the bougainvilleas which hung in festoons of purple and scarlet at the entrance. He hurried along to the hot-house and flung open the door. The clamour of the falls assaulted him with an almost personal violence; but it was not this that made him step back and clutch the railing by his side. It was something far more important.

The moonflower was in full bloom.

He stayed there, staring at a cluster of pale, luminous petals that shone from their background of dark green leaves. Then he went forward, stepping on tiptoe, as though the flower were asleep, and he feared to wake it.

It was of incredible beauty. There were three eight-petalled blooms, each of them over six inches across. They had not only the colour but the quality of snow, for the outer rim of each petal was frosted with the palest silver. This sheen was echoed in the calyx, but far more brightly, so that it shone like a device of exquisite craftsmanship. In the depths of each centre was a faint powdering of gold.

It was not a flower, it was a jewel. And yet . . . it was a flower of flowers, for the essence of its beauty lay in its very transience. Like the morning glories, from whose family it had evolved, it was born for a few hours only, for a single golden noon, to droop at dusk. Even now, as he stood before it, he knew that its crowning moment was passing, that there was a subtle fatigue in the pale fabric of the petals, as though it had made some supreme effort at self-expression.

Mr. Green looked his last; then he turned and retraced his steps, shutting the door behind him. At the door of the cool-house he paused and closed his eyes. He wanted to photograph those pale petals on the retina of his brain. He had a sense that they formed an essential part in the design of a drama that was eluding him.

There . . . the mental photograph was taken. When he opened his eyes again he was blinking, very rapidly.

A few moments after his return to the great hall he was blinking more than ever. For it was now that the drama took a sensational turn.

Superintendent Waller had already come down, leaving the photographer upstairs with the younger of the two policemen. He was standing by a desk, waiting while Sergeant Fisher laid out the finger-printing apparatus. The others were grouped about in various attitudes of dejection. They had been joined by Sandra, who was sitting in an armchair, staring into the fire. There were also three new-comers, whom he took to be members of the staff . . . a frail old lady in black bombasine, a gipsy-like woman in a blue serge dress, and a stocky young man in a green baize apron.

Then the telephone rang.

Kenneth lumbered off the edge of the sofa, where he had been sitting next to his wife, and went over to answer it.

"It's for you," he said, turning to Waller. "Scotland Yard."

The superintendent walked across and took the receiver.

"Waller speaking. Yes . . . I'll hold on." A moment's pause. "Good morning. sir. No, sir. Not yet. What's that? Good Lord!" He listened intently. "The eleven-thirty, you say, from Exeter last night? Well, sir . . . that lets him out. We'll have to think along fresh lines, and pretty quickly too. No, sir, I shan't have any need of Bates, I'm very well served down here. Yes, sir, I'll keep in touch. Good-bye."

He hung up. Then he turned towards them. His face was grim.

He spoke very deliberately. "Copper Jack," he said, "has been arrested."

Kenneth sprang to his feet. "Thank God! Has he confessed?"

"No, Mr. Faversham, it is not quite so simple as that.

48

He was found hiding on a goods train which he had boarded at Exeter at eleven-thirty last night."

"Well?"

"According to Dr. Rudyard, Mrs. Faversham was still alive at eleven-thirty or thereabouts. Copper Jack had stolen a bicycle, but even on a bicycle, in the best conditions, it is at least an hour from here to Exeter. It is therefore quite inconceivable that he could have been in any way connected with this crime."

Beryl stood up, holding on to her husband's arm. "What . . . what does it mean?" she stammered.

The superintendent answered: "It means, Mrs. Faversham, that we shall have to look nearer home." In the deathly silence that followed, he swept the room with a glance which had all the majesty, and the horror, of the law.

v

It was typical of Mr. Green that this revelation should cause him to fade even further into the background. If he had been a real detective, like Sherlock Holmes, he would doubtless have strode to the centre of the stage, and delivered himself of a caustic phrase which would have set the whole world wondering. But he had no caustic phrases to deliver; he was as much in the dark as any of them.

So he faded, gliding gently across to the wall that was in the deepest shadow, where he leant against a Knowle settee of dim green velvet. He had the quality of a chameleon; in his old green suit, with the rich and sombre tapestries behind him, he blended so completely with his surroundings that he might have been some curious little creature of threads and stitches, hanging from the wall.

He watched the scene through half-closed eyes.

It is like a ballet, he thought. All these figures coming and going. This low, urgent music of voices. With the muffled drumbeat of death echoing through from the floor above.

But his reactions were not merely aesthetic. He realized that once again he was caught up in a web which in due course he would be called upon to disentangle . . . if he chose to disentangle it. He was not sure if he *would* choose to do so; he was tired, and growing old; it might be better if he were to excuse himself and drift away, before it was too late.

But he had a tidy mind . . . that was the devil of it. And murder was an untidy business, till you had your finger on the criminal. Presumably the criminal was here, in this very room, within a few yards of him. . . .

He drew himself up abruptly, a tiny, grey speck against the looming glory of the tapestry. He no longer felt tired and old. Once more he became, of a sudden, the celebrated Mr. Green, author of *First Principles in Detection,* that massive work which for thirty years has been a "must" in the world's Scotland Yards. The first sentence in that book, as the reader will recall, runs as follows:

"After the commission of any and every crime, the discoveries of the first twenty-four hours are likely to be more rewarding to the investigator than those of the subsequent twenty-four hours."

Mr. Green bowed to his own philosophy. Like a small, alert chameleon, he crouched by the tapestry, blinking, making mental notes. Here are some of them.

Kenneth—Beryl—Scole—Pusey—Wilburfoss—Sandra. The principal actors in the drama. All of them, presumably, might have murdered Mrs. Faversham—with the exception of Sandra, who had spent all night in the next bedroom to his own at The Greyhound, playing her part of midwife. He would cross-examine these people in his own quiet way when Waller had done with them. In the meantime, who else was there?

He spied a new face—a thin, scared, elderly woman in black silk, standing next to Ackworth, the butler. Mrs.

Ackworth, no doubt. Yes, he remembered her now, from the old London days. A very minor character, he imagined. But he would talk to her later on . . . one never knew. He caught her eye, and she bowed to him, like a distracted duchess.

Another new arrival, coming down the staircase. Plump, forty-five and very smart, with his short black coat, his patent leather shoes, his striped trousers, and his grey satin tie. Far too smart, thought Mr. Green, for a country doctor —rightly assuming that this must be Dr. Max Rudyard. He should be in Wimpole Street, with a shiny black Daimler, flitting to and fro between the neuroses of the nobility. He frowned at this irreverent thought; he must not allow himself to be prejudiced. All the same, he feared that he might find it difficult to work in harmony with so sleek a person . . . a person, moreover, so obviously concerned with his own plumpness. See! He is holding in his stomach even as he goes up to Waller and asks him a question. He is worrying about his double chin even when he nods at the reply. He is pulling in his waistline even as he sits on the Knowle settee, with his black bag over his knees. A small soul, feared Mr. Green, entirely surrounded by plumpness, like a little sausage in an island of batter.

Still, one never knew. He might be competent.

Who else? The stocky boy in the green baize apron. Whispering in a corner with Wilburfoss. That must be young Meadows, whom Scole took with him on the moon-flower expedition. Yes—he remembers him now. A nice lad, and, according to Scole, highly competent. He steps aside as the gipsyish woman comes up and lays her hand on Wilburfoss's arm. Young Mrs. Wilburfoss, no doubt. No love lost between her and young Meadows, by the look of it; he glares at her with an expression of positive loathing. He must keep an eye on Meadows—on all of them, if it comes to that.

And what is happening now? Mr. Pusey has gone up to Waller. He has changed his opulent tweeds and is dressed for the city. In his hand he carries a brand new suitcase.

Mr. Green moved closer. As though a theme were suddenly isolated from the low murmur of an orchestra, he heard their dialogue.

Pusey. "I'm sorry. But I have a train to catch. The most urgent business."

Waller. "I quite understand, sir. But this is also urgent."

Pusey. "I fail to see. . . ."

Waller. "We cannot make exceptions, sir. It is not a question of any suspicion. But your evidence . . . and your fingerprints."

Pusey (explosively). "My evidence will be at your disposal at . . ." (with a glance at his wrist-watch) ". . . three-thirty, when I shall return from Exeter. My fingerprints you can take now."

It is perfect ballet, thought Mr. Green. See . . . he is holding out his hands, moving towards the table where the policeman is standing. He is followed by the reluctant Waller.

The dialogue continues.

Pusey. (Holding out his thumbs to be blacked). "I do not wish to appear unco-operative. But very considerable interests are involved." (A side-glance between himself and Kenneth Faversham.) "By midday the news of this tragedy will be published in London. It will affect the Stock Market. Considerably. The Faversham holdings are widespread . . . and most of the investments are in small companies. . . ."

A pause. A silence. Two big black thumbs are pressed on a sheet of white paper.

Kenneth steps forward. He says something to Waller in a low voice. Waller shrugs his shoulders. A moment later, Pusey has wiped his hands, gripped his suitcase, and hurried out.

Pusey was followed at the table by Sandra. Poor young thing, thought Mr. Green, she looks more affected than any of them. Her face was grey with fatigue, and as she pressed her fingers on the ink block she swayed as though she were about to faint. Mr. Green felt indignant that Waller did not seem to notice her condition. Did he not realize that the poor girl had been up all night?

Acting on a sudden impulse he hurried forward and offered her his arm. She turned to him with a faint smile.

"This young lady ought to be in bed," he said to Waller in reproving tones.

Waller, who was still smarting from his encounter with Mr. Pusey, made no comment; he merely handed her a cloth with which to wipe her fingers.

"That filthy old rag!" exclaimed Mr. Green. He pulled out his own handkerchief from his pocket. "Allow me!" Before she could protest he had taken her fingers and was wiping them clean. "There!" He gave her hand a gentle pat.

"Perhaps you would prefer to take charge of this business yourself?" demanded Waller, with heavy irony. There were times when Mr. Green irritated him acutely, particularly when he was afflicted, as at the present moment, by these ridiculous fits of blinking.

"Not at all," returned Mr. Green. "In fact I was hoping that you would give me permission to withdraw."

"Upstairs?"

Mr. Green nodded.

"I've no objection," grunted Waller. That was not quite true. He *had* an objection, based on a foreboding that as soon as Mr. Green entered the death-chamber he would discover more than he had discovered himself—which was, to be frank, precious little. However, he dismissed the thought as ungenerous. In a more friendly tone he said: "You'll find the young sergeant up there. You can send him down to me, if you like. I know you prefer to work alone."

"Thank you."

"D'you want a word with the doctor first?"

"Later, if I may. For the moment I'd rather have an open mind."

"I understand. Well . . . good luck."

53

Mr. Green turned and walked slowly up the great stair-case, followed by the awe-struck gaze of Sergeant Fisher. The little man had been his hero ever since the days of his boyhood; it might almost be said that he slept with a copy of *First Principles of Detection* under his pillow. What would he not have given to be with him at this moment?

He was recalled to his immediate duty by the querulous voice of Mrs. Ackworth, protesting against having to dip her fingers into "all that muck".

VI

Mr. Green dismissed the young police-sergeant, who seemed thankful to be relieved of his lonely vigil.

Then he closed the door gently behind him, and locked it.

For the moment he ignored the great four-poster bed, in which lay the body of the dead woman, covered by a linen sheet. He wanted to acquaint himself with the general geography of the room.

It was dominated by a tall bay window that gave directly on to the falls. Apart from the hot-house itself, which jutted out at an angle, this room was closer to the falls than any other part of the mansion. The uproar of the water was so great that Mr. Green wondered how any woman could have slept through it. It also occurred to him that this angry clamour was an ideal background for a crime of violence; the shrillest scream would hardly be heard in the next room.

He opened the window wider and leant out. A gnarled trunk of wistaria curled and twisted up the wall immediately below, forming a perfect natural staircase for even the least agile of criminals. Some fresh scars on the bark suggested that it had been recently climbed. Waller, of course, would have noted a detail like that. He observed that the ground immediately below the window had already been roped off . . . Waller again no doubt, making sure that no previous footprints were lost. He smiled reminiscently. Waller was a great one for footprints. Well—we all had our little ways.

Mr. Green himself had never set much store by them; he found that they too often led him in the wrong direction.

He turned from the window and walked over to the opposite wall. A wide gash in the panelling showed where the safe had been wrenched from its setting. It was almost incredible, thought Mr. Green, that any woman so shrewd —and so acquisitive—as the late Mrs. Faversham should have entrusted her treasure to so frail a deposit. The safe had not even been firmly cemented into the surrounding brickwork; a few deft strokes with a chisel would have been enough to loosen it.

If the old lady had sought her own death, with the idea of giving her executioner the least possible trouble, she could hardly have arranged it more expeditiously. The uproar of the waters, the open window, the climbing staircase of the creeper, the jewels—hanging, as it were, by a silken thread. It was folly on the grand scale. He sighed and shook his head. Well, she had paid for it, to the full.

And now he tiptoed across to the great four-poster bed. It was typical of him that he should walk on tiptoe, for though he had seen the dead in many guises, he had never lost his sense of reverence in their company—a reverence which he did not always extend to the living. Typical, too, that before he drew back the sheet which covered the dead woman, he should close his eyes and say a prayer for her soul. He knew that she would not have thanked him for it, when she was in this world, but now, maybe, she would feel differently.

He drew back the sheet and looked down. She was not a pretty sight. They had closed her eyes and folded her hands, but the angry contusions round her throat told their own tale. It was as though her neck had been held in a vice of steel. He bent down, and flexed her little finger. Nothing to be learnt from that. Death might have occurred at any time within the last ten hours. It seemed an obvious case of strangulation. And yet, there was something about the face that puzzled him. Something so elusive that he could not put a name to it—something that did not seem quite "right". It was like the subtle difference that exists in the faces of twins who are apparently identical, yet easily identified. However, he must not attach any value to such flimsy speculations; maybe it was merely a trick of the light. All the same, he would keep the memory of this little moment of puzzlement on one of the back shelves of his mind. Those shelves were crowded with similar memories, and they often came in handy.

He carefully replaced the sheet, and turned to go, when suddenly he paused, and sniffed. Here at last was something quite definite, something about which there could be no argument. It may be remembered that Mr. Green's nose was as sensitive as the palate of a tea-taster; he had once, for example, analysed the components of two extremely subtle perfumes on the handkerchief of a murderer even after it had been sent to the wash. And now, once again, it was a perfume that arrested his attention.

It seemed to come from the floor. He knelt down, and sniffed more keenly. The scent was stronger than ever, and it was centred in the fringe of the heavy brocade curtains with which the back of the bed was draped. He crawled forward, and very gently, between two fingers, drew the curtain towards him.

"Ah!" The exclamation came from him quite involuntarily. There, on the fringe, was a speck of white powder; there were several more specks on the carpet, as though somebody had shaken out a tin of talcum. The powder, to Mr. Green's remarkable olfactory sense, gave out a sweet, cloying odour which for the moment he could not identify, though he had a suspicion that somewhere, long ago, he had smelt it before. Here was another conundrum for the back shelf of his mind.

In the meantime, he must preserve this piece of evidence, if "evidence" it could be called. He drew out a pair of surgical scissors, and cut off a tiny fragment of the fringe, which he wrapped in tissue paper and transferred to his wallet. He had hardly risen to his feet again when there was a knock on the door.

56

He went across and opened it. The young policeman stood outside.

"Superintendent Waller's compliments, sir. When you are free he'd like a word with you."

"Would you tell him that I will be down in a few minutes?"

The young policeman departed. Mr. Green tiptoed back to the bed for a last look at the face of his old friend. He screwed up his eyes and tilted his head to one side, in an acute effort of concentration. Something was wrong. But what? It was a mere matter of expression . . . and on the faces of the dead, "expression" is even more difficult to translate and to interpret than on the faces of the living. He closed his eyes. He must photograph that expression. Elusive as it was, he must not let it escape him. It might prove the last dimly coloured fragment of the fantastic jig-saw puzzle that was confronting him.

Now he must go down to Waller. The good, kind, painstaking creature would doubtless try to pick his brains, and ask him what he had "discovered". How could he answer him? He had discovered nothing.

But he had made the beginnings of a fascinating collection of mental photographs.

A flower that had bloomed too soon. Why?

A young man downstairs (Meadows), staring with hatred at a young woman (Mrs. Wilburfoss). Why?

A middle-aged man with a suitcase (Mr. Pusey), in a desperate hurry to leave the house. Why?

A patch of white powder, with a strange perfume, immediately beneath the body of the corpse. Why?

An expression. Printed by the cold hand of death on the corpse itself. An expression that did not "fit". Why?

How could he explain these things to Waller? How could he even mention them? The good man would only laugh . . . as he had so often laughed in the past.

Mr. Green, as these thoughts raced through his mind, had been standing by the open window, and the air was chill. He had a sudden desire to sneeze. He drew out his hand-

57

kerchief and only noticed, just in time, that it was covered with black ink. With an impatient gesture he thrust it into his pocket again, and sneezed.

The sneeze cleared his brain. It was a call to action. He had dallied long enough. With a swift gesture he drew the sheet once more over the face of the dead woman and hurried out of the room.

4

WALLER met Mr. Green at the bottom of the staircase.

"Any news?"

"Really, Waller, I thought you had news for *me*."

The superintendent grinned. "No, my lad. I just couldn't bear the thought of you up there all on your lonesome. You might have got scared. But seriously . . . was there anything?"

Mr. Green's face was pink. There were occasions when his leg could be pulled, and there were occasions when it could not. This was one of the latter. So he decided to say nothing to the superintendent about the patch of white powder on the carpet. In any case, it might prove to be of no importance.

"There was nothing," he said shortly.

Waller nodded. "I'm glad in a way. At least it makes me feel I haven't made any major bloomers, to date."

Kenneth Faversham came up, with his wife leaning on his arm. "Are we still supposed to stay in the house?"

"No, sir. There's no need for that any longer."

"Thank God!" He turned to Beryl. "Let's get out of here, darling, and motor down to the sea. We could lunch at Torquay. Nobody need see us."

Scole joined them. "Could I come with you?"

"Of course. Would that be all right with you, Inspector?"

"Certainly, sir. I imagine you'll be back to-night, in case there are any developments?"

"Yes. We'll probably be home by tea-time." He turned impulsively to Mr. Green. "Why don't you and the superintendent stay and have luncheon here?"

Mr. Green began to murmur that he did not wish to put him to any trouble, but Kenneth stopped him.

"It won't be the least trouble. It'll take Ackworth's mind

off things. Besides, Dr. Rudyard's staying to luncheon, in any case. So you can have a talk to him, and prowl around on your own."

He gave them a fleeting smile. He seemed, of a sudden, to be co-operating with them, in a frank and friendly manner. It was a welcome change from his previous attitude.

"You are more than kind," said Mr. Green.

"That's settled then." He turned to his wife, "Come on, darling; let's get a breath of fresh air. There's a south-wester blowing up, and you can smell the sea."

II

The south-wester blew up with a vengeance, and an hour later, when they sat down to luncheon in the library, the windows were rattling.

There were three of them—Mr. Green, the superintendent, and Dr. Rudyard. The doctor at once proceeded to make himself at home, taking the head of the table, and diving his hand into a packet of starch-proof rusks which he had brought in with him. His fingers darted restlessly in search of preliminary titbits, such as salted almonds, which he managed to pick up by the half-dozen, and black olives, whose stones he concealed under one of the starch-proof rusks. All the time his eyes wandered in the direction of the serving-hatch, where Ackworth stood waiting for the first course. This proved to be an *œuf cocotte,* which disappeared down his throat with astonishing rapidity, leaving him to drum his fingers on the table, and to turn his head once more to the serving-hatch.

It might be difficult, thought Mr. Green, as he toyed with his egg, to direct the thoughts of so greedy a person to the matter at hand, but he must make the attempt.

"I am glad that we have this opportunity to talk . . ." he began.

"Not at all." The doctor turned to Ackworth with an ingratiating smile. "A little butter, perhaps?" he hissed. Then he went back to Mr. Green. "Forgive me, but naturally,

60

everything is disorganized to-day. You were saying?"

"He hasn't said anything yet," chaffed Waller, "but he wants to pick your brains."

"My poor brains!" he laughed affectedly, stretched for a rusk, and thought better of it. "Again! What question is it that you wished to ask me?"

"The question we are obliged to ask all members of your profession on these melancholy occasions . . . the approximate hour of death."

The doctor frowned impatiently. "Our old friend *rigor mortis*. I took an instant dislike to it as a medical student, and nothing that has happened since then has given me any cause to change my mind."

Mr. Green nodded. Here, at least, they had something in common. "You mean that it is an untrustworthy guide?"

"Not at all," snapped the doctor. "Within its limits it is infallible. Or almost infallible. But one must *know* those limits. Whenever I come across one of those ridiculous statements in a coroner's report to the effect that so-and-so had been dead for three hours, or five hours, or six and three-quarters, I feel. . . ."

What he felt was for the moment obscured. He broke off abruptly, and stared with dismay at the silver dish that Ackworth was handing him. "Curry!"

"I'm sorry, sir," said Ackworth, "but we didn't know you were coming till it was too late."

"Is there nothing else?"

"Well, sir . . . a little cold ham?"

"That will have to do. And a salad, perhaps? And if you *had* any of the Stilton? That would be delicious. And you won't forget the Vichy water? Thank you. But please . . ." waving a large white cuff towards the others, "serve these gentlemen first. I can wait. I am in *no* hurry." As he said this he seized a starch-proof rusk from his packet, and bit it so fiercely that fragments of it exploded on to his brocade waistcoat.

"We were talking of *rigor*," he continued, munching

rapidly. But it seemed that his mind was not on the subject, for his eyes followed with avidity each spoonful that Mr. Green was putting on to his plate. "Rice," he added, in the same breath, "is poison to me. Pure starch." He reached for another biscuit.

Mr. Green made no comment. The combination of *rigor* and rice was not one which he, personally, would have chosen as a topic of conversation. Indeed, it robbed him of his appetite. He sighed, and pushed away his plate.

Waller, who was not so delicate, came to his rescue. "You mentioned time limits," he said.

"I did."

"Which you suggested were infallible."

"Quite."

"Good. You examined the body at half past eight?"

"Or thereabouts."

"Very well, then. Can you tell us your conclusions?"

"Certainly. Ah! My ham!" Once again they had to wait, while he attended to more important matters. "Ackworth remembers everything!" he purred, his pudgy hands darting this way and that. "The salad looks delicious. And that is my own dressing, is it not? Wait . . . where is the pepper-mill? Ah, I see it, behind the french mustard."

At last he was appeased. At last, replete, he was able to sit back and devote his attention to the matter at hand. He lit a cigarette, and regarded Mr. Green with eyes that were shrewd and clear, in spite of their casing of fat.

"I am probably telling you nothing that you do not know," he said. "But I imagine that you wish to confirm the theories that you have already formed. Very well. I examined the body at eight-thirty. Mrs. Faversham had certainly been dead for *three* hours."

Waller leant forward as though to speak. The doctor checked him. "Or four, or five, or six, or seven, or eight, or . . . conceivably . . . eight and a half. No longer."

"Those are your limits?"

"They are the limits of any doctor who speaks from experience as opposed to theory. And I have had rather more

62

experience than my appearance might suggest. For two years I was the only doctor in one of the less luxurious Japanese prison camps. There were times when the supply of corpses was more than adequate. Which was more than one could say for the supply of food." He gave them a sudden twisted smile . . . which was less a smile than a nervous twitch, a grimace of pain remembered.

Mr. Green, of a sudden, found himself understanding Dr. Rudyard. Not liking him, but understanding him, which is the next best thing.

"There are some authorities," he suggested, "who might stretch your limit to ten hours."

The doctor shrugged his shoulders. "If you have some preconceived theory that demands such a period. . . ."

"I am not in the habit of forming preconceived theories."

"I did not intend to be rude. But when one is sure of one's facts, one is impatient. I am speaking from a very wide experience, and I am taking into consideration not only the time factor, but the physical make-up of the deceased, with which I was of course very familiar. At whatever hour Mrs. Faversham was killed, it was not before midnight."

He leant back, and drew on his cigarette.

"Satisfied?" demanded Waller.

Mr. Green did not appear to hear the question. He was staring straight in front of him, drumming his fingers on the table.

"I said . . . are you satisfied?"

Mr. Green blinked. "Of course, of course," he murmured. And with a little smile to the doctor . . . "Very grateful, too. In a case like this, facts are worth their weight in gold. And we seem, at least, to have a fact. Midnight."

"Can you pin-point it nearer than that?" demanded Waller.

"Pin-point would be hardly the word. I can make a rough estimate, which would probably be accurate within the hour."

"And that would give us . . . ?"

"At the inquest I shall state that death occurred between

two-thirty and three-thirty. For purposes of convenience let us say 3 a.m. Does that fit in with your theories?"

"At this stage of the game I am no fonder of theories than Mr. Green."

"But at least you have the *facts* . . . from midnight onwards. May we have them?"

Waller glanced at Mr. Green. He noticed that he was blinking in an agony of impatience. "Has my old friend any objection?"

"On the contrary," returned Mr. Green. "However, I should prefer that we began a little *before* midnight."

"Is that necessary? Surely we are all agreed that. . . ."

"Quite," interrupted Mr. Green, with less than his usual politeness. "But I cannot plunge into things quite so quickly as some people." He turned to the doctor with an apologetic smile. "I find it necessary, as it were, to set the stage. I am sure that the superintendent will understand what I mean."

Waller grunted uneasily. He knew, from long experience, that when Mr. Green assured him that "he would understand what he meant," it was better to pretend to do so.

"Very well. How do you propose to set your stage?"

"With the assistance of Ackworth—who, I see, is just arriving with our coffee."

"I've already interviewed Ackworth. He'll have nothing to tell you."

"No *facts*, perhaps," returned Mr. Green patiently. "But then I do not want Ackworth to provide me with any *facts* . . . I merely wish, as it were, to absorb the atmosphere."

And now Waller was very uneasy indeed. Whenever Mr. Green talked vaguely about "absorbing the atmosphere", it was a sure sign that he was on the trail of very definite information.

III

It needed no great persuasion on the part of Mr. Green to make Ackworth set down his tray and take a seat at the end of the table. The old man was pining to talk to somebody. His wife was a sorry confidante, who could only wring her hands and utter gloomy prophecies as to the fate which lay in store for them, now that her mistress was dead. It was a comfort to sit down and talk to Mr. Green, whom he had known in the grand old days of the London house. Even if he were a sort of policeman, he was a proper gentleman, for all that.

Besides, it wasn't as if he wanted to cross-examine him . . . oh no! He only wanted to pass the time of day, as it were, about that unhappy night and the last time he saw the old lady.

It was a proof of Mr. Green's uncanny tact that, at the end of the interview, Ackworth was still under the impression that he had not been cross-examined. It had all been "just a friendly chat".

This was how it went:

"What time was it that you served dinner?"

"At seven-fifteen sharp, sir."

"Had Mrs. Faversham any reason for being so punctual?"

"Only the television, sir. When she was going to watch, she liked to be settled down in her arm-chair in time for the play."

"Miss Wells dined with her?"

"That's right, sir."

"Can you remember the menu?"

"It was very simple, sir. A cheese *soufflé*, some blue trout, and a compote of pineapple. They drank a Traminer '39."

Mr. Green gave a little sigh of appreciation. "I remember it," he said. "Did you notice anything unusual while you were serving dinner?"

"No, sir. Mrs. Faversham was in very good spirits. At the end of dinner she lifted her glass to Miss Wells and she said: 'Only two days more!'"

Waller leant forward. "What did she mean by that?"

"I gather that she was referring to the moonflower, sir, and the time it was supposed to blossom."

"Undoubtedly," said Mr. Green. "Did they have coffee?"

65

"Only Miss Wells, sir. Mrs. Faversham never took it."

"Those were my orders," observed the doctor. "With her blood pressure, coffee would have been poison."

Mr. Green nodded. "Quite." He turned to Dr. Rudyard. "I suppose you had prescribed a sleeping draught?"

The doctor raised his eyebrows. "Yes. She took it in the form of drops."

Mr. Green turned back to Ackworth. "What happened after dinner?"

"I cleared away at seven forty-five. When I looked in, ten minutes later, they were both sitting by the fire with the lights out, waiting for the play to begin."

"Did Mrs. Faversham say anything?"

"Not to me, sir. But to Miss Wells she did. 'Two days more!' she said again."

"An obsession," grunted Waller.

"What was the next time you remember?"

"Just after nine o'clock, sir. Mrs. Ackworth and I have our television in the servants' hall, and we were watching too. Then suddenly it broke down. I didn't know whether it was just our set that was wrong, so I went along to the drawing-room. Theirs had failed too. They'd switched on the lights and were sitting in front of the empty screen. Just as I came in, the programme started again. Mrs. Faversham turned to me and asked me to bring her in a glass of hot water, as she wanted to take her sleeping draught."

"Was that the usual time she took it?"

"She had no fixed time, sir. Sometimes she'd take it immediately after dinner, sometimes she'd wait till she went to bed. It depended on the way she was feeling."

"When you brought the hot water, who poured out the sleeping draught?"

"Miss Wells, sir."

"Was it the usual amount?"

"I have no means of saying, sir."

The doctor looked up. "Are you suggesting that Miss Wells inadvertently poured out an overdose?"

"Not at all. But I suppose it would be possible?"

66

"Quite. But hardly probable. She is a highly skilled nurse, and exceptionally conscientious."

"In any case," demanded Waller, "what has this got to do with the crime?"

"Very little, I should imagine," returned Mr. Green, with a bland smile. "But when one is trying to recreate the *atmosphere*. . . ." He returned to Ackworth. "And so Miss Wells gave Mrs. Faversham the sleeping draught. And she drank it. Did she say anything as she did so?"

"Yes, sir. The same thing, over again. 'Two more days!' "

"And then?"

"Well, sir, then she said good-night."

"And that was the last time you saw her alive? At about ten past nine?"

"It was, sir."

Ackworth folded his hands and lowered his eyes . . . a picture of well-trained grief.

Waller drew nearer to Mr. Green. "Is this getting us anywhere?" he muttered.

"I should think it highly improbable," murmured Mr. Green. "But if I *might* be allowed another two minutes?"

Waller snorted and withdrew.

"Now, Ackworth," he continued, "I want you to try to remember things very clearly. What time was it when you returned to the kitchen?"

"Just on a quarter past nine, sir. I'm sure of that because it was the beginning of the serial."

"You continued to watch till the end of the programme?"

"Yes, sir. That would be about ten-forty, when they gave the news."

"Did anything happen while you were watching? Were any bells rung, or anything like that?"

"No, sir. Nothing."

"No sign of anybody prowling about anywhere?"

"None, sir."

"What did you do when the programme was finished?"

"I went along to the drawing-room. Miss Wells was there."

"Alone?"

67

"Yes, sir. She told me that Mrs. Faversham had gone up to bed and didn't wish to be disturbed. And she said that if the telephone rang, she would answer it herself."

"The telephone? Oh—of course. I had forgotten. She was expecting a call from the inn."

"Yes, sir. Mrs. Keswick's baby."

"When did the call come through?"

"Just on eleven, sir. Mrs. Ackworth and I were going to bed. A few minutes later we heard Miss Sandra driving off in the Morris."

"I see. And after that, I imagine, you went to sleep?"

"I did, sir. It had been a long day, and I was dog-tired."

"Quite. Well, that seems very clear." Mr. Green turned to Waller. "I don't think we need trouble Ackworth any more?"

"Not on my account."

"Thank you, Ackworth. That will be all—for the moment."

"Thank you, sir." A pause. "By the way, sir, I wonder if you would advise me regarding the press. Three reporters have telephoned already."

Waller chuckled. "It doesn't take them long to get on the war-path. If they ring again, tell them I'll make a statement this evening."

"Very good, sir." Ackworth turned and left the room.

IV

When Ackworth had gone, Waller pushed aside his coffee-cup with an impatient gesture.

"Have you got enough 'atmosphere' for the time being?" he demanded.

"More than enough, thank you."

"In that case might we revert to the matter at hand?"

"By all means."

"Good. Then let us have a few facts."

68

"Ah! Facts!" echoed the doctor, crossing his legs and smacking his lips, as though a fact were some delicious form of edible.

"We'll begin with the people staying in the house. As you know, there were only two resident servants—the Ackworths. All the rest of the work was done by daily women from the village. Well, you've seen Ackworth and heard his story. And I've seen Mrs. Ackworth, who has no evidence to offer, apart from the fact that she was the first to find the body in the morning. That leaves four people—young Mr. and Mrs. Faversham, Hilary Scole and Pusey."

"But what *motive* . . ." began the doctor.

"Fifty thousand pounds' worth of jewellery might be considered a motive," retorted Waller. "To say nothing of the will. As far as *that* is concerned, we shall have to await the arrival of Mr. Pusey, who is the only one who knows its contents."

"I still find it inconceivable that Kenneth or Beryl. . . ."

"That is unfortunate," snapped Waller, "for I shall have to ask you to conceive it. In a case like this we must begin by assuming that all these four people desired Mrs. Faversham's death, and did their utmost to contrive it. May I continue? Thank you. We were considering the two young Favershams, Hilary Scole, and Pusey. Well, for the earlier part of the evening, their movements are quite clear. They all left the house at seven o'clock to drive to Lady Pendlebury's; they all dined with her at eight; and they all went on to the dance at Launceston at nine-thirty. The first person to leave the dance was Kenneth, shortly after eleven."

"Why did he leave so early?"

"I don't know. He just told me that he was bored, but I don't believe him. Perhaps Pusey will be able to help us there. At any rate, he got home at midnight and went straight to bed."

"Do you believe that?" asked the doctor.

"I have no reason to think otherwise."

"Did he see anything or hear anything during the night?"

"He says not."

"Who were the next arrivals?"

"Pusey and Scole. They left the dance at about midnight —they can prove that, of course—and arrived here shortly after one. The same story. Up to bed. Nothing unusual."

"And Beryl?"

"She was the last. She stayed till the end, and some friends drove her back. They dropped her at the bottom of the drive at about four o'clock."

"Why at the bottom of the drive?"

"She said that the sound of the car on the new gravel might wake people up."

Mr. Green looked up. "That was most considerate of her."

"Quite," returned the superintendent.

"And she too went straight to bed, and slept the sleep of the just?"

"So she says."

"Do you believe her?"

"I do not."

"Why not?" It was the doctor who asked the question.

"I don't know. Maybe you'd call it instinct." He looked across at Mr. Green. "My old friend might be able to explain. He's listened to almost as many liars in his lifetime as I have myself. After some years at the job you get to know the genuine article. She was 'lying in her throat' as they say in the Old Testament. And she was scared stiff into the bargain."

There was a long pause. The wind was rising swiftly and the sky was darkening. The doctor shivered and rose to switch on the lights.

"It is fantastic," he said. "Beryl of all people!" He sat down again. "Have you interviewed the outdoor servants?"

"How many are there, by the way?" inquired Mr. Green.

"Wilburfoss, the head gardener, who lives with his wife in the stable buildings. And young Meadows, his assistant, who has rooms over the coach-house. The other gardeners, three of them, come from the village, like the daily women.

I've got a man checking up on their movements."

"No evidence from any of them?" inquired the doctor.

"Not a thing. The same old story. Silence. Sleep. You'd think the place had been a sanatorium, that night."

"Didn't even Wilburfoss have anything to say?"

Mr. Green sat up sharply. "Why Wilburfoss in particular?"

"Really!" The doctor gave a high-pitched laugh. "Surely I do not have to tell you that he and Mrs. Faversham were lovers?"

"What's that?" The explosion came from Waller; Mr. Green merely blinked.

"Oh dear! Have I said the wrong thing?" The doctor flicked a speck of dust from his lapel, in affected embarrassment. "It was all a long time ago, of course. I shouldn't imagine that there had been any . . . how shall I say? . . . any passionate relationship for at least ten years. But it was quite a scandal in London, at the time."

"Well, of all the. . . ." Words failed the superintendent. He swung round and faced Mr. Green. "I suppose you're going to tell me that you suspected this all the time?"

Mr. Green dropped his eyelids modestly. "Not at all. At least, not precisely."

"What do you mean . . . not precisely?"

"I mean that I *did* happen to remark . . . I think it was when I was talking about Wilburfoss to Mr. Scole . . . I *did* happen to remark that he might have sat for Praxiteles."

"And who the devil is Praxiteles, when he's at home?"

Mr. Green heaved a deep sigh. "For the moment," he said, "he appears to be the only person whom we have mentioned who quite definitely did not kill Mrs. Faversham."

v

Waller rose to his feet and strode across to the window. "It's growing darker," he muttered.

"In more senses than one."

The doctor gave a nervous giggle. "I do hope I haven't

71

been indiscreet. I wasn't suggesting that Wilburfoss *did* it."

Waller looked at him impatiently, but did not reply.

"It would be much more likely to be *Mrs.* Wilburfoss," he continued, still in the same high-pitched, nervous voice. "She obviously knew all about the affair. And she hated Mrs. Faversham. Even though she was thirty years younger, she was jealous of her."

Mr. Green looked up. "Are you sure of that?"

"Oh yes, quite sure. Madly jealous. Mrs. Faversham used to make naughty little jokes about it to me. (She used to speak to me a great deal more openly than to any of the others. Women like that always imagine that a doctor has no sensibilities.) Whenever she referred to Mrs. Wilburfoss she called her 'my hated rival'. One day she said 'I'm sure she'll put poison in my tea'. Not that she was afraid of her . . . it just amused her to see her suffer. She often used to send for Wilburfoss in the morning, when she was still in bed, and keep him there, talking about the garden, much longer than was necessary. Simply to put ideas into Mrs. Wilburfoss's head."

Mr. Green wrinkled his nose. "How extremely unpleasant."

"Yes, wasn't it? Considering her age and her position and everything. She wasn't really a very nice person, you know. All the same, I somehow don't feel that Mrs. Wilburfoss actually strangled her, do you?"

"I have hardly had time to give the matter serious consideration."

"Of course, she *could* have done it. She is as strong as a horse, and anybody could have climbed up that wistaria outside the window. What do *you* think, Superintendent?"

Waller did not appear to hear him. "There's a car coming up the drive," he exclaimed. "It looks like Pusey's. Yes, it is." He turned to Mr. Green. "Come along; let's go and meet him; he's the most important witness of the lot."

"Why is that?" demanded the doctor.

As though he were brushing away a tiresome fly, Waller retorted: "Because he's got the will."

"Ah! The will!" The doctor picked up a *marron glacé* from a silver tray and protruded a small pink tongue at it, before biting it in half. "Yes," he murmured, as he munched, "I expect that will be *full* of surprises!"

It was.

5

Looking back on the Faversham case in after years, Superintendent Waller always remembered his interview with Mr. Pusey as the moment in which the whole drama came to life and took a definite shape and purpose. Till then, a confused mass of figures had been drifting aimlessly on a darkened stage. Suddenly, certain individuals were spot-lit from above, subjected to a pitiless scrutiny. At last he had something definite to follow.

As soon as he had marshalled him into the library, followed by Mr. Green, he set him down in front of the fire, took out his notebook, and proceeded to subject him to a rigorous cross-examination.

He began with a polite skirmish.

"I hope, sir, that your business in Exeter was brought to a successful conclusion?"

Mr. Pusey made a deprecatory gesture. "I could hardly describe it as concluded. The Faversham interests. . . ."

"I gather that you have been in touch with the Stock Exchange?"

"With Mrs. Faversham's brokers, yes. We were able to dispose of a number of important holdings at a very satisfactory price before the news of her death was known to the Market."

"Did the news have much effect on the value of her securities?"

"Less than I thought. It is all sound stuff. However, I flatter myself that by taking prompt action this morning I have saved her estate over £50,000. Which will come in very handy when we are paying death duties."

"My congratulations. And now, there are some questions I should like to ask you about the will."

Mr. Green leant forward. "If I might interrupt for a

74

moment . . . are we right in assuming that the will was kept in the wall safe behind Mrs. Faversham's bed?"

"Yes. Together with her jewels. She had it specially installed for that purpose. Very foolishly, in my opinion."

"Were there any other papers in the safe?"

"I couldn't say. Even if there were, they could hardly have been of comparable importance."

"No?" queried Mr. Green. "No?" He seemed to be addressing the question to himself.

"Well really, my good fellow, what other document *could* have compared in importance?"

Mr. Green nodded, and studied his fingernails. "As you say," he murmured.

"May we continue?" Waller's voice had an edge of irony. He was impatient with Mr. Green for wandering, so obviously, from the point. "What was the date of this will?"

"It was made last August, immediately after Mrs. Faversham's serious illness. As soon as she was well enough to attend to business, she sent for me."

"There was no other will?"

"None."

"Could you recollect the terms?"

"I could, but I see no reason to do so."

Mr. Green leant forward. "It might be of great assistance to us if we knew them."

Mr. Pusey hesitated, then he beamed and nodded. "Very well. If *you* say so, Mr. Green. As one gentleman to another . . . eh?"

Mr. Green winced. He glanced at Waller to see how he was responding. To his relief, he was answered by a cheery wink.

"Quite," he said.

"It was a complicated document," continued Mr. Pusey, "but there were only six principal beneficiaries. Firstly Kenneth, and secondly, in the event of his decease, his wife. Thirdly, Hilary Scole, fourthly Dr. Rudyard, fifthly Mr. Wilburfoss and lastly . . ." he toyed for a moment with his monocle . . . "and lastly myself."

75

"May we have some idea of the respective amounts?"

"Kenneth receives precisely what he was obliged by law to receive, under the will of her late husband. Not a penny more."

"How much is that?"

"The estate of Candle Court and its contents. And approximately half a million in securities."

"That should keep the wolf from the door," grunted Waller.

Mr. Pusey shot him a reproving glance. "It will be considerably reduced by death duties."

"And the others?" prompted Mr. Green.

Mr. Pusey appeared to suffer from a momentary embarrassment. Then he said: "Fifty thousand apiece, with the exception of Wilburfoss, who receives ten."

There was a moment's silence. Neither Mr. Green nor Waller could think of any tactful comment with which to greet this revelation.

"The other legacies," continued Mr. Pusey, "are mainly to charitable institutions, botanical societies, and the like. They amount to well over a hundred thousand pounds. There will be more than enough to cover that."

"Is Miss Wells a beneficiary?" Again it was Mr. Green who spoke.

"No, she is not."

Waller frowned at Mr. Green. Why should the little man keep wandering from the point?

"Well, sir," he said, "that was very helpful."

"In the sense that you now know that six of us had an excellent motive for murdering Mrs. Faversham?"

"Indeed, sir. . . ."

"Ha! Ha!" Mr. Pusey's laugh was forced and stagy. "You must forgive my little joke. Is that all you wanted to know?"

"No. It is not."

"Of course . . . my movements. They are quite simple, and easily verified."

"I have already verified them, up to the time when you arrived at the ball. I am more interested in the later hours of the evening. I believe that Mr. Faversham was the first to leave?"

"Yes. At about eleven."

"Did he give any reason for going so early?"

Pusey hesitated for a moment. "He was in an extremely bad temper. There had been some sort of argument with one of the stewards about paying for the tickets . . . but I don't suppose that would interest you."

"It would interest *me* very much," said Mr. Green softly.

Waller heaved a deep sigh. There he was . . . interrupting again!

"It was a pitiful little business," explained Pusey. "The tickets were half a guinea each. Apparently he thought that his mother had paid for them, but she hadn't. She was inclined to be . . . er . . . careful, about matters like that. When the steward came up and asked for the money, he hadn't got enough. I suppose he felt humiliated."

"Not unnaturally. Had he taken much to drink, by the way?"

"He has a very strong head."

"Yes. But was he drunk?"

"I should prefer not to commit myself, beyond saying that if I had taken as much myself, I should have hesitated before attempting to drive home."

"Thank you."

Waller took up the thread. "You left the dance at midnight, with Mr. Scole?"

"That is so. Beryl . . . Mrs. Faversham, I should say . . . stayed till the end, as I believe you know."

"Was Mr. Scole's behaviour in any way unusual?"

"In no way. He was greatly fatigued, and slept most of the way. The drive was quite uneventful. We arrived here shortly after one. And we went to bed."

"And then?"

"What usually happens when one goes to bed?"

Waller gave a polite smile. "And then?" he repeated.

Pusey did not answer, nor did he look at Waller. He stared straight ahead of him, as though he were pondering some course of action. His eyes were clear and keen, in spite of the pouches beneath them.

"And then . . ." he began.

He rose to his feet. "I would like a moment to think. And I might think more clearly if we had some fresh air." He strode across the room, pulled back the curtains, and pushed up the window with an impatient gesture. The sound of the falls, which had been a muted undercurrent to the conversation, flooded into the room, clear and strong. They had a dark, angry note, cold and cruel, harsh and hard and relentless—as though they had some bitter tale to tell, and were speeding on their way to tell it.

"If only," thought Mr. Green, "if only one could read the language of the waters!"

Then Pusey turned and spoke.

II

"It will all have to come out sooner or later," he said, "so there is no point in prolonging the agony. I need hardly say that I speak with reluctance. However. . . ."

He sat down, leant back, and ran his hands through his hair. It was the action, not of a *poseur,* but of a man who was genuinely puzzled. He had suddenly become human.

"When we entered the house," he continued, "I was immediately struck by something unusual. Mrs. Faversham's dog—or rather, the absence of Mrs. Faversham's dog. It was a small but extremely alert Pekinese which she had christened King Kong. It usually slept in the corridor connecting the main hall with the annexe—a strategic position in which it was monarch of all it surveyed. Last night it was not there.

"I was puzzled by this, but I did not attach much importance to it at the time. I imagined that Mrs. Faversham might have taken it to sleep in her room, for a change . . . particularly as she knew there was a dangerous convict at large in the neighbourhood.

"I said good-night to Hilary, who went straight to bed.

He looked desperately tired, and I fancy he had a touch of fever. Then I went up to my room . . . the yellow room. It is by far the most beautiful bedroom in the house, and was previously occupied by Beryl and Kenneth, but for some reason or other they had grown tired of it, or so Mrs. Faversham told me. I fancy it is more likely that they had grown tired of one another. At any rate, Kenneth had moved to the Chinese room at the end of the corridor.

"I slipped on a dressing-gown and went along to see him. You must remember that I was anxious because of the mood, and the condition, in which he had left the dance. I was afraid that he might have done something foolish—woken up his mother, made some scene. I wanted to reassure myself.

"I knocked at the door. There was no reply. I knocked again. Then I opened the door and switched on the light. He was not there. The room was empty, and his bed had not been disturbed."

He broke off suddenly, and looked across towards the open window. "That damned waterfall," he muttered, as though to himself. "On and on and on. . . ."

"I will close the window," said Mr. Green. He went across and did so. The angry clamour faded into a dark muttering of liquid voices.

"Thank you," said Pusey. "I am sorry to seem temperamental, but water in such large quantities. . . ." He gave an apologetic smile. "Which reminds me that I would very much like a drink." He rose and helped himself to a whisky and soda. "Will either of you gentlemen join me?"

They shook their heads. He swallowed his drink and continued. . . .

"Looking back on all this—and particularly on what I am about to tell you—it seems to me incredible that I did nothing about it. I had not the excuse of telling myself that Kenneth might have been delayed, that his car might have broken down; the Rolls was standing outside the front door when we returned. He had certainly come home, but he had disappeared. Yet I did nothing."

79

"What could you have done?" interposed Mr. Green, kindly.

"I am glad you asked that, because it was the question I asked myself. I suppose I might have gone in search of him, but what would have been the point of that, even if I had found him? If he had decided to quarrel with his mother, the damage would already have been done, and I should only make it worse. If he had not, if he had merely gone out to cool his temper, so much the better. I hoped that was in fact what he had done. I still hope so. Indeed, I believe so. I should like to make that quite clear, Inspector."

"Quite clear, sir." Waller's tone was very dry.

"In any case, I did nothing about it. I went back to my room, and got into bed. But I could not sleep. The whole evening had been too upsetting. When I heard the stable clock strike two, I switched on the light and began to read. I read for an hour. The clock struck three. I became impatient. I decided to force myself to sleep. I thought that perhaps the sound of the falls would help me—besides the room was stuffy—so I went to open the window. As I did so, I looked out, over the terrace and on to the valley. It was a brilliant night and the moon was riding high. The air was as clear as crystal, you could see every branch of every tree in the woods. And in the shadow of the woods I saw . . . I saw Beryl."

"How did you recognize her, sir, at that distance?"

"She was wearing the scarlet cape that she had worn to the dance."

"What was she doing?"

"Nothing at all. She was standing still, as though she were waiting for something."

"People usually are," murmured Mr. Green, "when they stand still. Which is all too seldom."

Waller tapped his pencil impatiently. "But what could she have been waiting for?"

"It is your function to discover that, not mine," retorted the lawyer.

"Did you make any movement . . . call out to her?"

"Certainly not. For one thing, she was at least fifty yards away, and she would not have heard my voice above the falls. For another, it was none of my business." He gave Waller a glance of defiance. "I had no reason to suppose that a tragedy was about to take place, if indeed it had not already taken place."

"So what did you do?"

"I went back to bed, and fell asleep."

"And then?"

"I was awakened—it was just after four—by gravel being thrown up at my window. I got up and looked out. . . ."

"Did you switch on the light?" It was Mr. Green who spoke.

"As it happened, I didn't. It is hardly of any consequence, is it?"

Mr. Green resisted the temptation to retort that he was not in the habit of asking questions of no consequence.

Pusey continued. "There she was again, standing under the window. I put on my dressing-gown and hurried down to let her in."

"How was she . . . I mean . . . did she appear in any way unusual?"

"Yes, she did. She appeared astonished."

"That, of course, was to be expected." Mr. Green murmured this cryptic remark so softly that the others did not hear him.

"Astonished?" echoed Waller.

"Exactly. She stared at me as though she had seen a ghost. Then she pulled herself together, said something about forgetting her latchkey, and being sorry that she had woken me up."

"Did you ask her where she had been in the last hour?"

"I did not. It was none of my business, as I said before. Besides, there was no time. She said good-night, and went straight upstairs."

"To her own room?"

"Presumably. I did not follow her, if that is what you mean."

81

"And that was all, until the morning?"

"That was all. If I may be forgiven for saying so, it was quite enough."

Waller made a final note, and put away his book. He turned to Mr. Green. "Well," he said, "after that, I suppose you know most of the answers."

"Hardly. What is even more important, I do not yet know most of the questions. But there is one question I would like to settle at once, for my own peace of mind." He turned abruptly to Pusey. "Was it a *nice* little dog? I did not see it when I came over to luncheon yesterday."

"What? King Kong? No. It's a perfect beast of a dog. It's always yapping and snarling at everybody."

Mr. Green sighed heavily. "Still, a dog is a dog. And death is death."

"You talk as if the dog had been murdered, too," grunted Waller. "It's probably gone off rabbiting."

"If there were rabbits in the Elysian Fields," observed Mr. Green, "I should be inclined to agree with you."

Which was his sole, and not very helpful, contribution to the solution of the problem.

6

IT IS usually said of great men of research—whether in science or in crime—that they "never leave anything to chance". Mr. Green was not of this school of thought; he left much to chance. Chance, to him, was the supreme improviser, to whose tunes it was well worth listening; no man could tell down what strange and often rewarding avenues they might lead him. A flying feather, borne on the wind over a summer field, might conduct him to romance, to tragedy, even to death. It might also, of course, do none of those things; it might merely land in a bed of thistles. Still, one would have had the pleasure of the chase, and there were times when Mr. Green felt that the pursuit of feathers, drifting over summer fields, was more honourable than some of the races in which mankind had been lately engaged.

It was a feather that he followed on this occasion . . . or rather, a kitten chasing a feather.

It was on the following morning. The day was sullen and overcast, with a rising wind. At ten o'clock he had accompanied Waller to Candle Court—not because he had any definite role to play, but because Waller had insisted on it.

"I don't mind telling you," growled the superintendent, as they panted up the hill, "that this case has got me flummoxed. I don't even know where to begin. Let alone what to believe." He shot a side glance at Mr. Green. "I suppose *you've* got everything nicely labelled already?"

"Then you suppose too much," retorted Mr. Green. "I have nothing labelled. I mistrust labels, at this stage of the game; they usually send one to the wrong address."

"Who would *you* get working on, if you were me?"

"If I were you? That is an impossible assumption."

"But seriously?"

Mr. Green's forehead creased into a frown, as he tried to think of himself stepping into Waller's shoes. The conception refused to materialize; they were two totally different people, physically and spiritually. A graph of Waller's progress, in any case he was investigating, would have shown a series of firm, straight lines, drawn with military precision along certain well-defined routes. In the majority of cases these lines converged into the scene and author of the crime; but there were occasions when they went completely off the map. A graph of Mr. Green's progress, on the other hand, would have shown a strange collection of zigzags, leading in no specific direction, and often only faintly pencilled in. But invariably . . . for he had never known a failure . . . these febrile tracings were linked together in the final stages, knitting themselves into an ineluctable web, in the centre of which, at last, the culprit was discovered, like the last stroke in a design of exquisite delicacy.

How could he suggest such comparisons to his old friend? If he were Waller, indeed! The idea was grotesque. Yet he did not wish to offend him.

"If I were you," he said at length, "I do not think that I should actually 'work' on anybody at all. Have you seen young Mrs. Faversham since we talked to Pusey?"

"No. I was going to try to talk to her this afternoon."

"And challenge her with Pusey's statement?"

"Naturally."

"I think you would be ill-advised. She will only deny it."

"Maybe she will. But sometimes one can learn as much from a denial as from a confession."

"That is true."

"All the same, I suppose you're right. You usually are. It's your old technique . . . keeping the suspect guessing."

"Do you regard her as a suspect?"

"They're *all* suspects. There was no love lost between Kenneth and his mother. Nor between Beryl and her mother-in-law. As for Pusey and Scole . . . Pusey knew the contents of the will, and Scole must have had a pretty clear idea—apart from the little matter of the jewellery. Then

84

there's the doctor. Not a pleasant type at all, and quite capable of shinning up a wistaria, with malice aforethought. Entirely apart from Wilburfoss . . . which brings in the *crime passionel*, and Mrs. Wilburfoss, the woman scorned. Hell! It's getting more like a whodunnit every minute."

"You have omitted one person."

"Who?"

"Sandra."

"I omitted her for the same reason that I omit yourself. When that old woman was strangled, Sandra was half a mile away. Can anybody deny that?"

"No."

"*You* certainly can't. She was practically lying in your arms all that night."

"There is no occasion to be ribald. She was doing nothing of the sort. She was being an extremely efficient midwife."

"Then why pick on her?"

"I merely fancy that she has something to tell us."

"O.K. I'll get cracking on her."

Mr. Green sighed, very audibly.

"Well, what's wrong with *that*?"

"Nothing, my dear Waller, nothing. It was just your phrase —'get cracking'. I would ask you to remember that you cannot open the mind of a woman with a jemmy."

"Meaning that you'd prefer to keep her to yourself?"

"Not at all. My position in this affair is far too invidious."

The superintendent kicked a stone out of his path. He felt, as he had so often felt in the past, an urgent desire to take his old friend by the shoulders and shake him till he rattled . . . till something came out of him . . . till the penny dropped. However, such a procedure would have been a proof of his own inferiority. Besides, for once in a way, Mr. Green might not have picked up the penny.

They had reached the entrance to the drive. The house looked gloomy and forbidding with its drawn blinds.

"Well, here we are. I'm going to have another talk to Ackworth. I fancy he may have a few things to tell me about young Mr. Kenneth's past life. Want to come along?"

"I should prefer to leave it to you."

"What have you got up your sleeve, you old rascal?"

"Nothing," replied Mr. Green, in all innocence. "Nothing at all. I merely have a fancy to listen to the falls."

II

But he did not listen to the falls, for a feather blew across his path, and in its wake was a kitten with a crooked tail, and he noticed that the kitten was pitiably thin.

Now Mr. Green was one of those pleasant old gentlemen who liked his kittens fat; he liked them to be bulging and bursting with the good things of the world; a thin kitten was to him a challenge, a call to action. So he followed it.

It darted round the corner of the house, still chasing the feather, with Mr. Green panting in its wake; the feather nearly came to rest in a puddle beneath the great arch that led to the stable buildings, but another puff of wind switched it along. Kitten and feather disappeared. A moment later Mr. Green was standing under the arch, very out of breath, staring about him.

Where had it gone? The stable premises were larger than one would have expected from the front of the house, for they stood on falling ground, and were partly concealed by the great conservatory. Their original function had long been forgotten, and to-day they were given over to purposes of horticulture; there were mushroom beds in the stalls where hunters had kicked their heels, and spades and flower-pots and bulbs in fibre where the stable-boys had slept.

It was—one would have thought—a kitten's paradise, with warm straw, and a hundred dark exciting corners in which mice might be lurking. And yet, the kitten had been terribly thin. Where had it gone?

Then he cocked his ears. From a doorway on the left he heard the voice of a young man.

"Sambo!" he was saying. "There's a good Sambo! Wait a minute, my pretty, it won't be long. Yes Sambo, it's rabbit, and it's all for you. There you are, Sambo."

There was the sound of a plate being set on the stone floor. Mr. Green stepped softly forward. What he saw gladdened his heart. The kitten was bent over a heaped-up plate of rabbit, which it was gobbling with ecstatic haste, its tail raised high in the air. Watching it was a figure in a green baize apron whom he recognized as Meadows, the young under-gardener who had accompanied Scole on his recent expedition. To his surprise he saw that he was engaged in cleaning boots.

The young man looked up and started violently. The tropics, thought Mr. Green, seem to play havoc with people's nerves. He must reassure him.

He stepped forward. "I very much approve," he said gently. "It was what I wanted to do myself."

Meadows blinked, as though he could hardly believe his ears. Mr. Green noticed, to his distress, that he was trembling.

"Did you call him Sambo?" inquired Mr. Green, trying to put him at his ease.

"Yes, sir," he stammered. "Nobody else calls him nothing, nothing except bad names. They don't feed him, neither."

"He looks very thin."

"Yes, sir. He's been gone away, these past few days. And I've been. . . ." He paused, and a flush spread swiftly over his pale cheeks. "I've been busy, busy—what with one thing and another." He bent down to give the kitten a stroke. "But it's going to be all right from now on, isn't it, Sambo?" His voice seemed to have an undertone of earnestness, as though he were indeed seeking an answer to the question.

"You seem to be pretty busy now," observed Mr. Green, glancing towards the pile of dirty boots.

"Yes, sir."

"I shouldn't have thought that was part of your job."

"It's not, sir. It's not indeed. But. . . ."

He was interrupted by the sound of a woman's voice calling angrily across the yard. "How much longer are you going to be with them boots, Meadows?"

For a moment the young man did not reply. He stood staring straight ahead of him, his thin, dark face transformed by an expression of extraordinary malignancy.

"D'you hear me, Meadows?"

Still he stood there, a silent portrait of sheer hatred. Mr. Green studied him closely—noting every detail, the vein that stood out on his forehead, the tight pressure of the lips, the twitching muscle of his right arm, which was holding a black patent leather shoe whose heel was thickly coated with clay.

"D'you hear me, Meadows?"

He took a deep breath. "Yes, Mrs. Wilburfoss, I hear you."

"Are you getting on with them boots?"

"Yes, Mrs. Wilburfoss."

"Then look slippy about it."

There was the sound of a window closing, and silence for a moment. Then Meadows lifted his arm and hurled the shoe at the wall.

"One day," he muttered, "she'll go too far, that woman. She'll go too far!"

He turned in sudden dismay; he had forgotten that he was not alone.

"Beg pardon, sir," he stammered. "I don't know what's come over me to-day."

"That's quite all right," murmured Mr. Green in the gentlest of tones. "But you frightened Sambo, when you threw that shoe."

He pointed to the kitten, which had retreated behind a pile of boxes.

Meadows stepped across to the corner. He knelt down and flicked his fingers to the kitten. "Sambo . . . come, my pretty . . . come to me."

He is an endearing lad, thought Mr. Green, but he is very unhappy. He wondered why.

The kitten jumped into Meadows' arms, and was soon purring happily again.

"I wouldn't have frightened him, sir, not for anything.

But I've not been myself lately. Not since we got back."

"The change in the climate perhaps," observed Mr. Green, in so flat a voice that anybody who knew him would have realized that he was speaking for effect. "It must be very trying."

"Yes, sir."

"And that would not be the only change, of course," he continued. "Change of diet, change of soil. All very upsetting. Soil particularly. I imagine that the soil where the moonflower grows is largely decomposed leaf mould with a basis of spagnum?"

The young man looked up sharply. "Yes, sir," he began. "But there are other. . . ."

"Quite," interrupted Mr. Green. "Entirely acid, of course?"

"Yes, sir. As acid as you'll find."

"A sort of tropical edition of the soil you have around these parts?"

"That's right, sir."

"Ideal for rhododendrons, of course?"

"Yes, sir. 'Tis indeed."

Mr. Green sighed. "It makes me very envious. My own garden has veins of chalk. Not everywhere, but enough to make it impossible to grow rhododendrons. Or azaleas or ericas, or half the things I want to grow."

"That's bad, sir," said the young man, regarding Mr. Green with genuine sympathy. "If I ever had a garden of my own, I'd fly from chalk like the plague, I would."

"You would be well advised," said Mr. Green, "and from clay too, unless you had such a passion for roses that you never wanted to grow anything else. No clay about here, I suppose?"

"A few patches in the woods, sir," said the young man. "Up above the falls, where there's that clump of elms." He frowned and scratched his hand. "That's a tree I can't abide, sir."

"I wonder," murmured Mr. Green, "if you have the same aversion to it as I have?"

"Pardon, sir?" The young man's brow was deeply furrowed. He knew the old gentleman was not laughing at him. But he was not quite sure of the meaning of the word "aversion".

"Pardon, sir?" he repeated. He wished he was educated. He lowered his eyes, and went on cleaning the boots.

"All I know, sir," he said at length, "is that elm-wood's good for nothing. Except for making coffins."

Mr. Green nodded. "That was precisely what I meant."

Their eyes met . . . the old eyes and the young eyes, the calm, kind eyes, and the wild, frightened eyes, in which a flicker of hatred still lingered. But not hatred for Mr. Green; the young man felt, in a dim, instinctive way, that he had found a friend.

"I must be going now," said Mr. Green. "But perhaps we may meet again."

"I should like to, sir."

"I am sure there is a great deal you could tell me . . ." he paused for a fraction of a moment . . . "about your adventure."

"It would be an honour, sir."

III

The kindly features of Mr. Green, as he passed through the stable arch, and made his way towards the noisy river, were very grave indeed. In the last quarter of an hour he had changed his spiritual companions. He no longer walked with Chance—that airy and unpredictable divinity, tripping on light, fantastic toes; he was in step with Destiny, a lady of a very different aspect. For Destiny walked with feet of clay.

Literally, with feet of clay. The same clay as he had noticed on the heel of the shoe which that poor, frightened boy had been cleaning.

Well, if Destiny must be his companion, so be it. He would learn her purpose very soon.

The wind was rising every moment; he had to clutch on

to his old green hat. He turned sharp left, towards the granite bridge that spanned the falls. As he crossed it, the roar of the water was deafening.

He climbed the hill swiftly, with a surprising agility, brushing aside the sweeping branches of the rhododendrons and the wild azaleas. He was in search of different flora. He found it on the crest of the hill. There was a little clearing where, of a sudden, his feet struck harder ground. The soft, spongy leaf mould met a streak of clay. The rhododendrons and azaleas faltered, drew back, died . . . leaving the soil to a clump of dark, stocky elms, through whose ugly branches the wind clamoured in a wild lament.

Yes, he knew what he wanted. It was all too obvious. A little patch of newly turned earth, of freshly stamped elm-leaves. Most of them had blown away. What fools men were!

He knew what he would see. It was hardly worth while turning the earth. It would only hurt him. But he supposed he had better turn it.

He knelt down, and his podgy little hands delved into the cold, clinging soil. They touched something. He shuddered. He braced himself. Evidence was evidence. He delved deeper. The last layer of soil was thrown away. He looked down. He saw what he had known he would see. A patch of beige fur . . . a spot of red on a broken neck.

Mr. Green made a last sweeping gesture. The mound of earth tumbled in. He rose to his feet and stamped on the earth. He had a ludicrous feeling that somebody, somewhere, should be whispering . . . "ashes to ashes, dust to dust".

For after all, a little dog is a little dog. Even if it had not always been a very nice little dog.

7

MR. GREEN went straight back to the inn. He felt that this latest development should be put before Waller without any further delay.

The train of argument seemed childishly simple.

(a) On the night of the murder, the dog had been buried by a man wearing patent leather dress shoes.

(b) Presumably the man who had buried the dog was also the man who had killed it.

(c) Presumably, again, the man who had killed the dog had done so for a definite reason, of which the most obvious seemed that it had disturbed him, or might have been expected to disturb him, in some criminal undertaking.

(d) There were only three men wearing patent leather dress shoes on the night in question, Kenneth, Hilary and Pusey. According to Pusey, Hilary went straight to bed in a state of exhaustion. Again according to Pusey, he himself went straight to bed.

That left only Kenneth.

What could be more convincing?

However, Mr. Green did not like his solutions to come too easily; not because he enjoyed the exhilaration of the chase but because . . . well, life was not like that. Life did not run in straight lines.

Consider (b). Why, for example, was it so certain that the man who had buried the dog had also killed it? Why was it so impossible that two men might not have been working in conjunction?

Consider (d). They had only Pusey's word for it that Hilary had gone straight to bed . . . or for that matter, that he had gone to bed himself. Of course, there was his story of seeing Beryl, and if that could be proved it would lend strength to his assertions.

But he was not at all inclined to take Mr. Pusey's word as though it were Holy Writ. (Incidentally, he would very much like to have seen the contents of the suitcase which Pusey had taken with him on his trip to Exeter. It seemed a remarkably large affair if it contained only "papers"—as apparently he had told Waller.)

There was one thing about this dog business which disturbed him more than anything else. It was . . . how could he put it? . . . *emotionally* wrong. A man who had just committed a brutal murder of an old woman would not, surely, go to the pains of burying her dog? He would be more likely to throw it into the river, to put it behind a bush, or, for that matter, to leave it where it was.

So Mr. Green reasoned, as he walked back to the inn. His (*a*), (*b*), (*c*) and (*d*) were just a little too good to be true. They *seemed* to point to Kenneth, but they might in fact point to somebody quite different.

In order to make certain, he decided to employ a little conjuring trick, which he would use that night. He had been invited to dine at Candle Court—rather reluctantly, he suspected, by Kenneth himself. He had been inclined to refuse, for apart from Hilary he had little in common with the other members of the party. However, it would be different if he had a purpose, and the little trick would provide him with one.

It might, indeed, be quite diverting.

And now, to tell his tale to Waller.

II

But before he could speak to Waller there was another crisis to be surmounted.

As he entered the lounge, the young landlord hurried forward. He was evidently in a state of some agitation.

"Excuse me, sir, but were you going up to see Mr. Waller?"

"I had intended to, yes. . . ."

"Well, sir, I took the liberty of sending him to your room, seeing as it is a bit further from the missus. You see, sir, Mrs. Faversham arrived only five minutes ago, and she was in such a state that. . . ."

Even as he spoke there was the sound of angry voices from behind the door at the top of the staircase.

Mr. Green raised his eyebrows. "I will go up at once," he said.

When he opened the door, Beryl's anger seemed to fill the room. Women who are normally cold and restrained are especially alarming when they lose control of themselves, and Beryl was on the point of doing so.

"Don't tell me you can't sue the police for libel," she was crying, in choking accents, with her face so near to Waller's that her nose almost touched his chin.

"My dear madam," he began. Then he noticed Mr. Green standing in the doorway and an expression of ineffable relief spread over his features.

She turned. "Oh, it's you," she hissed. "Creeping in, as usual!"

"As this is my room," replied Mr. Green, in the mildest of tones, "it did not occur to me to knock."

"Who cares whose room it is?"

Mr. Green made no reply to this very rude question. He merely blew his nose. He was well aware that although a soft answer may turn away wrath, no answer at all is sometimes even more effective.

So it was in this case. His mildness, and his obvious determination to remain unmoved, began to act as a sedative.

"It's outrageous," muttered Beryl. "The whole thing."

Mr. Green nodded politely. "If you were thinking of sitting down," he observed, "the most comfortable chair is by the window."

She glared at him, but she sat.

94

"I am afraid that Mr. Waller will have to sit on the bed," he continued. "Those long legs of his! I myself shall be quite happy on this stool."

"You are very clever, Mr. Green," she remarked, with a sneer. "You have a way of treating every situation as though it were a tea-party."

"If that were true," he replied, unruffled, "I should regard it as a very high compliment. The standard of behaviour at tea-parties is usually excellent. And now, may I know to whom I owe the honour of this visit?"

She was about to speak, but he was looking pointedly at Waller.

"I've been following up Mr. Pusey's statement," he said. "I couldn't get this lady at the house, but I left a message for her, at which she seems to have taken offence. She followed me down here. As the argument was getting a bit heated in the bar parlour, I took the liberty of borrowing this room."

Mr. Green beamed at him. "With, I hope, fruitful results?"

"The lady has refused to make any statement at all."

"That's a lie," she exclaimed loudly. "I have made a very definite statement. I have stated that if I am accused of murdering Mrs. Faversham. . . ."

"There was no question of accusation. . . ."

Mr. Green held up his hand. "Please! At the end of the corridor there is a young lady nursing a baby. They are both trying to sleep."

His reproof had the required result. The ensuing dialogue, though tense, was no longer shouted.

Mr. Green continued: "I imagine that the point at issue is your own movements, between the hours of three and four on the night of the crime?"

She made no comment.

"And that Mr. Waller has informed you of Mr. Pusey's statement that he saw you, at three o'clock, standing in the garden?"

"Pusey!" she retorted contemptuously.

Mr. Green ploughed gallantly on. "And that it was not

95

till an hour later—that is to say, at four—that you signalled to his window and that he let you in? Do you deny that?"

"I do not deny that I entered the house at four."

"But you do deny that you were in the garden at three?"

She did not reply.

"She refuses even to comment on it," interposed Waller. "In her original statement, she told us that she returned from the dance at *four*. Naturally we had to check up on that. She was driven home by a Mr. and Mrs. Brockhurst, who stated that they dropped her at the bottom of the drive at *three*. So the evidence of Pusey and the Brockhursts. . . ."

She turned on Waller with extraordinary vehemence. "How *dare* you bring the Brockhursts into all this?"

"Really, madam, I have my duty. . . ."

She swept him aside. "Mrs. Brockhurst is the biggest gossip in the county. Apart from that, she absolutely loathes me. What she will be saying, I can't imagine."

Mr. Green suddenly realized that they were confronted with a situation which was by no means new to him in his career; it was a situation where the motivating forces were far more trivial than the circumstances would suggest. The violence of Beryl's reaction to Waller's inquiries was not—at least primarily—due to the fact that she was hiding a guilty secret. It was due to the fact that, in her opinion, Mrs. Brockhurst was a cat.

He raised his left hand, and behind it he managed to give Waller a wink that contorted his plump cheeks. One had to be rather obvious with the dear chap, when one was dealing with women.

"If I know the inspector," he said, "I should think it highly improbable that we have any trouble with the Brockhursts. I am sure that you cautioned her?"

Waller took the cue. "Naturally, sir."

A gleam of pleasure came into Beryl's eye. "You cautioned Eva Brockhurst?"

"Of course."

"As though she were a criminal, or something? Whatever did she say?"

96

Mr. Green intervened, for Waller might have found it difficult to reply to this question in the right mood.

"Whatever she may have said, I think we can be fairly certain that she will not say anything more. When the inspector gives people a warning, they usually heed it.

"And now," he continued, "as we were saying, you returned at three o'clock?"

III

There was an infinitesimal pause. It was as though she were reluctant to leave the subject of the possible humiliation of Mrs. Brockhurst. But there was something in Mr. Green's tone of voice.

"Yes."

"And you walked straight up the drive to the house?"

"No."

"Why not?"

She seemed to be wrestling with herself. Suddenly her mouth twitched into a smile. "I suppose I'd better tell the truth, though it will probably sound ridiculous. I wanted to see the falls."

"That does not sound at all ridiculous to me."

"Doesn't it?" she asked eagerly. "I'm glad. They can be incredibly beautiful by moonlight. All ghostly and silver. I've loved them all my life. You see I was born at Candle Court. The sound of the falls was the first music I ever heard. . . ." She stopped abruptly. "I'm sorry. You were asking for facts."

"You seem to be giving them to us." Mr. Green shot a warning glance at Waller, whose definition of "facts" was somewhat more solid than his own.

"So you went to look at the falls," he continued. "And after looking at them, you turned to go back to the house?"

"Yes."

"And . . . something happened?"

"Yes. I saw somebody."

A fact at last. Waller leant forward—a big, solid, black

shape, coming into the picture. Mr. Green surrendered the helm to him.

"You saw somebody?" he repeated.

She clenched her hands very lightly. Her resentment against the inspector was still alive. But she could not fight any longer.

"Yes. A man."

"Could you recognize him?"

"No. I was too far away."

"What was he doing?"

"He was hanging on to the creeper outside her window."

"Was he climbing up towards the window or down to the ground?"

"I didn't stay to see."

"You didn't stay to see?"

"No."

"So that for all you know, at that moment, he might not yet have committed the murder?"

"I suppose so."

"Mrs. Faversham might still have been alive?"

"Perhaps."

"And if you had raised the alarm. . . ."

She turned on him angrily. "It's all very well to say that now! But if I had raised the alarm I might have been murdered myself. For all I knew, it might have been that convict."

"What did you do when you saw this man?"

"I . . . I stepped back into the shadow of the trees."

"And then?"

"I tiptoed away down the path."

"You didn't stay to see which way he went?"

"No. I was terrified that he might see me standing there."

"Was that very likely, if you were in deep shadow?"

"Well . . . in any case, he might have come my way."

"To do so, he would have had to walk across the whole length of the lawn, which was in bright moonlight. Surely that was the last way he would have come?"

"I suppose so. But I didn't think of that at the time."

"Even if he had seen you, isn't it more likely that he would have made off into the woods, where it would have been almost impossible for you to follow him?"

"I really don't know. I . . . I couldn't say. It was all so unexpected."

"After you had tiptoed away, where did you go?"

"Further upstream."

"How far?"

"I'm not sure. It may have been a quarter of a mile."

"What did you do then?"

"I just sat down and waited."

"For how long?"

"For an hour—or so it seems."

"Why did you wait so long?"

"I wanted to be sure that the man wouldn't come my way."

"Is that the only reason?"

"What other reason could there be?"

Waller's honest face, as he looked at her, was unusually grave.

"Somebody has to make a very unpleasant suggestion at this point," he said. "And I suppose it had better be me. I am going to suggest to you, Mrs. Faversham, that the real reason you waited so long was because you wished this man —whoever it may have been—to succeed in whatever crime he may have been committing."

She made no answer.

"I am also going to suggest that you were not afraid of him, that you had no need to be afraid of him, and that in fact you wished him well."

She threw back her head. "And what if I did?"

She turned on Mr. Green. "I suppose you think that very terrible, don't you?"

Mr. Green merely sighed.

"All right. Perhaps it is. But I did wish him well. I didn't know that he was going to commit a murder. . . ."

"But if you had known, you would not have stopped him?"

99

"No," she cried bitterly. "I would not have stopped him. And if I were in the same position again, I would act in the same way."

She rose swiftly to her feet. "There! You've got what you wanted. I hope you're satisfied."

Mr. Green also rose. "There is just one small point," he said. "I understand that you returned to the house, without your key, and were obliged to throw gravel up to the window in order to gain admittance?"

"Yes."

"Why did you choose Mr. Pusey's window?"

"Because it was not Mr. Pusey's window at all. It was my window—our window." She spoke with heat. "I was born in that room. It is the most beautiful room in the house. It was because I loved it so much that Mrs. Faversham turned us out of it. She was that sort of woman."

"So you had forgotten—for the moment—that Mr. Pusey was sleeping in it?"

"Of course I had forgotten. Is that all?"

"As far as I am concerned, yes."

She turned to Waller. "What is the next step? When do you bring out the handcuffs?"

He did not see the joke. "We shall continue our investigations, madam."

"That will be jolly for everybody." She glanced at her watch. "I must be going. I'm sorry if I have seemed faintly hysterical, Mr. Green. But I'm not used to this sort of thing. By the way, you're dining to-night?"

"If I may."

"At eight o'clock. Black tie, if that's all right? Till then!"

Waller opened the door for her, and she went out.

IV

"We live and learn," said Waller, sitting down on the bed with a heavy sigh.

It still needed half an hour to luncheon. Mr. Green went

100

to the cupboard, and produced a bottle of Tio Pepe which he kept for "emergencies".

As they sipped it, he told Waller about the discovery of the dog.

Waller permitted himself a low whistle. "It looks as though we shall have to keep a weather eye on young Mr. Kenneth. You're sure they *were* his shoes?"

Mr. Green flushed faintly. Waller had put his finger on the one weak point of his argument.

"No, I am not," he said. And before Waller could protest ... "There was a pile of shoes and there were three pairs of patent leather shoes, all of the same pattern."

"Couldn't you have given them one of your celebrated sniffs?"

Mr. Green ignored this sally, which seemed to him extremely vulgar. "What is more," he said, "I was anxious not to arouse any suspicions in the mind of young Meadows. He might come in useful later on."

"How?"

"One never knows."

Waller merely grunted at this unhelpful observation.

"It seems to me that you're slipping," he said.

This was too much for Mr. Green, particularly as there was an element of truth in it. He *should* have found some excuse to examine the shoe and establish the identity of its owner. But he was only human, and he sometimes made mistakes. He also sometimes lost his temper.

"I do not think that you are the person to speak of slipping," he remarked.

"Why do you say that?"

"If I had been conducting this case I should not have permitted possible suspects to leave the house carrying suitcases large enough to hold the crown jewels."

It was Waller's turn to bristle. "Do you mean Pusey?"

"I do."

"How could I have stopped him?"

"Are the powers of the police so limited?"

Waller gave an angry snort—all the angrier because, in his

secret heart, he agreed with Mr. Green. That suitcase of Pusey's had worried him. It had certainly been big enough to hold, if not, the crown jewels, the safe containing Mrs. Faversham's. And he had permitted it to be carried off under his very nose.

"It's all very well for you to talk about the powers of the police," he retorted, "but you know quite well that they have to be exercised with discretion if we're ever going to get any results. I suppose that in theory I could have had everybody stripped naked the moment I got into the house. . . ."

Mr. Green suddenly smiled and lifted his glass.

"Let us call pax," he said.

"That's all very well, but . . ." then Waller too grinned. "O.K. You win."

"We neither of us win. I should certainly have noticed the shoe. You *might* have done something about the suitcase—though it would obviously have been embarrassing. However, I don't imagine that in either case our negligence will prove absolutely fatal. Another glass of sherry?"

"Not before lunch. Coming down?"

"I think not. I shall have some soda-water and a digestive biscuit up here."

Waller groaned, and went to the door. "By the way," he said, "Sandra Wells wants to see me this afternoon. Care to come along?"

"If you will allow me."

"I can't imagine it can be very important. But as you say, one never knows."

8

A FEW minutes after Waller had left, Mr. Green was called to the telephone.

It was Kenneth, speaking from Candle Court. "I say, old chap," he said. "I'm awfully sorry about this Beryl business."

Mr. Green murmured that it was of no importance.

"No, but really. She shouldn't have come down and made a scene like that. She's just told me all about it."

"The information she gave us may be very valuable."

"Let's hope so. All I mean is—carrying on like that makes it look as though we were hiding something. You don't feel that, do you?"

"Not at all."

"That's what I wanted to be sure about. I mean—I want you to feel that you can sleuth about here as much as you like, without bothering to ask me."

Mr. Green winced. The word "sleuth" was not one of his favourites.

"That is very kind of you. As a matter of fact there is one little thing I should like to do this afternoon."

"Yes?" Was it fancy, or did he hear Kenneth catch his breath?

"I should like to pay another visit to the moonflower."

"Oh, that old thing!" There seemed to be a note of relief in his voice. "I thought you meant something to do with the murder. By all means come and see it again, though I must say it's beginning to look like the morning after the night before. Would you like Hilary to be with you?"

"It would be a great privilege.'

"I'll tell him. Round about three? Good. And I say . . . you might say a word to Waller, about Beryl? That's a good chap. I'd hate him to get the wrong impression."

With which he rang off.

Mr. Green did not consider it necessary to pass on Kenneth's message to Waller. It would hardly be likely to modify the superintendent's "impression"—or indeed, his own.

II

Mr. Green's soda-water and digestive biscuits were soon disposed of, and since the rising wind had blown away the rain he decided to go up to Candle Court before three o'clock in order to familiarize himself once more with the terrain of this most elusive mystery.

He took a roundabout route, which he imagined must roughly coincide with the path followed by Beryl on the fatal night. It turned to the right at the bottom of the drive, followed a deep plantation of pines and wild rhododendrons, and emerged at the far end of the lawn, with the falls immediately ahead.

Yes, he thought to himself, the story certainly fits, as far as it goes. This is where Beryl would come out, and this is where she would stand. From here she would have a clear view of the window of the bedroom, and on the other hand, she would herself be plainly visible from Pusey's window.

And as Waller had pointed out, it would have been highly improbable that any criminal, even if he had noticed her, would have taken the risk of pursuing her across the open lawn, for he would have been in full view of any possible spectators.

On the whole, he was inclined to believe her story, as far as it went. That is to say, he did not as yet see any logical reason for doubting it.

He moved closer to the falls, until he was partly sheltered by the group of stable buildings which joined the domain of Wilburfoss. How enthralling was the rush of the water! The strong south-west wind swept through the pines and flecked the surface of the river with tiny silver feathers; and as the wintry sun peered through the clouds a tiny rainbow hovered on the edge. He could stay here for ever. . . .

Even as he toyed with this agreeable notion, he heard a shrill scream, borne on the wind. It seemed to come from behind the stables. He turned and ran in the direction of the sound, as swiftly as his short legs would carry him. So strong was the force of the gale that he was half-blinded, and it was not till he came to the great arch leading into the courtyard that he realized he had stumbled upon yet another tragedy, even if it was only a minor one.

He drew back into the shadow of the arch. It was an extraordinary scene that met his eyes. Against the door leading to the conservatory stood Wilburfoss, his face blazing with anger. In front of him, stepping in a tipsy sort of dance, was young Mrs. Wilburfoss, her arms on her hips, her hair streaming on the wind. As she danced, she sang, in a husky, drunken contralto . . .

> *Tom Pearce, Tom Pearce, lend me your grey mare,*
> *All along, down along, out along lee,*
> *For I want for to go to Widdicombe Fair. . . .*

A hiccup stopped her.

Wilburfoss raised his fist. "Get back in the house, damn you, get back in the house!"

She danced a step nearer. She was obviously very drunk, and Wilburfoss took a quick step forwards. His movement seemed to sober her.

"Touch me and I'll scream," she cried. "I'll scream louder than the falls!"

Wilburfoss looked round him apprehensively. Mr. Green, feeling acutely embarrassed, shrank further into the shadows.

"Want to see moonflower," she cried, in a whimpering tone. For a moment the fierce wind seemed to choke her.

"Want to see moonflower," she repeated.

"Get back," he shouted again.

She answered with another catch of the old song—

> *So Tom Pearce's old mare, her took sick and died*
> *All along, down along, out along lee . . .*

She broke into a shrill, choking laugh. "Her took sick and died. Ha, ha, ha . . . ho, ho, ho! Her took sick and died all right!"

Wilburfoss could stand no more. He ran forward and put one hand over her mouth and one hand over her wrist. But she was a big woman, and she had the unnatural strength of the drunkard. She struggled free, and stood there swaying, half-weeping, half-laughing, pointing her finger at him.

"I did it once," she screamed. "I'll do it again. You'll see . . ."

And once again. . . .

> But this isn't the end of this shocking affair
> All along, down along. . . .

And now Wilburfoss stepped forward and gave her a stinging slap on the cheek with the flat of his hand.

At the same moment, a fierce gust of wind blew over a sheet of corrugated iron which had been propped up against the wall where Mr. Green was standing. The din it made in falling caused them both to turn round sharply.

The woman, stung with pain and shocked by the sudden clatter stared wildly at Mr. Green, as though he were a ghost. And then she stumbled back into the house, with the insane laughter of one for whom all reason for laughter has been lost.

All this had happened in the space of a single minute.

III

Wilburfoss stood stock-still. He was not looking at Mr. Green. He had turned towards the house, as though to assure himself that his wife was safely inside.

Mr. Green, at that moment, was reminded of his first impression . . . "he might have sat for Praxiteles." There was something statuesque about his figure, so grave, so suddenly still. Were it not for the greying hair, he might have been a young man.

Then he came to where Mr. Green was standing.

"I feel a bitter shame about this, sir."

"Please do not distress yourself," murmured Mr. Green, who was looking greatly distressed himself. "I hope you do not think that I . . . that is to say, it was entirely by chance. . . ."

"I'm sure, sir. In any case, you'd have probably found out sooner or later."

Mr. Green nodded. "Perhaps I should," he said. "There is not much that you can tell me about drunkenness. My own father. . . ."

The eyes of the two men met. "So you know what it is?" he said.

"I know. It is the ultimate curse."

"Aye. It's that all right." He sighed deeply. "She's not often as far gone as this, and it's only once before that I've had to raise my hand to her. It's not so bad when she stays in the house. But these last few days have been a bit too much for her. She's got a lot of crazy notions in her head— about the flower, I mean. It's a bit of bad luck, you seeing her like that."

"I shall try to put it out of my mind."

"Will you, sir?" He looked at him keenly, and then he shook his head. "Aye, that's what you say now, sir. And it's mighty kind of you. But you don't strike me as a gentleman as would like to put a thing like that out of his mind."

Mr. Green could think of no convincing reply to this very true observation.

"You heard what she said, sir?"

"I heard her singing, yes."

"That wasn't what I meant, sir. I meant the other."

Mr. Green nodded.

"That must have sounded pretty queer to you, sir?"

"I can't say that I understood it."

"No, sir. But you might remember it, mightn't you?"

"I might."

"And you might connect it with . . . with the other business?"

107

Mr. Green made no reply. Everything that Wilburfoss was saying was perfectly true; but he liked the man, and at the moment he would have preferred to comfort him rather than to cross-examine him. Besides he was too emotionally disturbed, himself, to think clearly.

"Would it not be better," he said gently, "to talk about this at some other time?"

Wilburfoss looked him straight in the eyes. "You're a kindly man, sir," he said. "And I thank you for your consideration."

"There is nothing to thank me for."

"I beg to differ, sir. I know what you must be thinking . . . after what you heard."

Mr. Green gave a faint smile. "Then you know more than I know myself."

Wilburfoss ignored this little sally. "But I'd ask you to think twice, sir, before you start adding things up."

Mr. Green held out his hand. "I always think twice, Wilburfoss," he said. "And then . . . well, then I think twice again."

The grip he received made him wince. But he had a curious feeling that he had made a friend.

He turned, and made his way back to the great house, where Hilary Scole was waiting for him in the hall.

IV

It was one of Hilary's "bad days", and Mr. Green was shocked by his appearance; he had not realized how sick a man he was. His face was drained of all colour; even his lips were white. His hand, as he gave it to Mr. Green, was limp and hot.

"You are sure you feel up to this?" he asked.

Scole gave a faint laugh. "As much as I feel up to anything."

"But if you have a fever. . . ."

"I always have a fever. That is why I feel quite at home in hot-houses. Let us go straight inside."

108

They passed down the corridor. Nobody else was about.

Hilary threw open the door of the first house, paused for a moment to take a deep breath of the temperate air, and then led the way to the hot-house, the Holy of Holies.

And now Mr. Green had yet another shock. For the moon-flower did look, indeed, "like the morning after." The dark glossy leaves which he recalled, swirling upwards in an arrogant sweep of vitality, were lack-lustre and drooping. True, some new growth had started at the base of two of the plants, but it was feeble and sickly. Only one flower was in bloom, on the longest plant, but even this was pale and pinched, with only a trace of that miraculous silver sheen which had made the earlier flowers so memorable.

"But what has happened?" he exclaimed.

"That's what we'd all like to know." Scole sank heavily on to a chair which was a relic of the days when old Mrs. Faversham used to come and gloat over her treasures. "All I can say is, thank heavens I got a full collection of photographs when they were at their best."

"Did you expect anything like this?"

"Certainly not. Mind you, I didn't imagine that we'd keep up to the standard of the first blooming. This sort of plant never does. You probably know that from your own Morning Glories, of which the Moonflower is really only an exotic development. The later Morning Glories are never as fine as the first." He smiled. "There might be an idea for a lyric, there."

Mr. Green shook his head. "It is really . . . most, most disturbing. Has Wilburfoss any explanation?"

"None."

He bent down to examine the plants more closely. "One would almost think that they had been poisoned."

"I think one may leave that out of account. Wilburfoss is hardly likely to have watered them with weed-killer."

"Or subjected them to some sort of . . . of deliberate ill-treatment." He glanced up to the roof. "Could it be a question of a draught?"

"No. We've gone into all that."

Scole rose to his feet. "As a matter of fact the whole thing is even more mysterious than you yet realize."

"In what way?"

"Well, look around you."

Mr. Green peered through his glasses at some of the lesser glories of the house. For a moment his face registered no particular expression. Then he began to frown. "Dear me!" he murmured. He stepped to the door of the temperate house, took off his glasses, polished them, and put them on again. "Upon my soul!"

"Do you see what I mean?"

"I believe so. It isn't only the moonflower that is affected. Everything in the two houses looks . . . looks. . . ."

"Off colour?"

"Exactly. Even the bougainvilleas look unhealthy. And those beautiful silver ferns. . . . Could there be something amiss with the heating apparatus?"

"I fail to see how. It's extremely efficient and Wilburfoss is quite meticulous about that sort of thing. Besides, the mean level of the house must have been pretty accurate during the past five weeks."

"Why?"

"Because of the period of germination of the moon-flower. It was precisely as we expected, to within forty-eight hours. Admittedly, the actual *flowers* came out with a bit of a rush but. . . ."

He paused. "I say, is there anything the matter with your eye?"

Mr. Green had suddenly began to blink violently.

"Yes," he murmured, "I think I must have got something in it."

"Let me have a look."

Mr. Green submitted himself patiently, while Scole pushed up his eyelid. "Can't see anything," he said at length.

"Perhaps I was mistaken," said Mr. Green. "Perhaps it was merely the heat beginning to affect me. Would you mind if we went outside?"

110

V

They strolled back to the house, and after a desultory conversation, Scole went upstairs to rest. Mr. Green, encountering Ackworth in the hall, inquired if he might use the library for the next hour, to write a few letters.

"Yes, indeed, sir." Ackworth had a soft spot for the little man. "There's nobody in this afternoon, though Miss Wells will be back to see the inspector at five o'clock."

The library was very quiet, and was one of the few rooms in the house where the sound of the falls was heard only as a low murmur.

Mr. Green's suggestion that he wanted to write letters was only an excuse; in fact, he wanted to think. What a day it had been!

First, the encounter with Meadows, and the episode of the boots. And the look of extraordinary malignancy on Meadows' face when Mrs. Wilburfoss had called to him across the yard. And his muttered exclamation . . . "One day she'll go too far." Even at that hour of the morning, she must already have been drinking heavily. She was obviously a woman who might arouse very fierce emotions of hostility in any hot-blooded young man, particularly as—in her sober moments—she had a curious, smouldering sexual attraction. "One day she'll go too far." Was that remark fully explained by the mere fact of her drunkenness?

It might be. But again, it might not.

And then . . . the discovery of the dog. That had been a neat piece of work, he flattered himself, of quite a classical simplicity. However, he would never fail to reproach himself for failing to identify the shoe. That had been a blunder . . . of equally classical simplicity. He only hoped that he would be able to retrieve it this evening, with his little conjuring trick.

After that, the Beryl outburst. The more he thought about her story, the more he was inclined to believe it. For one thing, there was an element of the ridiculous in it, which could hardly have been invented. Her fury at Waller for checking her movements with Mrs. Brockhurst—"The biggest gossip in the county"—was patently genuine. And there had been nothing false about her confession that she had taken a fancy to look at the falls. It was the sort of thing she would do, for her feeling for Candle Court was akin to fanaticism. For that matter, it was the sort of thing he might have done himself.

Equally convincing had been her frank admission that she would have done nothing to prevent the murder of Mrs. Faversham—that in a negative way she actually connived at it.

And what was he to make of the Wilburfoss episode? And should he tell Waller about it? He supposed he ought to do; it would be unfair to keep it to himself. Up till now they had not seriously considered either Wilburfoss or his wife as possible suspects. Had they any right to dismiss them? After all, Wilburfoss was probably aware of the fact that he had been left a legacy. Ten thousand pounds was a great fortune to a man in his position—apart from the value of the jewels. Mrs. Wilburfoss would also, almost certainly, be aware of it. She was a passionate, powerful woman; she cherished a bitter hatred for Mrs. Faversham; and in moments of drunkenness she was obviously not quite sane.

Those words of hers rang through his brain. *"Her took sick and died."* It seemed pretty certain that they referred to Mrs. Faversham herself. And then . . . *"I did it once— I'll do it again."*

That was what worried him. The phrase sounded sinister; it had a ring of death; and it was quite evident that Wilburfoss himself was afraid of the interpretation he might put on it.

Waller—needless to say—would think the worst. "She was drunk," he'd say. "She couldn't be expected to choose her words. What she meant was that she'd killed one person and that she might kill another." He decided that he would not tell Waller—not yet.

Finally, the moonflower. And the bougainvilleas and

112

the silver ferns. And the strange sickliness of all these lovely things. Once more he began to blink. . . . Mr. Green's outward and visible sign of intense, inner cerebration.

At that moment the door opened and in walked Miss Sandra Wells, followed by Waller.

And once again, the whole story took a new twist.

9

WALLER, it may be remembered, had suggested that the interview with Sandra Wells would probably be only a "matter of form".

It proved to be anything but that.

To begin with, she insisted that it took place out of doors. She came into the room, wearing a tweed overcoat, and politely but firmly suggested that they took a stroll in the garden. When Mr. Green raised his eyebrows and looked out at the weather, which was rapidly worsening, she smiled and said: "It will do us good, Mr. Green. We all need a breath of fresh air."

"*Quite* so fresh, Miss Wells?"

"I think so, Mr. Green. Apart from that, walls have ears."

She waited, holding open the door. He realized that, in spite of her outward docility, this young lady had a will of her own. They followed her.

She led the way across the terrace and over the lawn, towards the low wall that gave on to the swiftly running river. When they reached it, she sat down and beckoned to them to follow her example.

"We can raise our voices here," she said, "without any fear of being overheard. And I have always hated talking in whispers." She turned to Waller. "Have you made any progress?"

"Very little, I'm afraid, miss. We were hoping you might help us."

"Have you any reason to suppose I could?"

"Yes, miss. Though it's a rather negative reason. You're the only member of the household who couldn't have committed the crime, even if you had wished to do so."

She nodded. "That thought had occurred to me."

"And also," added Mr. Green, "you are the only member

of the household for whom it seems impossible to imagine any sort of motive."

She raised her eyebrows. "Really? Does that mean that I'm the only person who has been left nothing in Mrs. Faversham's will?"

"I'm afraid so. Even the servants have legacies. Not you."

She sighed, and then shrugged her shoulders. "Oh well, it doesn't matter . . . though she did drop little hints that she wouldn't forget me, when the time came. I can't say that I set much store by it, because I never imagined that the time would come so soon."

"Are you quite sure you never imagined that, Miss Wells?" It was Waller who asked the question.

"What do you mean?"

"Were there not some occasions, in the past few weeks, when you felt that Mrs. Faversham's life was in danger?"

She paused for a moment. "Yes, there were."

"From whom?"

Again she paused. "If you are asking me who killed Mrs. Faversham, I cannot tell you. I can only tell you this. That on the night she was killed, there was a murderer staying in the house."

"I do not quite follow. . . ."

She faced him; her eyes were clear and unflinching. "A murderer staying in the house," she repeated. "A man who already had one death on his hands."

"And his name?"

"His name is Hilary Scole."

They both stared at her.

Suddenly she shuddered and put her hand over her eyes. "Now that I've said it, I wish that I hadn't. But what else could I do?"

"If you have proof of this allegation . . ." began Waller.

"Do I strike you as a person who would say such things at random?"

"Perhaps you would like to tell us the particulars?" suggested Mr. Green.

115

"That is what I came out here to do. That is why I wanted to be sure that we were not overheard."

She glanced over her shoulder at the great house, in which the lights were beginning to be lit. In the gathering twilight it had a curiously insubstantial quality, as though it were a mere façade, a painted screen, behind which men and women moved like shadows, holding their secrets to them.

"There is a light in his room," she whispered. "I wonder if he is watching us?" She saw that Waller was offering her a cigarette. "Thank you. That is just what I needed." Her hands did not tremble as she cupped them over the flickering match.

"This young lady has nerves," thought Mr. Green, "but she is certainly able to control them."

She drew her coat more closely round her. And she told her story.

II

"I don't know how well you knew Mrs. Faversham," she began. "I'm not sure how well I knew her myself. She wasn't a very nice person. I often used to wonder why I went on staying with her. I suppose it was because . . . well, she was fond of me in her way, and when one's been lonely for a long time, one welcomes any sort of affection. Apart from that, I was well treated and I lived in great comfort. And sometimes she amused me. She had a very pretty wit, at other people's expense.

"But sometimes she shocked me, too. There were . . . cruelties. I won't go into them; they're over and done with, now. But this particular cruelty is not over and done with.

"It was on the evening of 18th December. I am sure of the date because I remember saying to her that it was only a week to Christmas Day, and asking if I might have the next day off, as I hadn't had time to buy any Christmas presents. We were sitting by the fire after dinner, watching a very dull detective serial on the television. Suddenly she got up and switched it off. Then she asked me to fetch her bag from the next room. When I gave it to her she was chuckling to herself in a rather horrible way. She said: 'Sandra, darling, I've got something in here which is much, *much* more interesting than any murder on television. This is a *real* murder, my dear, and I want you to enjoy it with me.'

"Out of the bag she drew a letter. 'Read that to me,' she said. 'Read it aloud, my dear. I think it will amuse you.'

"I took the letter, thinking it was some sort of joke. It was written in green ink, in long, sloping characters, and some of the words were blurred and running, as though it had fallen into water. The writer had evidently been in great haste; some words were almost indecipherable, some were omitted altogether, but after a few sentences the general meaning was appallingly clear.

"I put the letter down. 'Who is this from?' I asked. Then she told me. Hilary Scole. I could hardly believe my ears. Hilary Scole! I said to her that I had better not read any more. 'Oh, but I insist,' she said. 'You read so prettily. And it's such a pretty story.' It was the sort of thing she *would* have said. So I read on."

She paused, and plucked at a patch of lichen on the rock. She seemed, for a moment, to be speaking to herself. "I wonder what would have happened if I had thrown that letter into the fire?"

III

"You read on?" prompted Mr. Green.

She recollected herself. "Forgive me. Yes. I read on."

"Can you give us an outline of the story?" asked Waller.

"I'm afraid that's all it will be—an outline. I suppose that if I were a heroine in a novel I should say that every word of it was engraved on my memory. That wouldn't be true. When I'm shocked or upset, words don't engrave themselves on my memory; they get confused and mixed up. But the main facts of the story are quite simple.

"Hilary Scole had murdered a native girl whom he had picked up on the expedition. It was at a village called

117

Rosaria, which is where they pitched their last camp before climbing the mountain where they found the moonflower. I looked it up, afterwards, on the map, but of course, it wasn't marked; all I can remember from the letter is that it was a group of huts on the banks of the Uruguay river, with the jungle creeping up on it, and the mountains beyond. And that it was always raining. And that all the undergrowth was full of leeches. It sounds horrible.

"You remember that they found the moonflower among the ruins of an old temple, on the lower slopes of the mountain? Yes—it was in all the papers. Well, apparently the natives still used the temple for some primitive form of worship, in spite of anything that the Catholic missionaries could do or say, and this girl was the daughter of one of the temple priests. I should imagine that it was all very crude and squalid; in fact, he said so quite definitely; but he also made it obvious that this religion was a very real thing to these people. . . ."

She seemed to hesitate. . . . "And that this girl meant everything to him; it was a sort of obsession. . . ." She broke off with a nervous laugh. "I find this rather embarrassing."

"Take your time, miss," grunted Waller kindly.

"It mightn't be so bad if I'd never met him. But to think of that shrivelled little man, in love. . . ." She shuddered, and shook her head.

"He was not always a shrivelled little man," sighed Mr. Green. "Even a year ago, he could cut a fine figure. It was the tropics, taking their toll."

"That's what makes it all the more horrible. Mrs. Faversham's reaction, I mean. You see. . . ."

They waited for her to go on. She threw away her cigarette. From now on she spoke more quickly.

"Here are the main facts. I'll try to be brief. They became . . . they became lovers. It was a secret to everybody but young Meadows. That boy worshipped Hilary. The girl didn't go with them on any of the expeditions—that would have been too dangerous—but he used to come back to her

118

every two or three days, when they returned. One night he found her in the hut with another man. It was the night they discovered the moonflower—the first moonflower."

"The first?" interrupted Waller.

"Yes. There were two. Didn't you know?"

"I heard some rumours," observed Mr. Green, "but never any facts."

"But that was the whole point. Or rather, Mrs. Faversham's *belief* in it was the whole point. I suppose that she never mentioned it to the press because she didn't want anybody to think that the expedition hadn't been an unqualified success. And if she were proved wrong . . . but in her opinion she *couldn't* be proved wrong. . . ."

"What was the special quality of this flower?"

"It was scented."

Waller broke into an ironic laugh. She turned on him. "It's not so amusing, when you hear the rest of it."

"Beg pardon, miss. But it seems—sort of—out of proportion."

"It was," she retorted. "Hideously out of proportion. The whole setting. The characters, the climate—everything. As I told you, he came back to find this girl in the arms of another man. The man escaped, but he stabbed her to death. From then on, it was a matter of minutes. As far as I could gather from the letter, it was Meadows who saved the situation. It was Meadows who carried the body to the canoe, to take down the river and throw over the rapids. It was Meadows who packed up the few things they needed, and dealt with the natives, who were growing suspicious. And it was Meadows, when they escaped, who went on ahead, with a letter for Mrs. Faversham. They decided it would be better if they each travelled alone. Meadows reached home a week ahead of Hilary."

"That letter," interrupted Waller. "It beats me how any man of intelligence could write it. It was practically a death-warrant."

"For whom?" inquired Mr. Green, innocently.

"For himself, of course." Waller shifted impatiently on

the stone parapet; there were times when Mr. Green's irrelevancies were very irritating.

Mr. Green nodded. "Of course," he echoed. "For himself, as you say."

"I suppose it *was* a death-warrant," said the girl thoughtfully, "but I don't see how he could have avoided writing it. After all—Mrs. Faversham was his employer. She had invested thousands of pounds in his expedition. There had been a great deal of publicity. If he had abandoned everything, and turned up in England without a word of explanation. . . ."

"There's something in that," agreed Waller.

"Besides, it wouldn't have been a death-warrant if it had fallen into the hands of a decent woman; she'd have understood the tragedy of it all; she'd have destroyed it, forgotten about it. As it was, she used it as a weapon. Or rather, she intended to use it as a weapon."

"For what purpose?"

"To satisfy her ambition. To find the moonflower. The scented moonflower."

"You mean . . . she was going to send him back?"

"Yes. To the Uruguay river."

There was a deep frown on Mr. Green's face. "That would have meant certain death."

"*Certain* death?" she wondered. "Could they have proved that the girl had been killed?"

"I was not thinking of the girl; I was thinking of the colour of his eyes. And the texture of his skin."

She stared at him for a moment. Then she nodded. "Yes. I see what you mean. He couldn't have stood it." She laughed bitterly. "But that wouldn't have mattered . . . not to her. She would have killed more than Hilary Scole, for the moonflower . . . the scented moonflower. She was a fanatic about it. It meant more to her than the most fabulous jewel. There was something not quite sane about her obsession for it . . . something almost indecent . . . it was a sort of lust. And I had to watch the whole business. It was sickening. Hilary would come down to dinner, looking like death, and she would deride him because he wasn't eating. 'We must fatten you up,' she'd say. 'You'll need all your strength, Hilary dear, in the next few months. . . .' "

She broke off abruptly and stared over to the great house. "The light's gone out in his room."

She seemed suddenly very frightened, very feminine.

"He may be coming down—out here. He may have guessed what we were talking about."

"Even so . . ." began Mr. Green.

She rose swiftly to her feet. "Even so, I don't want to speak to him, not at this moment. I don't think I could look in his eyes, after telling you this."

She started to go, and then she turned again. "But I had to tell you, didn't I? It was my duty, wasn't it?"

It was to Waller that she addressed the question.

"Yes, miss," he said gravely. "It was your duty. And we are grateful."

She gave them a fleeting smile, and made away.

IV

They walked back to the inn together.

"Motives—motives!" growled the superintendent. "The air's thick with motives." He threw himself into a chair in the cosy parlour and ordered himself a pint of bitter.

"If there's one thing that's worse than no motive, it's too many. There's hardly one of 'em that isn't better off now that old woman's out of the way."

Mr. Green stared into the fire. "Hilary Scole's motive would seem to be the strongest of them all."

The superintendent nodded. "From now on, we'll have to make some pretty exhaustive inquiries about him." A thought occurred to him. "This doesn't make Pusey's story any the more convincing, does it?"

"Hardly."

"He seemed very insistent on the fact that Scole went straight to bed. How did he know? He also rubbed in the fact that he was physically exhausted. I wonder why?"

"I have been wondering why, too."

"There's no reason why Scole shouldn't have done it. Nor Pusey either, for that matter. Nor both of them together. Nor . . . hell, the whole collection of 'em."

Suddenly Waller leant forward. "Would you like to take a bet?"

"What about?"

"About the jewels in that safe?"

For once in a way the superintendent was a step ahead of Mr. Green.

"But I have no theories about them," he said.

"Well, I have. I bet you ten to one that before we're much older, those jewels will be returned."

Mr. Green raised his eyebows. "That is a very interesting assumption."

"And a quite possible one."

"Quite possible. I congratulate you."

"If they *are* returned, it makes the case against Hilary blacker than ever. It would be a proof that the motive of the robbery was the letter, which nobody else knew about."

"Except Miss Wells."

"Quite. But we can count her out. Thank the Lord there's somebody we *can* count out."

Mr. Green glanced at his watch. "I think I shall go up-stairs to rest. I've got an hour before dinner."

"You'll come in to see me before you go to bed?"

"Of course."

"With the whole story?"

"If there is any."

"No aces up your sleeve?"

Mr. Green blinked at him reproachfully. "My dear Waller," he murmured, "have you ever known me to keep an ace up my sleeve?"

10

KENNETH was waiting for him in the drawing-room. By night it was even more beautiful than by day. Its pale elegance, its symphony of silver and grey, was enhanced by the golden light of the candles.

"Evening, Green," he blustered. "Glad you could come along. What'll you drink?"

"A glass of sherry, if I may."

He handed it to him. "Got any new ideas?"

"None that are worth mentioning, I'm afraid."

"Let's hope you don't take too long about it."

Mr. Green flushed, ever so slightly. "Is my presence in the neighbourhood so embarrassing?"

"Good Lord, no!" He made an awkward gesture of dissent. "In fact, it would be a good deal more embarrassing if you were to go. That's why I telephoned to you this morning. You know what people are. They'd think we hadn't wanted you prowling around . . . that we were afraid, or something. It's merely that. . . ." He paused. "Well, Beryl thought perhaps you would like to come up and stay in the house?"

"It is very kind of you. But I am quite comfortable at the inn."

Kenneth gave an audible sigh of relief. "If you don't want to stay, perhaps you'd like a latchkey?"

"That might be useful."

"All the same, I hope there won't be any more cross-examinations?"

"Not as far as I am concerned."

"Thank the Lord for small mercies." He took a gulp of neat whisky. "You can't imagine how that sort of thing gets on Beryl's nerves."

"Naturally."

He finished the glass; he was already a little thick in his speech. "I mean . . . I shall never forget that night. It was all so extraordinary. Everybody wandering about the place, for some reason or other."

"Or other," echoed Mr. Green.

"Are you suggesting anything?"

"Not at all."

"I mean—you do understand about Beryl, for instance, coming back late and then going for a walk? It sounds crazy but it's Beryl all over."

Mr. Green nodded. "The romantic type," he observed, without a flicker of irony.

At that moment "the romantic type" entered the room in person, followed by the rest of the party.

As soon as Mr. Green had greeted his hostess, his eyes sought a lower level. He seemed momentarily interested in the carpet. He was, in fact, studying the gentlemen's shoes. It was with a sense of relief that he saw that they were all of identical pattern, of roughly the same age, and with no appreciable difference in size.

He felt quite consoled. He had not missed any chances after all.

A boring dinner party it was, in which the conversation dragged leaden feet through four courses of colourless food. Mr. Pusey pontificated about the law, Kenneth grumbled about the weather, Beryl made small talk about her neighbours in the county, and Hilary, for the most part silent, ate little, occasionally taking a sip of wine.

"Poor devil!" thought Mr. Green, who never lost his sense of pity, even for the most ruthless of criminals. "How ill he looks!" And indeed, he was only too obviously a sick man. His skin had the colour of a candle of which the flame is flickering.

The only person who began to show any sign of life was Sandra. She was sitting on his left. At first they had little enough to say to one another, for every subject of conversation seemed to be overshadowed by the stormy interview of the afternoon.

And then, Mr. Green accidentally spilled the salt. An unusual lapse on his part, for he was of all men the most delicately fingered.

"Oh dear!" cried Sandra. "You must take a pinch of it and throw it over your left-hand shoulder, three times."

He smiled amiably. "Is that really necessary?"

"But yes! Everybody knows *that*. If you don't, it means terribly bad luck."

"For whom?"

"For yourself."

"Very well, I will oblige you."

He complied with her wishes. "So you are superstitious?"

"Aren't all women?"

"You believe in the stars?"

"I never stop having my horoscope read."

"Crystal gazing?"

"My favourite amusement."

"Palmistry?"

"Of course."

He nodded. "As a matter of fact, there *is* something to be said for palmistry. It is not merely an idle amusement. I have even used it in some of my cases. Now, your own palm, for instance. . . ." He held out his hand. "Might I glance at it?"

"By all means."

She stretched out her hand. But alas—clumsiness seemed to be the order of the day; in doing so she overturned her glass of claret. And by the time that a plate had been put under the tablecloth, and salt spread on the stain, the subject of palmistry had apparently escaped her mind. For the rest of the evening she talked, with heroic determination, to Mr. Pusey.

II

The clock struck seven. The pale, elegant drawing-room presented a scene that was very near to a still-life, so bored, so inanimate were the figures round the fire.

Mr. Green knew very well that he had outstayed his welcome; it was painfully obvious that all of them, with the possible exception of Sandra, wanted him to go home. But he was not quite ready; he had still to do his little conjuring trick. Now, he decided, was the moment.

This little trick, which has been mentioned before, was aimed at discovering the identity of the man who killed the dog. This man, as Mr. Green had pointed out to Waller, need not necessarily be the man who committed the murder. But it seemed almost inevitable that he should have some connection with it, and until he had pinned him down Mr. Green would feel restless and unhappy.

His attention was therefore fixed firstly on Hilary. It would have been physically possible for him to kill the dog, if he and Pusey were collaborators. Apart from that, Sandra's story of the afternoon—which he was inclined to believe—had loaded the dice heavily against him.

Secondly on Kenneth, for reasons too obvious to be enumerated.

Thirdly on Pusey, because it was Pusey who had first mentioned the absence of the dog on the fatal night.

He walked across to the window. As he passed Pusey, who showed signs of somnolence, he kicked him sharply on the ankle.

"Really!" cried Pusey. "You might look where you are going!"

Mr. Green was all apologies. It was inexcusable of him. But he continued on his way to the window, now that Pusey was thoroughly awake.

"The wind is rising again," he said. "From the west."

And indeed it was. It moaned round the old walls in rising protest.

"Sign of rain," grunted Kenneth from his arm-chair. "Hope it doesn't start before you get home."

Mr. Green ignored this most obvious hint. "There are clouds coming up over the hills," he observed blandly, "but they are still a long way from the moon. One can see quite clearly."

126

He heard the sound of a syphon splashing. He looked round, and saw that it was Hilary, filling up his glass. Good. It would be all the better if he had a glass in his hand.

"Quite clearly," he repeated. He pressed his little nose against the pane. "Why," he exclaimed, "I believe I can see something moving on the lawn!"

Sandra's light laugh echoed across the room. "Really, Mr. Green, you'll be giving us the creeps!"

"But I can see something . . . and it's moving closer."

"What do you mean by 'something'?" demanded Beryl. She made no effort to stir from her chair, and if her yawn was artificial, it was very well done.

"Yes. What do you mean?" It was Hilary speaking. Out of the corner of his eye Mr. Green could see that he had risen from his chair and was stepping slowly towards him.

"It's still not quite near enough to tell."

He could see them all reflected in the glass of the window, Beryl and Sandra by the fire, Mr. Pusey leaning forward tensely, Kenneth at the drinks tray, and Hilary coming nearer step by step.

Kenneth's voice broke the tension. "Hell's bells," he said, in exasperation, "are you trying to tell us it's a ghost?"

Mr. Green paused; he wanted his timing to be perfect.

"Now I can see!" he exclaimed. "No. It's not a ghost. It's a dog. A little dog. Running towards the window . . . a Pekinese with a black tail!"

He swung round; his face was within a few inches of Hilary's; they were eye to eye; and for one baffling moment he realized that Hilary—unless he was the greatest actor of all time—was quite unmoved. He was not even looking at him. He was merely staring out of the window, in befuddled curiosity.

From behind came a sharp crash and a cry of anguish. Kenneth had fallen to the floor, bringing the tray with him. He lay there, with a twitching mouth.

Mr. Green was the first to get to him.

"Sandra . . . Sandra . . ." he was whispering.

Slowly a decanter of brandy gurgled its contents on to the lapel of his coat. It was not a very pretty sight.

III

"So you see," said Mr. Green, "the ace up my sleeve seems to have changed the whole course of the game. In a direction which neither of us had anticipated."

Waller grunted irritably. "It's like a damned game of blind-man's-buff."

"It is," sighed Mr. Green. "But it wouldn't be the first of those games which we had played, with some success."

It was an hour later, and they were sitting in the little parlour of The Greyhound, fortified by two tankards of mulled ale, supplied in defiance of the licensing laws by Mr. Keswick. The young landlord was still enthralled by the adventure of paternity, and was in a mood of perpetual celebration.

Mr. Green had made his departure from Candle Court with mixed feelings. Among them was a sense of guilt at having aroused false hopes about the return of the dog. True, none of them had greatly cared for the dog, but his pretended discovery must have put them to a great deal of inconvenience; even when he finally bade them good-night he could hear the voice of a disgruntled Ackworth, calling to it across the terrace. And in spite of his protests, Hilary had insisted on wrapping himself up and joining in the search.

He only hoped that none of them would guess that there never had been a dog. None of them, of course, except Kenneth, who must *know*. Unless, by a million to one chance, his fainting fit had been a mere coincidence.

"Could it have been?" he murmured aloud.

"Could it have been what?"

"A coincidence? That sudden collapse?"

"Don't ask me. I wasn't there. In any case, I don't understand these melodramatic methods of yours."

Mr. Green bridled. "My dear Waller, at least they seem to get results."

"What's the use of results if you can't interpret them?"

"You haven't even tried to interpret them."

"A fat lot you give me to go on! Looks—glances—whispers!"

Mr. Green gave a perceptible snort. He was feeling very tired, and very baffled. He had played a beautiful conjuring trick, and nobody seemed to appreciate it. "You are talking," he said, "like a policeman."

It was Waller's turn to snort. "That may be better," he retorted, "than talking like a half-baked psycho-analyst."

The two old friends glared at each other in the light of the dying fire. And then the glares gave way to slow, affectionate grins.

"I deserved that," admitted Mr. Green.

"No you didn't. I *was* talking like a policeman."

"I'm glad you were. You were right about the 'looks and the sighs and the whispers.' I was being altogether too atmospheric."

"Crashing on to a tray of drinks sounds concrete enough. And even if he only whispered Sandra's name it was pretty significant."

"Of what? Can you sum up the situation?"

"As a policeman?" he chuckled. "Very well." He took a long draught of ale, smacked his lips, and set down his glass.

"We seem to have established two things," he said. "Firstly, that Kenneth killed the dog. I suppose it might have been Beryl, but Beryl didn't faint, and from what you tell me she seems to have believed that there really was a dog there."

His voice grew harder. "A man who could kill a dog like that would kill anything. In my opinion."

"And in mine."

"Now we come to the second thing, the strangest thing of all. The whisper. There was no doubt about it, I suppose?"

129

"None whatever."

"Then it establishes a far more intimate relationship between Kenneth and Sandra than we had any cause to suspect. In public Kenneth invariably calls her 'Miss Wells.' He makes a point of it. He makes it sound almost offensive; even his wife calls her Sandra. The point is, what sort of relationship?"

"Exactly. It might be passionate . . . or criminal."

"I don't see how it could be criminal. This may sound like a policeman, but it does seem to me that the one person in this whole set-up who could not possibly have climbed into that room and choked the life out of Mrs. Faversham is Sandra. Do you agree?"

"I do." There was no question of the sincerity of Mr. Green's comment.

"The only way she could have done it would have been if she'd had a twin sister who took her place at the inn. Or if she'd been able to assume an astral body."

"I think," said Mr. Green drily, "that we may ignore both those assumptions."

"So the criminal relationship seems to be out. She couldn't have done it herself, and there's no conceivable reason why she should have helped anybody else to do it. Or is there?"

"None that we know of."

"And there the matter rests for the moment, with confusion worse confounded. What's the next step?"

Mr. Green paused for a moment. Then he said: "I understand that they're going up to London tomorrow."

"Who?"

"Sandra and Kenneth. Beryl mentioned it—rather pointedly I thought—when I was saying good-night."

Waller sat up abruptly. "Good Lord! Why didn't you tell me before?"

"It slipped my memory." Mr. Green lowered his eyes as he told this little fib.

"I'll get through to the Yard at once, and have them followed."

"I rather hoped you would. It may lead to nothing, but one never knows."

"Did you find out which train they were taking?"

"Yes. I checked with Ackworth. It's the only good train of the day—the eight-thirty."

Waller strode across to the telephone in the alcove, and demanded trunks. He got through to the Yard with surprising speed, and a few moments later was talking to the faithful Bates.

"Look here, my lad," he said, "this is important. Have you got the photo-file of the Faversham case? All right— I'll hold on while you fetch it."

Mr. Green, listening to this conversation, reflected that though Waller might be only a policeman, he was a very enterprising one. It was his habit, in all big cases, to obtain photographs of every person who could conceivably be connected with it. To him, these photographs were as important as finger-prints. "People have an awkward habit of drifting away from the scenes of crimes," he used to say.

"Got it? Good!" He glanced at his notebook. "Turn to Number 3 and Number 12 . . . yes, 12. Those two will be on the eight-thirty from Exeter to-morrow, arriving Paddington twelve-ten. I want them followed and a full report on their movements. What? Yes, of course you'll want another man . . . they mayn't keep together. They mayn't even arrive together. How long shall you follow them? Well—give it till midnight and then use your discretion. What's that you say?" Waller's voice suddenly became explosive. "Listen, young man," he barked, "when I want immoral suggestions from you I'll ask for them. Good-night."

He banged down the receiver. But there was a broad grin on his face when he turned to Mr. Green. "Young devil," he muttered.

Mr. Green rose to his feet. "It is past my bedtime," he said.

"Mine too. You go on ahead—I'll see to the lights."

"That's very kind of you."

"Pleasant dreams!" He slapped Mr. Green on the back,

so heartily that he winced. "It's been a long day, but it's been worth it."

"Let us hope so."

"And for once in a way we seem to be walking in step."

"For once in a way? Surely we always walk in step?"

"Oh yeah? There *have* been occasions when you've kept an ace up your sleeve."

"Really!" retorted Mr. Green. And that was his only comment. For he was very tired and longing for his bed.

But as he undressed, in the small white bedroom that always gave him such pleasure, because of its exquisite combination of scents . . . the tang of the moorland air, the sweetness of the freshly laundered linen, the pale, elusive essence of the smoke from the pine-logs on the hearth . . . he had a faint feeling of guilt.

No ace up his sleeve? Was he being quite honest in his denial?

For after all, he had spilt the salt. On purpose. Perhaps he should have told Waller why he had done so. And Sandra had spilt her glass of wine. On purpose? Aye—there was the rub. *Had* she spilt it on purpose? In any case, whether it had been by chance or by design, it had spoiled his plan.

He heaved a deep sigh, tied his pyjama tape round his plump little tummy, sank into bed, and turned out the light. "Really," he thought, as he closed his eyes, "this business of detection becomes more and more complicated. It was much simpler in the days of Sherlock Holmes. *He* had an easy job. Just a phial of morphia, a violin, a dressing-gown . . . and that nice Doctor Watson. Such a helpful man, I always thought. I wonder if Sherlock Holmes would have told Dr. Watson about the salt? I wonder. . . ."

And then he ceased to wonder, and fell asleep.

11

On the following day, Mr. Green had Candle Court largely to himself. Kenneth and Sandra duly departed to London by the early train. Beryl and Pusey motored to Exeter on family business. Hilary decided to stay in bed.

Waller, awaiting further developments from London, took himself to Princetown prison, some fifteen miles away.

After all, that was the principal reason for his existence at the moment; the Faversham case was in the nature of a luxury; and if it had not been for his friendly rivalry with Mr. Green, he would not have devoted so much attention to it. Besides, during the night there had been yet another attempted escape which—largely thanks to the innovations he had suggested—had come to nothing. However, it had been a near thing, and he was not taking any chances.

"You'll have the field to yourself," he said to Mr. Green, as he struggled into his overcoat. "Which means, I suppose, that you'll have it all cut and dried by the time I get back to-night—if I do get back."

"No doubt," replied Mr. Green, with a polite bow.

"What are you going to do?"

"I might play a little Mozart, if Mrs. Ackworth is not dusting the drawing-room."

"I'm sure you might—what else?"

"Some of the simpler Schubert impromptus, perhaps."

"I don't want your entire musical repertoire. What else?"

"Oh, I see!" Mr. Green blinked innocently. "You are interested in my methods?"

Waller merely snorted.

"Well," said Mr. Green, "as it's such a pleasant day, I might take a few snapshots with my little camera."

With which Waller had to be content.

Mr. Green's camera, though small, was powerful and piti-less. In his secret heart he rather disliked it. He mistrusted all mechanical things, particularly when they strayed into the domain of art—or what some fools called art. Moreover, it had caused him months of irritation, learning how to work it. He would probably never have learned to work it at all if it had not been for his stubborn refusal to be outwitted by a wretched little box which could be mastered, in half an hour, by an intelligent boy scout.

It was surprising how many things, round and about the house, he found to interest him this morning. The view from Sandra's window seemed especially fascinating. "So charm-ing—such a wonderful vista," he murmured to Mrs. Ackworth, much to that lady's astonishment, because the room in question had one of the narrowest views in the house, consisting largely of the backs of the stable roofs. However, Mr. Green was such an old favourite that if he had told her he wished to photograph the dog kennel she would not have demurred.

It was not only the view from Sandra's window that absorbed Mr. Green. When Mrs. Ackworth had departed, he seemed to develop a great curiosity about everything in the room, although to the casual observer there was little to attract attention. There was only one photograph on the mantelpiece—a snapshot of a grey-haired, weather-beaten man in the uniform of a captain in the Merchant Navy. That must be her father, of course, who lived in retirement at Teignmouth. Waller had already checked up on him. Most of her rare holidays were spent with him. Nothing rewarding in that quarter.

It was a curiously impersonal room, with few of those small oddments and knick-knacks which, one would have thought, a lonely woman would have had about her. Her toilet things were sparse and almost masculine in their simplicity, and afforded Mr. Green few opportunities for sniffing. There was a lavender talc powder (one sniff), a bottle of *Eau-de-Cologne* (two sniffs), a cheap cold cream (half a sniff), and various other bare essentials of the female toilet on which Mr. Green did not waste any sniffs at all.

Even her small library of books gave no clue to her identity; there was the *Oxford Book of English Verse*, the collected stories of Somerset Maugham, two detective novels, an American volume entitled *Eat and Grow Beautiful*, and a pile of magazines, varying from *Vogue* and *Woman's Own* to *The National Geographic* and *The Knitting Weekly*.

Mr. Green raised his eyebrows. He had not realized she knitted. She certainly never took any of her work downstairs . . . if she *did* work, and if her interest was not purely academic. He turned the pages idly, momentarily lost in the mysteries of purl and plain. There was only one page which she seemed to have studied in any detail; it bore several pencilled notes, and a query, Mr. Green bent down to examine it more carefully, and as he did so he began to blink very rapidly. He gave the page another scrutiny, then he put the magazine back in its place. So Miss Wells knitted, did she? And that was the sort of thing she knitted! A very versatile young woman!

After the house, the stables. It was remarkable how many picturesque "angles" and "approaches" Mr. Green seemed to discover in this group of buildings, and how many rooms he found himself obliged to enter in order to get the right "perspective". Fortunately for him, he found an unexpected ally in Mrs. Wilburfoss, who had quite recovered from her drunken fit, and seemed, indeed, only too anxious to make amends for her behaviour.

Did Mr. Green want to go up into that room over the archway? Well—that was their bedroom, but of course he could go. She was afraid he would find it a little untidy, but she hoped he would excuse that. She would take him up herself, only she was busy with the washing. And the room under the clock tower? That was Meadows'. He certainly wouldn't object. She'd have something to say if he did! And the room at the end? That was just a lumber-room where all Mr. Kenneth's old school things had been put away—cricket bats, boxing gloves, and the like. Even all the glass cases containing his birds' eggs. She'd like to have a real good clear out one of these days. It must be nearly a year since anybody had gone into it.

So off he went, and from time to time his round, benevolent face might have been observed, peering out of lattice windows, taking shots at every conceivable angle. An exceptionally observant person would have noticed that from time to time a bright flash was visible, showing that Mr. Green specialized in interiors as well as exteriors. Such a person might also have noticed that, in spite of his enthusiasm, Mr. Green was strangely careless, for in a large number of his outdoor shots he appeared to forget to click the lever at all.

Fortunately for Mr. Green, however, the few people who were aware of his presence among them were not of the observant type. Such as Mrs. Wilburfoss. She had said that it must be nearly a year since anybody had gone into the lumber-room. Mr. Green, whose inquisitive footsteps happened to stray into this room, thought otherwise. It seemed to him that somebody had been in this lumber-room very recently—only a few days ago, in fact. And that this somebody had not left empty-handed.

III

At last his artistic endeavours were completed, and he took himself off, after another word with Mrs. Wilburfoss, in which he promised to let her have copies of any photographs which were particularly successful.

But just as he was about to re-enter the house, he saw a figure hurrying to meet him. It was Wilburfoss.

"May I have a word with you, sir?"

"By all means."

"Perhaps you'd like to come across to the stables, sir? We can be quiet there."

Mr. Green omitted to mention that he had only just come

136

from that direction, and fell in by his side. Wilburfoss walked in silence.

Glancing at him, Mr. Green was again struck by the rugged beauty of his features; he was like a dark Viking; one felt that he was a man of storm and wind and open water. A man for whom many women would commit the most dangerous follies.

"Here we are, sir."

He threw open the door of the main store-room, which was also used for office-work. Its walls were lined with shelves for rare bulbs and seeds; underneath were larger compartments for special fertilizers. At one end of the room a pile of boxes reached to the ceiling. Underneath the window ran a bench, the length of the wall. It was littered with papers, accounts, labels, and nurserymen's catalogues.

Young Meadows looked up from the desk as they entered.

"No—you needn't go, Meadows," said Wilburfoss. "We may want you." He turned to Mr. Green. "You don't mind, sir?"

"Not at all." He perched himself on a high chair. "Meadows and I are old friends. Please go ahead. I am all attention."

Wilburfoss leant against the bench and folded his arms.

"You remember, sir, you told me to report to you if anything out-of-the-way was to happen—no matter how small it might seem to be?"

"I did."

"Well, something *has* happened. It mayn't mean much, but I don't like the smell of it." He jerked his head towards the pile of boxes at the other end of the room. "One of them boxes is missing."

Mr. Green cocked his head on one side.

"They're the regular boxes we use for sending our stuff every week. Hybrid orchids, lily corms, camellia cuttings, azalea seedlings, and the like. Mrs. Faversham was a great one for swopping plants with other collectors. Heavier stuff, too, sometimes. We've a specially treated loam she was very keen on . . . we must have sent out cartloads of it."

137

"When did you discover about the missing box?"

"It was like this, sir. The lorry goes down to the station every Monday morning. Meadows drives it, and helps me to pack the boxes at the back. Well, on the morning after . . . after it happened . . . we packed the boxes as usual." His voice grew gruff. "Seemed as how we ought to carry on, in spite of everything. There were twenty-eight boxes, going to various addresses all over the country. That's right, Meadows?"

"Yes, sir. Twenty-eight. We checked 'em together."

"Meadows drives off to the station, delivers the boxes, and gets the receipt . . . for twenty-eight. I've got it here."

He handed Mr. Green a flimsy sheet of paper, stamped with the formal acknowledgment of British Railways, Lustleigh Station.

Twenty-eight boxes, per express passenger service. There followed a list of addresses.

"Are these the addresses to which the boxes were to be sent?"

"Yes, sir."

"And is this your handwriting?"

"That's right, sir."

"Very neat," commented Mr. Green. His manner was as polite as ever, but there was no ring of interest in his voice.

"The boxes went off, sir; Meadows came home, and we thought no more about it. Till this morning. And then I get this telegram." He pointed to a telegram slip lying on the desk before him. "I won't trouble you to read it, but it's from a lady in Exeter, complaining that her box had not arrived. And that made me fair wild, sir, because it was a hybrid odontoglossum we set great store by. . . ."

"Not one of the white ones?" demanded Mr. Green, with sincere anxiety.

"I'm afraid so, sir."

"Dear me—that is a tragedy. If it had been one of the common yellow. . . ." He checked himself, with an obvious effort. "But I am interrupting your story."

"So naturally, sir, I went down to the station, right away, to see what could be done about it."

"I should think so, indeed. One of the white ones!" He shook his head. "Please go on."

"The first thing I did was to ask to look at their ledger. You see, sir, they copy out this list of mine . . ." he pointed to the flimsy . . . "check the addresses with the boxes, and then enter them in their own ledger."

"Quite." Anybody who had known Mr. Green, and had marked the droop of his eyelids, would have suspected that he was somewhat bored.

"Well, there were twenty-eight addresses, all right. But the lady in Exeter wasn't among them."

Mr. Green looked up sharply. And blinked. "Not among them?"

"No, sir. But that's not the funniest part of it. There was one address which I'd never written."

Mr. Green blinked three times. "Can you remember it?"

"Certainly, sir. It was addressed to Paddington Station. In the name of 'C. C. Smith'. To be called for."

And now Mr. Green's face was indeed a study. It was so contorted with blinks that it gave the impression of a close-up in an old-fashioned film. It positively flickered.

"To be called for!" he whispered, staring at Wilburfoss. "To be called for!" There was a moment's silence. "You fool!" And he crashed his podgy little fist on the desk in front of him.

"I beg pardon, sir . . ." muttered Wilburfoss, stepping back.

"It is I who should beg yours," wailed Mr. Green, not looking at him. "I did not mean you; I was addressing myself. Fool . . . fool . . . fool! To overlook a thing like that! I should be certified."

He slid off his seat. "If you will excuse me for a moment," he murmured. "I would like a breath of fresh air, to clear my brain . . . if I may still lay claim to one."

IV

When he returned, some three minutes later, the two men were standing as he had left them, at the bench. On both their faces was an expression of bewilderment.

"You must excuse me for that exhibition of temperament," he murmured, with an apologetic smile. "But I hate stupidity in myself even more than I hate it in others. Now, may I ask one or two questions?"

"Of course, sir."

"The first is for Meadows." He turned to the young man. "When you arrived at the station, did anybody help you to unload the boxes?"

"Yes, sir. Same porter as always does. Name of Wallace. Been there nigh on forty years."

"Had you far to carry them?"

"Only a few yards, sir—just through the gate and on to the platform."

"Where I suppose they would be in full view of everybody?"

"That's right, sir."

"When you gave Wallace your list to be stamped, did he check the addresses on it?"

"No, sir; he only made sure that it tallied with the number of the boxes. Twenty-eight."

"But you left him a copy of the list?"

Meadows shifted uneasily from one foot to the other. "That's the funny part, sir. I did leave him a copy of the list. I always do. Mr. Wilburfoss gives me a carbon copy. And Wallace always puts it on a spike just inside the office door, by the side of the ledger, to enter it later on. But this time, when he went for it, it had gone."

"Gone? Are you quite sure you gave it to him?"

Wilburfoss intervened. "If Meadows says so, sir, that's good enough for me. He wouldn't make a mistake about a thing like that. What's more, Wallace says so, too."

"Then how did Wallace get his list of addresses at all?"

"From the labels on the boxes themselves, sir. Luckily there was plenty of time before the train came in."

"I see." Mr. Green was beginning to blink again. "So that when he came to the box marked 'Paddington, to be called for', he had no means of knowing that it had been substituted." He turned again to Meadows. "Were there many people on the station that morning?"

"About a dozen, sir."

"Anybody you knew?"

Meadows hesitated. "Well sir, there was Mr. Pusey."

"Did you speak to him?"

"No, sir. He was in a bit of a temper, sir."

"Why was that?"

"Well, sir, when I saw him at the stables after breakfast. . . ."

Mr. Green raised his eyebrows. "At the stables? What brought him there, I wonder?"

"That's what I wondered too, sir. So naturally I went up and asked him if I could help. And he seemed to take it quite badly, sir. Told me to mind my own business, sir. So of course I did."

Mr. Green nodded reflectively. "Could any of these people—apart from Mr. Pusey, of course—have substituted the box after you arrived at the station?"

"Well, sir, I suppose they could. But they'd have had to look pretty nippy about it."

"What's more," added Wilburfoss, "it'd have to be somebody who knew his way about this place. They were special boxes and special labels."

"You mean, you think the box must have been substituted up here . . . and that it was actually among those that Meadows drove to the station?"

"Looks like it, sir."

"Would that have been possible?"

"Not easy, sir. But possible, yes. The lorry was standing open in this yard for a good half-hour, unattended. And there were a lot of people about that morning, coming and going."

Mr. Green nodded. "Well. It seems fairly clear. Some person or persons unknown, early on the morning of the murder, was in possession of a *twenty-ninth box* and a *twenty-ninth label*. That box was either substituted here, or at the station. Here would seem more probable. But whichever it was, he—or an accomplice—must have been at the station to remove the carbon copy of the list from the spike." He sighed. "That is very elementary deduction, but it is all I can manage for the moment."

"But *why*, sir?" It was Meadows speaking. "Why should anybody want to send a box to Paddington like that? When they could have given it to me in the ordinary way?"

"Perhaps it contained something dangerous."

"But *what*, sir?"

Mr. Green looked him straight in the eyes. They were good eyes, he thought to himself, young and clear and brave. But they were filled with a strange sadness, a deep bewilderment. He put his hand on Meadows' shoulder.

"Your guess," he said, "is as good as mine."

v

"So that's how the safe got away! Under our very noses!"

Waller rose from his chair and gave an irritable kick to the log on the fire before which they were sitting.

It was late that same night. As soon as the superintendent had returned from Princetown, Mr. Green had taken him upstairs to his little room, set a bottle of whisky before him, and told him the latest developments.

It was a time when he felt the need of sturdy common sense. So many strange theories were forming in his own mind, so many shifting conclusions, half-truths and conjectures, that he wanted to test them against a simpler mentality, to watch them being assessed by a man to whom black was black, white was white, and all the intervening shades of small account.

Needless to say he did not take Waller fully into his

confidence. Not because he had anything in him of the dog-in-the-manger but because some of the theories which were being forced upon him were so fantastic that Waller would undoubtedly have laughed them to scorn, particularly when they were still young and unformed; they were like delicate plants that might wither in the blast of adverse criticism.

"You agree that the box *did* contain the safe?" he suggested tentatively. He himself was convinced, but he needed Waller's affirmation.

"A thousand to one," grunted Waller. "Everything points to it. As a matter of fact, it's the way I'd have chosen myself if I'd had the brains to imagine it. Put yourself in the murderer's place. He's got a large, heavy object, more dangerous than dynamite. He daren't hide it in the house, because he knows that the whole place will be searched—as it *has* been searched. He could bury it in the garden, or some such place, but it's no use to him, buried. Sooner or later, he's got to open it; probably sooner than later. Even if he did bury it, there's still a chance of discovery. In this part of the world, so close to the prison, people have the bloodhound mentality. They've seen 'em too often, scouring across the moors, to treat them merely as comic animals of fiction."

Mr. Green nodded. Everything that Waller said was in accordance with his own convictions; it was comforting to have them confirmed.

"It's the opening of the darned thing that must have given him his main headache," continued the superintendent. "You can't open a safe like that in five minutes, and you can't do it with a pair of nail scissors. Moreover, you can't do it in silence—you'll make a hell of a noise. You need time, you need privacy, and you need some pretty hefty tools. Which reminds me, we ought to make a check-up on the tools in this place. . . ."

"I have already done so," interrupted Mr. Green.

"Any result?"

"None, I'm afraid. There is a positive ammunition dump

of tools in a big shed adjoining the stables. Gardening tools galore, to say nothing of all the tools of all the motor-cars which Mrs. Faversham has owned in the last twenty years. She never could bear to part with anything. One could have taken fifty tools, which might have been useful, without anybody being any the wiser."

"Out of luck again." He helped himself to another small whisky. "Hell's' bells! When I think that I let Pusey get away with that suit case! Yet I can't imagine Pusey . . . can you?"

Mr. Green merely sighed.

"Well, *can* you? As you don't say anything, I suppose you mean you can. And I suppose you're right. In this sort of affair, one mustn't concentrate on what's probable, but on what's possible. Pusey *could* have murdered Mrs. Faversham; he *could* have stolen one of the boxes and put the safe in it; he *could* have done this shift at the station, lifting the invoice off the spike. . . ." He broke off abruptly. "But what about the other end of it? What about when the box gets to Paddington?"

"You mean—who was the person who collected it?"

"Yes. There must have been an accomplice. Pusey himself wouldn't run the risk of being recognized. Nor, for that matter, would anybody in this household."

"Unless he—or she—were exceptionally foolish."

"How *could* anybody be so foolish?"

Mr. Green smiled. "I agree that it seems very unlikely. But as you said a moment ago, we must concentrate not on what is probable but on what is possible. And in the field of folly, anything is possible."

Waller nodded. "O.K., that settles it. We must find out who were the booking-clerks at the clearing office at Paddington Station on 5th February. We must present them with a rogue's gallery of all the inhabitants, staff, and hangers-on of Candle Court, including a studio portrait of Wilburfoss's mother, who's been bedridden for fifteen years. After that, we must rub their noses in the aforesaid portraits and wait for a startled gleam of recognition. Whereupon we

144

arrest the criminal, return the jewels, put on the black cap, and Bob's your uncle. Sounds simple, doesn't it?"

Mr. Green had every sympathy for Waller's irritation. This was the sort of tedious, heart-breaking spade-work which was apt to wear down a man's nerves. He often thought that if he had to do it himself, he would lose interest in a case long before it was finished.

"All the same," he said, "it has to be done."

"By *me*. While you sit back and sniff."

Mr. Green flinched. Instantly Waller was all contrition. "Sorry, old chap." He put his huge hand on the little man's shoulder. "I didn't mean that."

"It is perfectly true," agreed Mr. Green. "I do sit back and sniff. But we must all do what nature shaped us for. And that reminds me. . . ."

He rose, went over to his desk, and opened a drawer. From it he extracted a pile of photograph spools—the undeveloped snapshots which he had taken that morning. He referred to a list, extracted one spool, and handed it to Waller.

"What is this?"

"An addition to your Rogues Gallery. When you get to the Yard to-morrow, please have it developed at once. Is that possible?"

"Of course."

"And please ask Bates—or whoever interviews the booking-clerks—to draw their special attention to the third picture."

"What *is* the third picture?"

"The third picture," said Mr. Green, with one of his maddening moments of mystery, "is a hunch. . . ."

Whereupon he helped himself to his second whisky and soda. It was dissipation, but he felt that he deserved it.

VI

And now it was the superintendent who had something to tell Mr. Green.

"When I was over at Princetown," he said, "Bates rang up from the Yard."

"Ah! Any news?"

"Plenty. Kenneth and Sandra got into a taxi together. And where do you think they went?"

"The Victoria and Albert Museum?" suggested Mr. Green with a faint hiccup. It was naughty, but he had suddenly begun to feel hilarious.

Waller merely scowled at this inanity. "They went to The Farmers' Bank in Soho Square."

Mr. Green, once more, was all attention. "Both of them?"

"Kenneth went in. She waited outside. After about twenty minutes he came out and handed her a package. Then they got back in the taxi, and drove to the National and Colonial Bank in Throgmorton Street. This time, she went inside. Kenneth took the taxi on, and drove to his club. The rest of his movements for the day are of no particular interest."

"And Sandra?"

"That's the devil of it. She came out, after about ten minutes, and walked down to the tube station entrance. Where, without so much as a by-your-leave, she vanished."

"Gave Bates the slip?"

"It wasn't Bates, it was the other man, Spencer. A bit of a mutt."

"Do you think she did it intentionally?"

Waller shrugged his shoulders. "Couldn't say. I don't suppose it matters much, but a routine job's a routine job and it should be done efficiently. There'll be some telling off to be done at the Yard, to-morrow."

"You're going up in the morning?"

"I certainly am. For one thing, I want to interview those two bank managers. For another, I want to get cracking on the staff at Paddington Station."

"You won't forget to take along my little snapshot?"

"No. Is that all you want me to do for you?"

Mr. Green hesitated. He had drunk far too much whisky —(two small singles, drowned in soda-water, over a space of three hours)—and it had gone to his head. Sometimes, in this spirituous condition, he longed to play with the idea of being Sherlock Holmes. It was an absurd weakness; he was unworthy to fasten the latchet of that great man's shoe; but there it was . . . he had this kink, and sometimes his craving to indulge it overcame his better judgement.

"Is that all?" repeated Waller.

"No," said Mr. Green—and the room seemed to swim round him as he prepared to indulge his little vice—"as a matter of fact, it is not."

"What else?"

"Well . . . just three things." (How wonderful if he had been tall and cadaverous and addicted to morphia, with the immortal Watson sitting before him!)

"Such as?"

"They are almost too obvious to mention. But in case they have escaped your attention. . . ."

He steadied himself against the table. His conscience told him that he would have to pay for this indulgence in the morning; but he was enormously enjoying himself.

"Firstly," he said, "and most obviously, I should like to know if Mr. Pusey collects butterflies."

Waller sat up sharply. He had been through this sort of thing before. The little man was drunk—according to his lights—but the little man was probably making brilliant sense. Automatically he stepped into the rôle of Dr. Watson.

He took out his notebook. Not a flicker of a smile crossed his face.

"Pusey. Butterflies. Yes?"

"Secondly," said Mr. Green . . . and, oh what a friend was Waller! . . . "secondly, though not quite so obviously, I would like to have a list of Indian boys of approximately nine years old, who have been entered at schools in the Hampstead district in the last nine months."

This was almost too much for Waller to swallow, just as it had been almost too much for Mr. Green to enunciate!

However there was something tense and almost sublime

about this moment, for both of them. He rose to the occasion. He wetted his pencil.

Aloud he murmured . . . "Indian boys . . . Hampstead district . . . nine months." He would have liked to add a dry "of course" but that might have broken the spell.

"Lastly," said Mr. Green, whose eyelids were beginning to droop, "I would like you to go to 369 Harley Street and ask Sir Ernest Steegeman how long Hilary Scole may be expected to live."

12

HOWEVER innocent he may be, the spirits of the average man are inclined to sink when he is informed that a gentleman from Scotland Yard has called to see him. And Mr. Stanhope-Forbes, manager of The Farmers' Bank in Soho Square, was a very average man indeed; he was a positive Gallup Poll of normal, middle-aged, respectable humanity. So it was with a deep sigh that he examined the card which his secretary handed to him, on the following afternoon.

"Superintendent Waller," he murmured. "Dear me," another, deeper sigh. "Did he say what it was about?"

"No, sir. He merely said that it was urgent." The secretary, who was a smaller and dimmer replica of his employer, sighed in sympathy.

"We must see him, I suppose?"

"It might be as well, sir."

Mr. Stanhope-Forbes nodded. "Very well. Ask him to wait. When I am ready I will ring."

The secretary went out.

Mr. Stanhope-Forbes had no valid reason for keeping Waller waiting; he merely wanted to delay the evil moment for a fraction longer, in the spirit of a man who takes a last turn round the block before ringing the dentist's bell. He had all too strong a suspicion of the reason for the superintendent's visit; it must have something to do with that dreadful Faversham case. It could have no other purpose. In all the long history of The Farmers' Bank, Mrs. Faversham was the only client who had ever been so inconsiderate as to be murdered. He still found it difficult to believe. It was the very last thing one would have expected of her, and it only went to show that no woman, even with a capital of £800,000, was to be trusted.

149

He pressed the bell. A moment later Waller was shown into the room.

Anybody who knew the superintendent, and understood the various methods which he was accustomed to employ in dealing with different types of men, would have had little difficulty in classifying the technique which he used at this moment. It came under the heading of Charm plus Firmness.

The charm was evident from the moment he sat down. This, he said, must seem an unwarrantable intrusion. He was only too well aware that he was interrupting the smooth running of a great organization. At the same time, he could see at a glance that Mr. Stanhope-Forbes was a man who would realize that duty was duty.

"One does one's best," murmured that gentleman, wondering when he was coming to the point.

He had not long to wonder. Firmness took command.

Waller sat bolt upright. "I am in charge of certain investigations in the case of the late Mrs. Faversham."

Oh, dear—here it came! "Indeed?"

"She was, I believe, a client of yours?"

"That is so. A very substantial client. The very *last* person whom one would have suspected of anything like this."

"Quite," interrupted Waller. "And her son, Mr. Kenneth Faversham, is also a client?"

"That is so."

"I understand that yesterday, shortly after two o'clock, he called at the bank."

"He did."

"May I ask the purpose of his visit?"

Mr. Stanhope-Forbes hesitated. "Am I obliged to answer these questions?"

Without an instant's hesitation, Waller switched off the Firmness and turned on the Charm.

"My dear sir," he replied, in the gentlest of voices, "you are not *obliged* to answer any questions at all. I am merely asking for your co-operation."

"I see. One has one's duty to one's clients."

"Of course. A sacred trust."

Mr. Stanhope-Forbes nodded. This policeman was really quite intelligent. A sacred trust. It was a phrase that he had used on more than one occasion himself.

"At the same time," said Waller, "one has one's duty to society."

Mr. Stanhope-Forbes agreed. One had indeed. He had often stressed the fact.

"And so I am sure you will not mind answering a few questions about Mr. Faversham's visit . . . which, of course, will involve an investigation of his current account."

"It is not our custom . . ." began Mr. Stanhope-Forbes.

"Quite," interrupted Waller. "It is not your custom to allow any investigation into a private account. And it is not the custom of the police to demand it. Except in extreme circumstances—when, of course, we can issue a search-warrant."

Mr. Stanhope-Forbes' jaw dropped. "Would that . . . would that be in order?" he stammered.

Waller chuckled amiably. "In a case of murder, if it were necessary, a search-warrant could be issued for Buckingham Palace. However, we needn't concern ourselves with such an unlikely situation. In your case, it never occurred to me for a moment to apply for a warrant, as I was quite certain that you would co-operate." He tapped his finger on the desk, as though to indicate that time was pressing. "All I need is the answer to a very simple question. What was Mr. Faversham's business here yesterday?"

Firmness was in full control. It echoed in the tone of his voice, it shone in the gleam of his eye. Mr. Stanhope-Forbes fluttered and trembled; he was torn between two conflicting duties . . . his trust to his client and his duty to society. Society, in the shape of the superintendent, won the day.

"He came to draw out some money," he said feebly.

"Was it a large sum?"

"A very large sum."

"May I know how much?"

"It was five thousand pounds."

The superintendent looked up sharply. "As much as that?

Well, well! What proportion was that of his total credit?"

"Fifty per cent. On the day after Mrs. Faversham's death, we received instructions from her solicitors to transfer ten thousand pounds to his account."

"Do you remember who gave you those instructions?"

"Certainly. Mr. Pusey . . . the head of the firm. If it had been anybody else, I might have hesitated. After all, I had not seen the will. However, in Mr. Pusey's case. . . ."

"Of course."

There was a moment's silence. Waller was staring at the carpet, thinking to himself. He seemed, for the moment, to have forgotten Mr. Stanhope-Forbes.

"Five thousand pounds," he muttered. "It's a lot of money." He looked up again. "In what denomination?"

"In five-pound notes. Ten bundles of a hundred apiece. If you wish, I can give you the serial numbers."

"Thank you. I don't think that will be necessary." He rose abruptly, and held out his hand. "Well, sir, I am much obliged to you."

"Will that be all?" faltered Mr. Stanhope-Forbes, accompanying him to the door.

"For the moment."

He went out. Mr. Stanhope-Forbes heaved the deepest sigh of all. "For the moment." What did that mean? Were there other, even more alarming developments, in store? It was all most distressing and irregular. His whole day was quite upset. So upset, indeed, that he spent the rest of the day dictating letters to clients who required increased overdrafts, informing them in the most acid terms that the bank was unable to grant them any further indulgence.

II

Meanwhile, Waller was speeding in a taxi towards the City, where ten minutes later, he alighted at the portals of the National and Colonial Bank in Throgmorton Street.

Here the setting was much the same, except that the walls were of marble instead of fumed oak. The manager, Mr.

152

Vernon, was not unlike Mr. Stanhope-Forbes, and his reactions were almost identical. So was Mr. Waller's procedure . . . Charm plus Firmness. The Charm we may take for granted; it was not till the Firmness stage that he came to the point.

"And yesterday," he was saying to Mr. Vernon, "this young lady—Miss Sandra Wells—made a cash deposit?"

"That is so."

"Was it a large amount?"

Mr. Vernon wriggled uncomfortably. "I am not certain that I can recall. . . ."

"In that case," interrupted Waller, in the most suave of tones, "perhaps I can refresh your memory. Was it in the neighbourhood of five thousand pounds?"

Mr. Vernon gaped. "How did you know?"

"We have our sources of information."

Mr. Vernon's world became, of a sudden, perceptibly darker. He saw spies in the accounting rooms, shadows over every ledger. Perhaps that new secretary of his, whom he had thought so reliable. . . .

"So you see," continued Waller, "there is really no point in withholding information—though I fully appreciate your motives in doing so."

Mr. Vernon capitulated.

"It was four thousand nine hundred and fifty pounds," he admitted.

"Presumably she kept fifty pounds for immediate use."

"That is possible."

"Was it in denominations of five pounds?"

"It was."

"Did she give you any explanation of how she had come into possession of so large a sum?"

"She said that she had been having a little gamble. And that it had come off."

"Did she say what sort of gamble it was?"

"No. I presumed that it must have been some exceptional stroke of luck in racing."

"What *was* her capital?"

He paused for a moment. "Let me think. There was £300 in Savings Certificates. £100 in Calcutta Electric. £100 in Consols. And a balance of about fifty pounds. The total assets were certainly never much more than £500."

Waller made a note of these investments. "Were there regular deposits?"

"Yes. A sum of three pounds a week, made by an arrangement with our Teignmouth branch. I understand that it was deducted from her father's pension."

Waller nodded, and made a final note.

"Well, sir," he said, "you have been most co-operative." And after the usual formalities he took his departure.

Although the two scenes had so much in common, and although the outward appearance of Mr. Vernon was so similar to that of Mr. Stanhope-Forbes, the result—as far as their respective clients was concerned—was very different. For Mr. Vernon was at heart a romantic. The departure of the superintendent left him in an exalted mood. He felt that he was moving in the centre of dark and dangerous deeds—as he certainly was. He spent the rest of the day dictating letters to clients who required increased overdrafts, informing them in the most glowing terms that the bank would be only too honoured to grant them the fullest indulgence.

III

Waller glanced at his watch. A quarter past three. He had just time to get to Harley Street to see Sir Ernest Steegeman.

He felt resentful at Mr. Green for having landed him with this particular chore. Not that "chore" was, perhaps, quite the right way to describe it. After all there was no need for him to see Sir Ernest at all; he was merely doing Mr. Green a favour. However, he did think that Mr. Green, in the circumstances, might have let him know *why* he was so anxious about the state of Hilary's health. When he had asked him, last night, he had merely replied that it "might prove important", which could hardly be described as helpful. Further cross-examination had proved impossible for

154

the very simple reason that Mr. Green had chosen that moment to fall asleep.

Well, there he was, at the massive front door of Number 369 Harley Street. Whereas most of the other doors to the houses in this forbidding street are covered with a rash of brass plates, indicating that their inmates, however distinguished, must content themselves with a single consulting-room, the door of Number 369 bore only one plate. Sir Ernest owned the whole house. And as a special mark of distinction, the brass plate still bore the legend

Mr. Ernest Steegeman

as though to prove that Sir Ernest was so aloof from the things of this world, so wrapped up in his task of healing suffering humanity, that he had no time to give to such things as earthly honours. Which was, in fact, not quite the case.

The superintendent sent in his card, and was almost immediately taken upstairs to Sir Ernest's consulting-room. It was a fine eighteenth-century room, with book-lined walls, and—unexpectedly—a Steinway grand piano. The floor was covered with Bokhara rugs of exceptional quality. A bust by Henry Moore was the sole compromise with modernity.

Sir Ernest rose, and asked Waller to be seated. He was a man of about sixty, tall and spare, with a deeply lined face of which the skin still bore traces of the yellow fever that had nearly been the end of him in his youth. Indeed, one of Sir Ernest's little jokes was that the reason why he was so successful in the treatment of tropical diseases was because, at one time or another, he had suffered from them all himself.

"I gather," he said, with a little smile, "that you have not come to me for medical advice?"

"No, sir."

"Then must I assume that I myself am under some sort of . . . er . . . suspicion?"

"No, sir. It is purely a matter of routine."

Sir Ernest nodded, and absent-mindedly tapped the blotting-pad in front of him.

"Quite. Quite. A matter of routine." He gave Waller a quizzical smile. "That is the phrase I always use myself, when the case of the patient is pretty hopeless."

"Before I go any further, sir, I may say that you are under no obligation to answer my questions . . . as yet."

Sir Ernest smiled. "The operative phrase, I gather, is in the last two words . . . 'as yet'."

"You may take it that way, sir, if you choose."

"Very well, I do choose. And I am grateful to you for putting it so clearly. What you mean is that . . . either I speak now, of my own free will, or I speak later, in a court of law?"

"Well, sir. . . ."

"Come, Superintendent, we are both men of the world. Have I misinterpreted you?"

"No, sir."

"Good. And who is the object of your inquiry?"

"Mr. Hilary Scole."

Sir Ernest raised his eyebrows. "Is he in any sort of trouble?"

"No, sir."

"Then I'm afraid I don't understand." . . . A light dawned on him. "Wait a moment. He was a friend of poor old Mrs. Faversham, wasn't he? In fact, she financed his last expedition?"

"That's correct, sir."

"Is it anything to do with that case?"

"Indirectly, sir."

"What does that mean?"

Waller hesitated. Then he gave Sir Ernest a single, swift appraising look. He decided that he was the sort of man with whom it would be best to lay all one's cards on the table —not that he had so many cards to lay.

"When I say it is indirectly concerned with the Faversham case, sir, I mean simply that everybody who was even remotely connected with Mrs. Faversham is, *ipso facto*, an object of 'interest'."

"You mean . . . of suspicion?"

"I said . . . of interest. If you, for example, had been Mrs. Faversham's doctor, you would also be of interest. When one is faced with a problem of this nature, one has to widen the field."

Sir Ernest began to trace designs on his blotting-pad. "You want to ask me questions about Mr. Scole's health?"

"That is so. . . ."

"I still feel reluctant. He is an old friend of mine."

"Perhaps that is all the more reason for your giving the information, sir."

Sir Ernest seemed to wrestle with his conscience. Then he said: "What is it precisely, you wish to know?"

Waller remembered Mr. Green's words. He repeated them. "I want to know how long he has to live."

Sir Ernest looked up sharply. "Have you been talking to him?"

"No, sir."

"Nor to any other of his medical attendants?"

"No, sir."

"Then your question is certainly to the point. If I answer it, will it harm him?"

"It will make no difference, one way or the other."

Sir Ernest nodded. "That, I think, is probably true. Very well." He rose to his feet and walked to the window, where a few desultory flakes of snow were beginning to spatter the panes.

"If he is lucky," he said, "Hilary Scole may live for six months."

"And if not?"

"For six weeks."

Waller tried to make his voice sound cool and official— but the sound of death's footsteps had never failed to strike a chill to his heart.

"And which do you consider the more probable?"

Sir Ernest turned. "Hilary was never a very lucky man," he said.

When Waller returned to Scotland Yard, young Bates—gigantic and rubicund—was waiting for him.

"The Deputy Commissioner's been calling for you, sir."

"What about?"

"Princetown, I believe." Seeing Waller's scowl of irritation he held up a massive hand. "It's O.K., sir, no cause for alarm. Only wanted to congratulate you. Seems that since you went down there the convicts wouldn't try to escape . . . not even if you left the front door open."

"That's enough of your cheek."

"All the same, he wants your report in, sir."

"Hell's bells. How many things am I supposed to do at once? I've got enough on my hands with this Faversham case, as it is."

A gleam came into young Bates' eye. "I couldn't take on some of that, could I, sir?"

"No, you couldn't," barked the superintendent. And then, seeing Bates' look of disappointment—like a dog who has been waiting for one to throw a stone—he relented. "Wait a minute. There might be."

"Yes, sir?"

Waller bethought himself of the second of Mr. Green's errands. It had been so fantastic that he had not bothered to do anything about it. Still—one never could tell.

"Know anything about Indian boys?" he demanded.

"What's that, sir?"

"Indian boys. Small brown creatures with two legs."

"Can't say I know much about 'em, sir."

"Well, now's your great chance to learn a bit more." He flicked open his notebook. "Ah, yes! Here we are. Indian boys. Approximately nine years old. Entered at schools in Hampstead district within the last nine months."

Bates scratched his head. "Any particular boy, sir?"

"Not that I know of."

"Anything special you want to know about 'em, sir?"

"No. Just where they are and what they're called." He

glared at Bates. "Well, what are you waiting for? If anybody had given me a job like that when I was your age I'd have caught a dozen of 'em by now."

Bates gulped. This was not the sort of job he had anticipated. Nothing glamorous about it at all. What's more, he hadn't the vaguest idea how to set about it. Talk about looking for a nigger in a woodpile—well, come to think of it, that was precisely what he was being asked to do.

He dared not risk his superior's wrath by asking for suggestions, but he made a last feeble effort to get Waller to throw a little more light on the subject.

"Nine years old, did you say, sir?" he asked, addressing the back of Waller's neck.

Waller turned sharply. "What, you still there? Yes, I did say nine years old. And I did say they'd got to have gone to school in the last nine months. And I did say in Hampstead district. And I do say scram."

Bates scrammed.

A sergeant entered with a portfolio which he laid on Waller's desk.

"Your photographs, sir."

Ah! Here was something at last—or might be.

"Which was the one I asked you to have enlarged?"

"This one, sir. On the top."

Waller looked incredulous. "Are you sure?"

"Quite sure, sir."

He took it between his fingers, and stared at it. It was the head-and-shoulders portrait of a benevolent old lady of about seventy. It had been taken somewhat sideways—Mr. Green was never very good at getting things quite straight—and it showed a portion of a silver frame. He had not the smallest clue to the identity of the subject; it reminded him of nobody he had ever seen before.

He gave a non-committal grunt. Then he said to the sergeant: "Get me another two dozen or so samples."

"Any particular age or type, sir?"

"No. As varied as possible. Half men and half women."

By "samples" Waller meant his own little collection of

portraits which he used, on occasions like this, when it was a question of establishing identity. They were chosen on the same principle as the characters on a "line-up" parade. Usually, half a dozen women sufficed, but in a case like this, where the net of suspicion was so widely spread, it was obviously necessary to have more.

While he was waiting for the "samples", Waller drew out the file of the Faversham case, and extracted pictures of all and sundry at Faversham Court, including even the least likely of those concerned, such as Mrs. Ackworth, Meadows, and the three daily women from the village. Might as well do the thing thoroughly while he was about it.

Then he stared, once again, at the portrait of the old lady. Was he sure he had not seen her before? Yes, he was. It was no use trying to kid himself. Was he quite certain that she reminded him of nobody? Yes, he was. She rang no sort of bell. He could not even place her socially, though he inclined to think that she was of the small shop-keeper class, possibly a countrywoman.

Well, before long, he might know a little more. Or again, he might not.

v

Even the strong arm of the law was incapable of animating the officials of Paddington Station with any sense of urgency. Mr. Waller waited, in a small ill-lit room on the west side of the station. On his way up he had called at the Parcels Office, examined the ledger, and established the fact that the box had been called for, round about 6 p.m. on the evening of 5th February. Opposite the entry in the ledger was a pencilled scrawl which might have been the mysterious, "C. C. Smith", or it might equally have been the Aga Khan. However, that was typical of the great majority of signatures.

Waller continued to wait, kicking his heels. He loathed slowness, and he felt that he was surrounded by it on all sides. He was apparently sitting in the room belonging to one of the station officials, but he had no idea who this official might be. Nor, apparently, had anyone else. All he knew was that it bore the word "Private" on the door. Who worked here was one of the dark mysteries of the British Railways.

At long last, however, the door opened, and in came a young man in horn-rimmed glasses followed by two young porters in uniform.

"These are two of your men," he said, in *blasé* and superior tones. "The other two are off."

Waller glared at him. "By the way," he said, "I didn't catch your name."

The horn-rimmed one raised his eyebrows and swept back his hair. "My name is Wilkins," he said, "if it's of any consequence."

"It may be," replied Waller, in such dark tones, that a faint shadow of apprehension fell over Mr. Wilkins' face. "And what, exactly, do you mean by 'off'?"

"Why having their tea," he replied shortly, as though to be "off" could admit of no other interpretation.

"Then, perhaps you will be good enough to fetch them at once."

Mr. Wilkins' jaw opened, as though he were about to argue, but Waller interrupted him. "Wilkins, I think you said your name was?"

The shadow of apprehension darkened. Why did this dreadful man keep on asking his name? What had he done? Oh, dear—it was all most irregular and disturbing, and the porters would be furious at being taken away from their tea, but what could he do?

"I'll be back in a moment," he said and swept out.

Waller turned to the two young porters, who seemed reasonably bright and forthcoming. They naturally assumed, with the optimism of youth, that a murder had just been committed in the vicinity of the station, and Waller was too tired—and too amiable—to disillusion them.

"Some of them trunks we 'as to 'andle," suggested one of them. "You never know what's in 'em. Might be a corpse, any day."

The other one gave a sepulchral guffaw. "Might be a couple of corpses, by the weight of 'em."

"Was it anything in our department, sir?" demanded the first one.

"Yes, it was."

"Wot? *Murder*?" He sounded as though he were cheering a goal at a cup-tie.

Waller nodded. However, he did not volunteer any more information.

They had not long to wait for the other two, who arrived in a breathless and slightly cowed condition, having evidently been warned by Wilkins that they were about to come into the presence of a Tartar. In a few swift questions Waller established the fact that one of the four of them must have handled the package on the afternoon of 5th February.

"What I want you men to do is very simple," said Waller. "Over there are a number of photographs. All types and ages. I want you to examine each of these photographs, and try to see if you recognize one of them."

"If we do," chirped in the youngest of the porters, who was inclined to be facetious, "will it be the one 'oo dunnit?"

Waller scowled at him with such ferocity that he lapsed into silence.

"If you do recognize one of them," continued Waller, "try to cast back your mind, and see if you connect him—or her —with the object which was being called for. I'm not going to tell you what that object was. It might be a trunk, or it might be a suitcase, it might be a crate, it might be quite large or it might be quite small. But please remember this. I don't want any shots in the dark. Don't try to recognize anybody just for the sake of it. Now get cracking."

The men went over, and began to examine the photographs. After a moment, the youngest porter gave vent to a "Coo!" and came over with one of the photographs. Waller glanced at it. It was one of his "samples", a certain Sergeant Cossor, of the vice squad.

He shook his head. "Sorry. No good."

"But, sir, I could 'ave sworn. . . ."

162

"Then you'd have sworn wrong. That's a dummy."

Deflated the young man returned.

Suddenly, the eldest of the porters turned round.

"I think I've got something here, sir."

"Yes? Bring it over."

He lifted a photograph from the pile, and walked across. He laid it on Waller's desk.

Waller's heart gave a sudden leap. He found himself staring at Mr. Green's old lady.

"Sure about this?"

"Quite sure, sir."

Waller nodded. He was a prey to a number of mixed emotions. It looked as though Mr. Green had done it again —though what precisely he had done, he could hardly guess. It was a bit tough on ordinary chaps, like himself, the way that little man swooped in and swept the board. However, he ought to be used to it by now. And anyway, there was still the question of the package to be identified.

"Do you remember what it was that she called for?"

"As a matter of fact I do, sir. Like a small wooden crate it was. About this size." He sketched it with his hands. "It was pretty heavy, and I remember asking her if she 'ad the crown jewels in it." He coughed apologetically. "That's a joke we often make with the public, sir."

"Did she have a porter?"

"No. She carried it away herself."

"Would you recognize her again?"

"Pretty sure I would, sir."

"I don't know if it will be necessary. If it is, I'll call on you again." He rose abruptly. "Thank you all for your assistance."

He gave a curt nod to Mr. Wilkins, and strode out.

VI

It was a very tired Waller who rang up Mr. Green that night. As soon as he had returned to the Yard, he had been hauled up once again, before the deputy commissioner, who was impatiently awaiting his final report on the measures to be taken at Princetown Prison.

"It's all very well, sir, but I can't do two jobs at once."

"Still worrying about the Faversham case?"

"Well, sir, you put me on to it in the first instance."

"I know. Getting anywhere with it?"

Waller hesitated. To say that he was "getting anywhere" would not be strictly true. He was not even sure that Mr. Green was "getting anywhere". True, they were not standing still, but whether they were going backwards or forwards or sideways, it was not for him to say.

So he contented himself with: "I think things are beginning to move, sir."

The deputy commissioner nodded. He was fully aware of what was passing in the superintendent's mind. He was also aware of the part that Mr. Green was playing. Between them, he was pretty confident that they'd get results; they usually did. In the meantime, he wanted his report.

"Well," he said, "that's good news. All the same, I dare say you could put it aside for twenty-four hours?"

Waller hesitated again. *Could* he put it aside for twenty-four hours? What about all the strange confusing discoveries of his crowded day? In particular, what about the mysterious old lady who had called at Paddington Station?

"After all," prompted the deputy commissioner, "you've got two quite good men down there, keeping an eye on things." (He deliberately did not mention Mr. Green; he did not want to wound Waller's *amour propre*.) "And if there are any special investigations, there's always young Bates."

Suddenly, Waller found himself in full agreement. Twenty-four hours out of this crazy business might be a welcome relief; it might clear his brain. It might even give *him* a chance, for a change, of sitting back and sniffing.

"Very good, sir," he said. "May I take it that I can have Bates exclusively?"

"By all means. Is he on anything special at the moment?"

If Waller had been in the habit of blushing, this would

have been his great opportunity. He simply could not bring himself to inform the deputy commissioner that Bates, at this moment, was scouring the highways and byways of Hampstead, in search of small Indian boys. It would have needed altogether too much explanation.

"Nothing very special, sir," he said. "Just an idea we had."

"That's settled then. D'you think you'll be able to get your report in by to-morrow night?"

"I'll have a good shot, sir."

With which, he went home.

It was ten o'clock before he was able to get through to Mr. Green. He told Mr. Green, briefly, of his interview with the deputy commissioner, and put Bates at his disposal. Then he said:

"Well, you were right."

"It *was* the old lady?"

"It was. No question about it."

A long, long sigh from Mr. Green, all the way from Devonshire.

"You sound depressed about it."

"Perhaps I am—a little." A pause. "What about the business at the bank?"

Waller gave him a brief *précis* of the financial transactions between Kenneth and Sandra.

"And Hilary?"

"Six months if he's lucky. Six weeks if he's not."

There was a longer pause. Then Mr. Green said: "I wonder if it should not be the other way round?"

"What do you mean?"

"Never mind."

Waller grunted. He was too tired for riddles. He wished Mr. Green good-night and rang off.

13

THE FOLLOWING day, for Mr. Green, began with a bang. And it went on banging, like a Christmas cracker, till the bitter end.

He had just had his first cup of coffee, in the little dining-room of the inn. With his first cup of coffee Mr. Green's life began; the overture started, the curtain rose, and the play went on. Until that moment he could neither think nor reason nor even perceive with any clarity.

It was lucky that he was thus fortified when the young landlord entered, bearing with him a large registered parcel. For its arrival made it necessary for him to employ his powers of perception to the full.

"This has just come for you, sir," he said. "It needs your signature."

Mr. Green signed his name in the postman's book. The landlord noticed that his fingers were trembling ever so slightly.

Mr. Green put the parcel on the floor beside him, closed his eyes, and began to think. As he thought, he frowned. He opened his eyes, and poured himself out another cup of coffee, which he drank at a single gulp. Then he closed his eyes, thought again, and frowned even more deeply.

After a moment, he rose quickly to his feet, picked up the parcel, and hurried out. In the doorway he met Ivy, the barmaid, coming in with his boiled egg. "I'm afraid I shan't have time for it this morning, Ivy," he murmured, to that young lady's distress. She had developed a fondness for Mr. Green, and she did not like to think of him going into the great world on an empty stomach. An empty stomach, in Ivy's opinion, was a treacherous and misleading organ, particularly when it was attached to an elderly gentleman. However, Mr. Green was already half-way up the stairs before she was able to protest.

Mr. Green took the parcel into his bedroom and set it down on his bed. For a moment he stood there staring at it. Then he took out his clasp-knife and cut the string, very carefully, sliding his knife under the seals, so that they were detached without breaking. He also made a note of the postmark. It had been sent off yesterday morning from Southwark; the district postmark was S.E.8 As, of course, one would have expected.

Then he prised off the top, using his clasp-knife. On a sudden instinct he got up, and locked the door. And then he took the box over to the bed and turned it upside down.

Out fell a clatter of leather cases, and a succession of objects wrapped in tissue paper. One of the cases came open as it fell, with a flash of gold and green and scarlet.

So there they were, the Faversham jewels, delivered into his hands. He had not asked for them, and he certainly did not want them, but he supposed that they might as well be with him as with anyone else. He went over to the mantelpiece, put on his gloves, and began to open the cases. He was not expecting any message to arrive with them, but he had better make sure.

No, there was nothing. For a moment he stayed there, watching them glisten in all their glory. The emeralds were perhaps the most valuable, in particular the famous tiara which had only recently been re-set by Boucheron. Then there was the necklace of star sapphires, and the rubies, of quite exceptional colour, so vivid that they seemed almost alive, like newly spilt blood.

He packed the jewels back in their cases. He would take them up to Candle Court at once; they were not the sort of things he could have lying about. Glancing at his watch he saw that it was already twenty minutes to nine. He must hurry; he wanted to catch them at breakfast, when they were all gathered together. It would be interesting to see their various reactions.

He was just about to put the cases into his own attaché case, when he paused, and thought better of it. He would put them back in the box in which they had arrived; he

167

would even refasten part of the lid, to give the impression that he had not emptied the jewels out at all. And then—if there were any of his watchers who were interested in something other than jewels, in, for instance, a letter—well, it would be instructive.

He put on his overcoat, clasped the box under his arm, and hurried out.

II

Meanwhile at Candle Court, breakfast was proceeding, none too amicably.

There were four of them, Beryl, Kenneth, Pusey and Hilary. The subject of discussion was Mr. Green himself.

"How much longer have we got to put up with him?" Beryl was asking.

"If it comes to that," said Kenneth, "how much longer have we got to put up with Waller?"

"I can stand him. He doesn't pretend to be a gentleman, and he usually keeps his place. But Mr. Green drifts in and out as though the house belonged to him."

"Well, I don't know what we can do about it. It'd look pretty queer if we suddenly told him to stop it."

"Why would it look queer?"

Kenneth threw his newspaper on the floor with a gesture of irritation. "If I've said it once, I've said it a hundred times. If we locked the door on Green at this stage of the proceedings, he might think we had something to hide."

"You needn't shout at me." She stared at him coldly. Kenneth had been behaving very strangely since his return from London last night. For some reason or other he seemed to be a bundle of nerves. He had obviously been drinking heavily, but would drink alone account for that queer, haunted look?

Aloud, she said: "I don't care if he does think we've got something to hide. Good heavens—he's had long enough to find it, if it exists. And he hasn't got a clue. Or if he has, he certainly hasn't mentioned it to any of us." She turned to

168

Pusey. "How long does that sort of person hang around after . . . after this sort of trouble?"

Pusey shrugged his shoulders. "I hardly know. In the case of the police, it may be for years. . . ."

"What? Do you mean to tell me. . . ."

He held up his hand to appease her. "Not actively, of course. Quiescently, shall we say? In the sense that the files of the case are kept open. . . ."

"But Mr. Green doesn't belong to the police? How long does *he* go on?"

Hilary spoke for the first time. He had apparently been paying little heed to the conversation. He had merely been staring out of the window, scanning the winter landscape with his hot, fevered eyes.

"He usually goes on," he said, "until. . . ."

At this moment there was a knock on the door leading to the conservatory passage.

"Yes?" cried Beryl. Wilburfoss came in. "What is it, Wilburfoss?"

"Just to know when Mr. Scole wanted to see me, m'lady."

"I'll come straight away." Hilary got up slowly, supporting himself with his hands on the table.

"But you were saying something about Mr. Green, Hilary. He usually goes on until . . . what?"

He gave her a curious smile. "Until he gets his man."

At which moment, the door from the hall opened, very gently, and a quiet voice murmured, "May I come in?"

III

Five minutes later, when the pandemonium had died down, and when Pusey—who had somewhat protestingly agreed to Mr. Green's suggestion that he should equip himself with gloves—was packing the jewels back in their cases, Mr. Green strolled to the window. He wanted a moment to register and catalogue his impressions while they were still fresh and vivid.

What were they, in the order of their importance?

Firstly, he had a very definite conviction that each and every person in the room had been quite genuinely startled by the arrival of the jewels. There was nothing bogus about their bewilderment. Whatever else they may have been expecting, they were not expecting *that*.

In short, none of them had sent the jewels, nor had any of them an accomplice who had sent them.

Admittedly, this was precisely the impression that Mr. Green had expected to receive, before he entered the room.

But it was satisfactory to have it confirmed.

Secondly, Hilary's reaction. He had just said three words. Staring at the jewels, he had stretched out his hand, very slowly, and said: "Is that all?"

Mr. Green was about to weigh up the significance of those three words, when Kenneth came up behind him. He seemed to have recovered his bluster and self-confidence.

"I say, old chap," he said, "this rather alters things, doesn't it?"

"In what way?"

"Well, really!" It was Beryl who spoke. "Surely the police won't be so interested, now that we've got them back?"

"Besides, there's the insurance people," added her husband. "Naturally, we shall have to withdraw our claim, so they'll be happy enough; they won't want to go on with it. As a matter of fact, the things were rather over-insured, so you might say, in a sort of way, that it's a loss to us, getting 'em back. But if it means the whole darned thing's nearer to being over and done with. . . ."

Mr. Green could scarcely believe his ears. Hard as the Favershams were, he had not been prepared for so blatant an exhibition of callous vulgarity. Unlovable as old Mrs. Faversham may have been, she was at least Kenneth's mother, and she had met a violent and cruel death. And the words in which he described this tragedy were "the whole darned thing!"

He checked the rebuke which he might well have delivered, and murmured something non-committal about informing the police.

170

Beryl drew him to one side. "May I have a word with you, Mr. Green?"

"What about?" demanded Kenneth, in a surly voice.

She gave him a hard, forced smile. "Nothing that concerns you, darling."

"We might go outside, if you have a moment?"

She took his assent for granted, and led the way into the hall, where, with some reluctance, Mr. Green helped her into a wrap.

"It's about Sandra," she said, when they were outside.

"Ah, yes!" Mr. Green blinked at her innocently. "Where *is* she, by the way?"

"She's staying in London till Saturday."

"With friends?"

"I'm sure I don't know. She never tells one anything. However, that's neither here nor there. What *I* wanted to ask you is . . . do you think we ought to do anything about her?"

"In what way?"

"Well, financially."

"It would be very generous of you."

"I haven't the least desire to be generous. I'm only thinking of what people will say. Like that ghastly Eva Brockhurst."

"Is it any business of hers?"

"Of course not. But she'll make it her business. So will the rest of them. They all know that Mother absolutely doted on her."

"What does your husband suggest?"

She threw back her head with an impatient gesture. "Kenneth says she's no right to anything at all, which is odd considering that . . ." She did not finish the sentence.

Mr. Green could barely repress a smile. Perhaps if Beryl were aware of the very large sum which had already passed into Miss Wells' possession, she might not think it so "odd" that her husband had no desire to increase it.

"I take it that she will be leaving very shortly?"

"Good heavens, yes. The sooner the better."

171

"In that case—perhaps—a hundred pounds?"

"That's what I thought. It'd have to be something like that. I couldn't resent it more bitterly, but anything less might look as though we were grudging it. I might throw in Mother's old squirrel coat, as well."

They had reached the low wall that bordered the path leading to the falls. By a common instinct they both paused, and watched the silver pageant of the water. The sight of it helped to restore Mr. Green's spirits. He had been beginning to feel slightly unclean, after this conversation.

Suddenly, a thought struck him. "By the way," he said, "I wonder if you could give me a little information?"

"Oh, dear! Is it about anything dreadful?"

"Not at all. It might almost be described as in the nature of light relief."

"We could certainly do with some of that. Well, what is it?"

"I wanted to know whether Mr. Pusey collects butterflies."

She burst out laughing. "Really, what an extraordinary question!" Then she looked at him more closely. "Is there anything sinister behind this?"

"On the contrary."

"Not that I've any great affection for Pusey." ("Nor," thought Mr. Green, as he noted the hard line of her mouth, "for anybody else.") "As a matter of fact, he does."

"Ah!"

"Why do you look so pleased about it?"

"It merely confirmed a little theory of mine. Has he collected them for long?"

"Yes, that's why I know about it. He was at school with Kenneth, and they were sort of rivals. Not too friendly, either; they used to have fights about it. But I should have thought that's all forgotten by now."

"No doubt," said Mr. Green.

Something in his tone of voice made her look at him again. "You're sure there's nothing sinister in your question?"

172

"Quite sure."

"D'you know, I'm almost sorry. I wouldn't mind seeing Pusey taken down a peg."

Mr. Green sighed and looked away. The pervading malice of her spirit seemed to poison the very river itself.

"Shall we go in?" he suggested. "It is none too warm."

She nodded. As they turned they saw a figure hurrying towards them. It was Meadows. He looked pale and distressed.

"Excuse me, madam," he said, touching his cap, "may I have a word with you?"

"Yes, Meadows. What is it?"

He hesitated, glancing at Mr. Green.

"Is it private?"

"Oh, no, madam, not with Mr. Green." He gave a shy, fleeting smile. Then his face grew grave again. "It's my old grannie. I've just got word."

"What about her?"

"She died in the night, madam."

Mr. Green noticed that Beryl's mouth twitched. Why was it, he wondered sadly, that the conjunction of death and grandmothers, when associated with the lower classes, was always regarded as a subject for humour? Why was it the pattern of the standard joke about the office boy who wanted to play truant? Old age—poverty—death . . . they seemed strange ingredients for laughter-making. But then, Mr. Green's sense of humour was sometimes sadly out of key with that of the crowd.

He heard Beryl saying, in hard, crisp accents: "Well, Meadows, I'm sure I'm sorry. I suppose that means you'll want to go up to London?"

"If it's convenient, madam."

"It could hardly be called *convenient*, could it?" she retorted. "However, things can't be helped. What train do you want to catch?"

"Well, madam, Mr. Scole . . . he said he'd take me in his car. He's going up this morning."

"Mr. Scole?" Beryl turned to Mr. Green. "Really, Hilary

173

is extraordinary. He never told me he was going up. I mean ... honestly ... sometimes I think he imagines my house is a sort of hotel." She recollected herself and turned back to Meadows. "Very well, Meadows. You'll tell Wilburfoss, of course."

"I've done so, madam."

Mr. Green had a sudden idea. "I wonder if Mr. Scole would be able to take me, too?"

It was to Meadows that he spoke, but Beryl chimed in: "Are you leaving us?" She made no pretence that she was sorry at the prospect.

He did not appear to hear her. "Do you think there would be room for me, Meadows? I have to be in London to-night."

"I'm sure Mr. Scole would be glad, sir. Shall I go and tell him?"

"If you would be so kind. In the meantime I will go down to the inn and pack my bag."

Meadows hurried off.

He was hardly out of earshot before Beryl said: "Really, you spoil that boy."

"In what way?"

"Well, you talk to him almost as though he were a gentleman."

There were many replies that Mr. Green might have made to this statement, but he did not make them; they would have been hardly suitable for the ears of a lady.

"I'm afraid it is a bad habit of mine," he murmured. Then, with a frigid smile, he extended his hand. "Till our next meeting."

"And when is that likely to be?"

"If all is well, the day after to-morrow."

"If all is well?"

Mr. Green looked her straight in the eyes. "Perhaps that is not quite the right expression. I am afraid that for some people it may not be well at all."

He turned and left her without another word. When he had gone, she clenched her teeth, and picked up a stone, and hurled it with surprising savagery at the river, as though an enemy were lurking in the hurrying waters.

IV

Mr. Green, as soon as he was out of her sight, quickened his steps considerably; indeed, it might almost be said that he ran.

He was out of breath when he reached the inn, but he put a call through to the Yard immediately. As luck would have it, there were no delays, and within a couple of minutes the cheerful voice of young Bates was echoing down the wire.

"Been trying to get hold of you, sir," he said, before Mr. Green could explain his business. "About your Indian boys."

"What about them, Bates?"

"The superintendent doesn't seem too keen on 'em, sir."

There was a long pause, in which Mr. Green refrained from saying a number of things that he was sorely tempted to say. It was too bad of Waller to take this attitude. Surely, after all these years of working together, in a sort of unofficial double harness, Waller knew him well enough to realize that he would not have asked him to follow up such a line of investigation without the most urgent reasons?

Then he realized that he was being unfair. Indian boys in Hampstead—it did sound, to say the least of it, far fetched. And if he were really honest with himself he must admit that he *had* been almost excessively obscure, simply because of his incurable tendency, from time to time, to toy with the role of Sherlock Holmes.

"Are you there, sir?"

"Yes, Bates. Forgive me, I was wool-gathering. About the Indian boys. You can assure the superintendent that in my opinion they are quite vital."

"That ought to be good enough for him, sir."

"Let us hope so. You have all the particulars, I believe?"

"Yes, sir."

175

"Then as soon as we have finished our conversation, I hope you will be able to continue your inquiries. And I should like a list of the names of the boys and their respective schools—you will only have time for that—delivered to me at the Travellers' Club in Pall Mall this afternoon, not later than four o'clock. You know the Travellers' Club?"

"Yes, sir."

"Good. Now please listen very carefully." Mr. Green glanced at his watch. Although so much seemed to have happened since breakfast, it was still barely half past nine. If they started within half an hour, and if Hilary drove at his normal speed, they should be there soon after four.

"I am coming up to London to-day and I shall be arriving at the Travellers' between four and five."

"By car, sir?"

"Yes. Mr. Hilary Scole's car. The registration number is HXR 830. It is a scarlet Jaguar sports model."

"A fast job, sir."

"Rather too fast for my liking," commented Mr. Green. "With Mr. Scole will be a young man called Meadows. I shall get out at the club, and I do not wish you to recognize me. The Jaguar will drive on, and I want you to follow it."

"Very good, sir." From the tone of Bates' voice it was obvious that he meant what he said. What healthy young man could fail to rejoice at the prospect of keeping on the tail of a Jaguar, particularly a scarlet sports model?

"Any idea where they'll be going, sir?"

"Mainly the London district, I think. Southwark for certain. But wherever they go, keep track of them."

"Very good, sir. Any messages for the superintendent, sir?"

Mr. Green paused. What message could he send to Waller, at a time like this? Nothing that would not sound totally incomprehensible.

"I don't think so, Bates," he said. And then: "But you might ask him to wish me luck."

176

14

MR. GREEN was just finishing breakfast the following morning when Bates telephoned with his report.

It was as he had expected. So much so, indeed, that for a moment he found himself wishing that the powerful little Jaguar had taken some strange turning that would have baffled him—that Hilary and his companion might have paid a mysterious visit to the zoo, or have been shadowed to a clandestine rendezvous at Madame Tussaud's.

This case, which had begun by seeming so baffling, was proving almost too simple.

Or was it? Mr. Green shook his head at the folly of allowing himself such a thought. It was tempting Providence. The moment a case gave the appearance of simplicity it was a sure sign that a surprise was round the corner.

Well, he would try to be ready for it, if and when it came.

He thanked Bates, wished him luck in his search for Indian boys, and went back to his perusal of *The Times*.

But the newspaper did not hold his attention. "Too simple, indeed!" Why had he allowed himself that momentary reflection? What imp of mischief had danced through his brain? Some aspects of the case might be simple indeed, but others. . . .

Besides, even if every piece of the puzzle were finally fitted, even if all the problems were solved, at the end there was the final problem of pain. Somebody was going to be hurt . . . mortally hurt. That was inevitable. And when the vast mystery of pain was involved how could one speak of simplicity?

Mr. Green had a sudden suspicion that this profession of his was making him callous, that it was hardening his heart.

He pushed aside *The Times* and walked rapidly to the

library. Then he sat down and began to write a letter. But it must have been a very difficult letter to write, for after each attempt he tore it up. Finally, he put his hand across his eyes, and if you had been watching him very closely, you would have seen that his lips were moving, as though he were murmuring a prayer.

After that, the letter came very easily. It consisted of only a few sentences, but they were sentences of comfort. He sealed it, and put it in his pocket. As he went out into the hall he no longer felt callous or hard-boiled.

II

Mr. Green, as might be expected, had friends in all trades and in all walks of society, and it was often his experience that the humbler their position, the greater their value. A lift-boy might prove a better friend than the owner of the mansion in which he worked, a news-vendor a more trusted ally than the press lord who owned the papers it was his job to sell.

So, at least, he felt as he passed through the swing-doors of the building which housed the vast concern known to all the world as Trans-Oceanic Airways Incorporated. He had more than a nodding acquaintance with the American millionaire who sat at the head of this international organization, and also with the peer who was his British counterpart. But he did not seek their co-operation.

Mr. Green knew exactly what department he wanted. It was a desk in the farthest corner, almost hidden by a soaring pillar of green malachite. Behind the desk the walls were decorated with a selection of particularly vivid posters, advertising the dreams of various South American states. Against this flamboyant background stood a little middle-aged woman in a grey serge dress. She was so mousy, so insignificant, that she reminded him of some small animal endeavouring to hide in the depths of a tropical jungle.

Her name was Miss Withers, and some years ago, in the case of the Bessingham diamonds, in which she had been

178

a very remote and minor witness, he had been able to save her from a few minutes of slight embarrassment. Her gratitude for this service could not have been greater if he had rescued her from the gallows, and ever since, at every Christmas, she had sent him a very expensive calendar.

"Well, Mr. Green—this *is* a surprise!"

And a very pleasant one, it seemed, from the tone of her voice and the pink flush of her cheeks.

Mr. Green, in a few graceful sentences, congratulated her on her appearance, and also on her taste in calendars. The last one, he assured her, had a place of honour on his mantelpiece—a statement which happened to be quite true. It had everything which, in his opinion, a calendar should have, including a great deal of poster snow and no less than six robins, of the most satisfactory corpulence.

After these compliments, he got down to business. Leaning over the desk, and speaking in a lower tone than was necessary—for he realized that she would be flattered if he made her feel that she was entering into a conspiracy—he said:

"Miss Withers, I wonder if you could help me?"

"Oh, Mr. Green, I *do* so hope so."

"It is not a business matter."

"Oh, no, I'm sure!" She spoke as though she would have been greatly disappointed if it *had* been a business matter.

"I am interested in the movements of Mr. Hilary Scole, and a companion of his."

Her face went blank.

"You do not know him?"

"Oh, Mr. Green—oh, I'm so sorry—but I can't honestly say I *do*."

"Never mind." He drew out his wallet and produced a snapshot. It was a duplicate of the official copy in Waller's file, and a very vivid portrait. "Does this convey anything to you?"

She stared at it intently. Then recognition dawned on her.

"Why, yes!" she exclaimed. "This is one of the two gentlemen who came in late yesterday afternoon."

179

Mr. Green nodded.

"I remember them distinctly, because we were really closing, and Miss Wilkins—she's that desk over there—had already closed her files."

"I see. What department does she deal in?"

"Miss Wilkins? She's on the Rio service."

"Is there a direct flight to Rio?"

"Oh, yes. Every Saturday afternoon."

"How long does it take?"

"Thirty-two hours, if there's no delay."

Mr. Green did a rapid calculation. "So that a passenger leaving this afternoon should be in Rio by midnight on Sunday?"

"That's right."

"Wonderful!" said Mr. Green, "this modern transport." But there was an absent-minded look on his face. He hurried back to Miss Withers. "Are you friendly with Miss Wilkins?"

"Oh, yes, we're quite chums, really!"

"Then I wonder if you could ask if she would very kindly tell you if either Mr. Scole or Mr. Meadows"—he spelt both names in full—"if either or both of those gentlemen are passengers on the flight to Rio to-morrow afternoon?"

"Of course, Mr. Green. I'll go right over."

She hurried off, leaving him to stare at pictures of the scarlet parrots of Guatemala, the golden cathedrals of Colombia, the purple mountains of Venezuela, and all the other allurements, which were displayed to entice the traveller to this singularly boring part of the world.

In a few moments she was back. She walked, as it were, on tiptoe, and her finger—metaphorically speaking—was to her lips, for she felt that she was indeed a conspirator.

"Yes," she whispered. "Mr. Scole is on the plane."

A shadow seemed to pass across Mr. Green's face. "*Only* Mr. Scole?"

"Only Mr. Scole."

Mr. Green blinked. And blinked again. "I wonder," he said to himself, "I wonder exactly what that means."

"Pardon, Mr. Green?"

"Forgive me. I was thinking aloud."

She beamed upon him. She was agog with curiosity but she could not summon up the courage to ask a direct question. However, she ventured: "Is it . . . is it in connection with something?"

"Yes, Miss Withers. It is in connection with something. Something very strange."

With that, she had to be content. A few more compliments and he was gone.

III

From the offices of Trans-Oceanic Airways, Mr. Green walked to Victoria Station, where he descended into the underground and bought a ticket to Southwark. He could have taken a taxi but he saw no reason to waste the money. Besides, he found that a journey by underground was always a good means of collecting his thoughts.

Judging by his puzzled expression when he reached his destination, and by the frequency with which he paused in the mean streets through which he walked, and stared at the pavement, and blinked at nothing in particular, there were still a number of thoughts in his head which had not yielded to collection.

However, he pressed on, and eventually found himself in a little grey street which bore the ironic title of Paradise Row. Half-way down was Number 117. He rang the bell.

The door was opened by an old lady. He took off his hat and asked her a question.

She shook her head.

He handed her the letter he had written at the club. He walked back the way he had come.

He had done his best.

IV

And so the day sped by for Mr. Green, with many and various calls, which need not concern us, for they were only very minor fragments of the puzzle which he was about to complete.

The last, and major fragment, was in his hand.

It was ten minutes to four, and he stood opposite a long, ugly, red brick building in a quiet road off Fitzjohn's Avenue, the broad sweep that bears the traveller so often from the mists of St. John's Wood into the comparative clarity of Hampstead.

However, Mr. Green, on this occasion, was not thinking of the weather . . . which was certainly inclement enough. He was waiting for the boys to come out of school—for that was the function of the building outside which he had paused. Not a very pretty school, he thought, as he strolled backwards and forwards on the opposite side of the road, and certainly not a very expensive one. But it was just the sort of school in which he would have expected to find the particular boy for whom he was in search.

A cracked bell in the porter's lodge pealed the hour, four o'clock, and even as it did so there came from inside the building the series of explosions and uproars which heralds the liberation of youth. There was the sound of slamming desks, and shouted challenges, and the scurry of young feet down stone staircases. Within the space of a few seconds the courtyard began to fill with small figures, some of them running helter-skelter for the entrance, by which he was standing, others strolling leisurely, with linked arms, a few walking alone, clinging to their satchels.

He moved closer to the entrance, half-hidden by the trunk of an ancient plane tree. Few of the boys glanced at him, and even those who did so did not look twice, so completely insignificant was his small figure. But he scanned every face with the keenest scrutiny. And then he found him.

He was almost the last boy to pass through the gate. He was smaller than most of them, and he walked slowly and quite alone, with his eyes to the ground. As he passed Mr. Green, he paused, and looked up to the sky, as though he were searching for a break in the clouds.

The boys in front of him turned round.

"Look at Blacky," shouted one of them.

"Blacky, blacky, blackamoor!" jeered another. The boy paid no heed to them, and they went on. He had heard the taunt only too often in his young life. For though his features were fine and sensitive, his skin was very dark—with the velvety texture of the Southern Indian.

Then he began to walk down the road, with Mr. Green in his wake. In spite of his years, his shortness of breath, and even more, his shortness of legs, Mr. Green was an expert shadower; he had a chameleon-like facility for fitting into his surroundings; and the fact that he always wore rubber soles to his shoes made him tread as softly as a cat.

However, even if he had desired to call attention to himself, it is doubtful whether the boy would have noticed him, so absorbed did he appear to be in his own thoughts. The road grew narrower and shabbier, and though it still bore traces of gentility, it had a melancholy air of coming down further in the world with every step they took.

At last the boy turned sharply to the left, and Mr. Green, still following, found himself in a *cul-de-sac* of old Regency houses from which the paint was peeling. The boy went to the last house in the row, climbed the steps, and let himself in through the front door with a latchkey.

Mr. Green prowled to the end and merged into the railings. He could not look into the house, for the blinds were already drawn. He noticed that against the window-pane of the room on the first floor there was a sign: "Basement Room to Let."

He walked up and down, twisting the fingers of his podgy hands with the same air of abstraction as he might have fingered a rosary, had his form of Christianity demanded such a symbol. He was far from happy. He was tired; he was rather hungry; his feet ached; and he felt a chill round his shoulders. Apart from these physical manifestations, he was mentally ill at ease. There were still—even now—some pieces of the puzzle that did not quite fit. Almost, but not quite. It was a question of an hour too soon in one place and an hour too soon in another. Sometimes it was even a question of a glance that seemed out of keeping, a turn of the head for which he could not account.

However, the principal cause of his depression was neither physical nor mental; it was spiritual.

What right had he—a little bachelor in late middle age, whose principal passions in life were his garden, his Siamese cats, and the sonatas of Mozart—what *right* had he to be prowling up and down this road on a mission which, if it succeeded, might only add to the misery of mankind?

Was it some abstract passion for justice? He could not lay such unction to his soul. Was it merely because he was piqued at the thought of being defeated—was he merely jealous of his reputation? No—he did not think that he was quite as petty as that.

Probably, he decided with a sigh, it was merely his passion for tidiness. He had been precipitated into a situation which seemed to make no sense, in which the laws of nature were apparently set at naught; and that disturbed him, filled him with a vague sense of outrage, almost of blasphemy.

For Mr. Green believed that the universe made very good sense, and that the laws of nature must be obeyed, even if, in obeying them, somebody got hurt.

He braced his shoulders, took a deep breath, and crossed the road.

He pressed the bell.

The door opened, and Sandra stood before him.

He took off his hat, and twirled it nervously in his hand. "I am afraid this must be a rather unexpected . . ." he began.

"On the contrary," she said, "I was waiting for you."

He went inside.

15

Come what, come may,
Time and the hour run through the roughest day.

IT WAS Mr. Green's favourite tag, which had been whispered to him by his mother, long, long ago on the day that he had set out for his first preparatory school.

Many were the times that he had recalled it, but seldom so fervently as to-day.

The train was just pulling into Exeter. In the next carriage to him was Sandra and the Indian boy, whose name, he now knew, was Krishna. So amazing was Sandra's sang-froid that even after their interview last night she had calmly suggested that they should travel down in the same carriage.

When Mr. Green had demurred, she had merely laughed, and suggested that he wanted to be by himself in order to perfect his case against her!

In a position where any other woman would have crumpled, or taken to flight, she became calmer and more resolute. She said to him:

"I admit that you have altered the situation and forced my hand. Perhaps it is just as well—for me. It will certainly clear the air. And it will be amusing to see Beryl's reaction, when she knows the truth."

To use the word "amusing"—at a time like this!

It was the same word that she had used to explain her insistence on their arriving at Candle Court unannounced. Almost her last words to him, on the previous night, had been:

"I am not going to run away, Mr. Green. Even if I wished to go, I am fully aware that it would now be quite impossible. A pair of figures like myself and Krishna can hardly vanish into thin air, particularly when eyes as keen as yours are watching them. You have me exactly where you want me.

"And so," she had continued, "you might at least allow me a little indulgence. It would amuse me to see Beryl's face, when she hears the news, and there has not been much amusement in my life, as you are probably aware—for you seem to know my whole history. If we give her warning, she will probably have heard the whole story from Kenneth before we arrive; she may even shut herself up in her room and refuse to see me. Apart from that, I believe in shock tactics. When people are suddenly confronted with a situation that alters their whole lives, they sometimes come out with some quite unexpected revelation."

It was really because Mr. Green also believed in shock tactics himself that he had consented to this plan. He too would be interested to see Beryl's face.

So here they were, getting out at the station, the accuser and the accused, making polite conversation.

"It is lucky that the garage where you left your car is so close to the station," observed Sandra.

"Yes indeed."

She turned round at the ticket barrier, and scanned the platform. "Mr. Waller was not on the train?"

"Oh, no. He is still at Princetown."

"Of course. Looking after the poor convicts. Still, he will be near at hand, which will be most convenient for you."

On the way to Candle Court, she sat with Krishna at the back, speaking to him in a low voice. She seemed to be giving him some sort of advice. From time to time he murmured, "Yes, I understand," and twice he repeated after her, "Whatever you do," as though he were learning a lesson.

Just before they entered the drive, she turned round to Mr. Green. "Whatever is going to happen will probably happen very quickly, so you had better come straight on with us, unless you want to miss something. I imagine that they will be in the drawing-room, as they always are at this time of day."

She jumped lightly out of the car, beckoning to Krishna to follow her. The front door was open and they passed inside. Sandra did not even trouble to take off her coat; she walked straight down the corridor holding Krishna's hand.

She had certainly been right in suggesting that what happened would happen quickly. Mr. Green had hardly hung up his hat before he heard voices from the drawing-room. They were not polite voices, and they were not murmuring conventional words of greeting. They were very angry voices and the angriest was Beryl's.

So the curtain was about to go up on a scene in a very ugly play. It was not a play that he would have witnessed, for choice; but life does not allow us very much latitude in the sort of dramas it presents to us.

II

Beryl's words rang out clearly as he walked along the corridor towards the drawing-room. As he turned the corner he paused. Sandra, holding Krishna's hand, was standing in the open doorway with her back towards him. Beryl was at the far end by the fireplace. She was saying:

"I think your behaviour is most extraordinary. Who is he?"

Sandra looked down at Krishna with a smile. She spoke quite calmly. "Just a relation."

"A relation of whom?"

"I suppose you might say of all of us."

Suddenly Kenneth came into the picture. He walked across to Beryl. "If you would only leave this to me. . . ."

She turned on him venomously. "I haven't the faintest desire to leave it to you. Sandra comes back to this house . . . *my* house . . . after a totally unexplained absence of four days . . . having apparently taken leave of her senses. She brings with her a . . . an infant . . . whose appearance I must say strikes me as hardly prepossessing. . . ."

"Just a moment!" It was Kenneth. His voice was very

187

harsh. He came quickly forward to Sandra. "There's no need for the boy to be in on this," he said gruffly.

She gave him a grateful smile.

"I'll get Ackworth to look after him for a bit. He could play in the garden, or something."

He took the boy's hand, and hurried out. He did not seem to notice Mr. Green, who walked quietly into the room.

Beryl looked up. "So Mr. Green is back, too! How delightful!"

"I would have let you know that I was coming, but. . . ."

"I wouldn't *dream* of asking you to go to so much trouble!" She was obviously almost hysterical with irritation. "Did you bring any other friends?"

"I did not."

"No black women, or anything like that?"

"That is not very amusing—Beryl."

It was Sandra who spoke. Beryl turned on her.

"What did you say?"

"You heard me quite clearly. I told you that you were not very amusing."

"How dare you speak to me so insolently?"

"Because I do not care to have Krishna insulted."

"Krishna? Is that the name of the black boy?"

"It is one of his names. He has another."

"Indeed? And am I likely to be interested in that?"

"You might be very interested."

"Why?"

"Because his name is . . . Kenneth Faversham."

The explosion came like that, in a few pistol shots of dialogue, and as always, after an explosion, the ensuing seconds seemed charged with an unnatural silence. One—two—three—four . . . on the dial of a man-made watch those would have been the number of seconds that would have been marked. But on the dial of time itself, whose measurements are of an infinite elasticity, a hundred shadows would have passed, and the seconds would have been multiplied by countless echoes. Of all these echoes Mr. Green, as he recalled this moment of drama in after

188

life, remembered most clearly the sound of the falls; their distant uproar was a perpetual comment on the futility of the petty dramas that passed within their ken. Men might come and men might go, straying this way and that, losing themselves, being swept into unnatural courses; but the falls knew what they wanted; the falls were strong, unswerving and relentless.

Then life took charge again. And even the sound of the falls was forgotten as Beryl began to laugh, high and shrill, on and on, in a fit of uncontrollable hysteria.

III

Come what, come may. . . .

It seemed impossible that time could run so slowly, that only two hours had passed since Sandra's revelation.

Mr. Green, as he looked out on to the lawns from the window of the library, to which he had retired, was astonished to see that they were still lit with wintry sunshine.

It was four-thirty. A family conference had been called for five-thirty. That was astonishing, too, when one came to think of it. And yet, what else was there to do? Here was a house in ruins, a family in a state of dissolution. It was a situation that demanded immediate action; it would have been intolerable merely to sit around and sigh.

One aspect of the whole affair was glaringly obvious. The crisis was economic rather than emotional. The deeper passions were not involved. Beryl's hysteria had its origin in outraged pride, not in a broken heart. Kenneth's panic was due, not to any dread of losing his wife, but to a fear of endangering his social position. As for Sandra—she had given no sign of having a heart at all, except where Krishna was concerned.

A soulless crew, reflected Mr. Green. It was fitting that Pusey should have been called in to sort out their problems. His own task would come later.

His attention was attracted by the sound of a car sweeping up the drive. He rose and walked over to the other side of the room, whose windows gave on to the main entrance. He peered out, and as he did so, his face was lit by a sudden smile. It was a radiant smile of pure happiness, the sort of smile one might expect on the face of a man who had seen a vision.

What, in fact, he saw, was Hilary Scole, emerging from his car, and passing into the vestibule.

So his guess had been right, after all. Hilary had not taken the plane. He had come back to face the music. And by doing so, he had lifted the whole drama on to a finer level. Some of the deeper passions *were* involved, after all.

It was consoling to think that the music would play a very different tune from the one which he had been expecting.

Four-thirty-five. Another car—this time, a sober black Wolseley. Waller had come at last. He went out to greet him.

IV

"What's all this about?" demanded the superintendent, lowering himself into an arm-chair by the fire.

Mr. Green, had he been in a flippant mood, might well have retorted, "You'd be surprised." However, he contented himself by murmuring, "There have been developments."

"Considering that you called me away from a meeting of all the higher-ups, they'd better be pretty startling."

"They are."

Waller sat up. Mr. Green was not in the habit of making false claims.

"Startling, eh?" He nodded. "Well, I'll take your word for it. Where do we begin?"

"We begin," said Mr. Green, "with the fact that Miss Sandra Wells is not Miss Sandra Wells."

"What's that?"

"Her real name is, of course . . ." (And here Mr. Green paused, with only the slightest twinge of self-reproach. He knew in his heart of hearts, that he should not have paused; he also knew that he should not have said "of course". But there were so very few times when he could pretend to be Sherlock Holmes, and they were so very enjoyable!)

He surrendered shamelessly to the temptation. "Her real name, of course, is Mrs. Kenneth Faversham," and before the bewildered Waller could reply, he leant forward and said: "I wonder if I might trouble you for a match?"

"Mrs. Kenneth Faversham?" echoed Waller, in block capitals.

"Exactly. And the Indian boy, needless to say, is Kenneth's son and heir. If you have not a match, perhaps I might borrow your lighter?"

"What the hell are you talking about?"

Mr. Green raised his eyebrows at this brusque question. Then he held out his hand. As though hypnotized, Waller groped in his pocket and threw across his lighter. Mr. Green flicked it open, with fingers which trembled ever so slightly. He took a long draw on his cigarette, and beamed placidly at the superintendent.

V

"You asked," he said, "for something startling."

There was a long pause. Then Waller said: "Have you known this all along?"

"For quite a while."

"You realize, of course, that if I am made officially aware of this situation. . . ." He finished the sentence with a shrug.

"It would be your duty to take action?"

Waller nodded.

Mr. Green gave him a gentle smile. "I was only hoping that you might take a generous view of your duty, at any rate, for the moment."

Waller made no reply.

"There have been times," continued Mr. Green, "when you have done so, in some of our previous collaborations."

"You're an old devil, aren't you?"

"I am not trying to seduce you from the path of honour. I am only asking you to hold your hand for a little while.

191

When you know the whole story, you must of course take what action you think fit."

"When I know it, maybe. But I don't know even the beginning of it. How did you find it out?"

"In a number of ways."

Waller grunted. He was feeling very small. "Including . . . sniffing?"

He could have kicked himself for making so cheap a crack. Mr. Green would have every right to feel resentment.

However, Mr. Green merely shrugged his shoulders. "As it happens," he said, "sniffing played its part."

"Am I to be let into the secret?"

"That is why you are here."

"Then supposing we get cracking."

"By all means. But first, let me explain the situation in this house at the present moment."

He glanced at his watch. "It is now a quarter to five. At half past five there is to be a family conference."

"Conference?" Waller snorted. "I should think it would be more like a free fight."

"That is quite possible. Between Kenneth and Beryl on the one side, and Sandra on the other."

"With you as the referee?"

"By no means. Pusey. This is not a fight for a woman's love, or anything so—so—touching as that. It is a matter of business."

"You mean of blackmail?"

"That is one way of putting it."

"Well—they'll hardly want me in on a business of that sort. Or you, for that matter."

Mr. Green frowned. "What they may or may not want is immaterial. We shall both be in on it. The only difference is that they will be aware of my presence, but they will not be aware of yours."

"How's that?"

"The library might have been designed for eavesdropping. There is a most convenient alcove by the door leading to the flower room, which is not in use at the moment. The entrance from the flower-room to the library is masked by a large screen. I have taken the liberty of placing an arm-chair behind it, where I hope you will be comfortable."

"You seem to have fixed everything very prettily. And when they've all branded themselves as bigamists and black-mailers, what do I do? Tiptoe away and pick a bunch of carnations?" He snorted indignantly. "You're not asking much, are you? Supposing I come out and arrest the lot?"

Mr. Green sighed. "I can only repeat, that is your affair, that is your affair. But before you lose your temper with me, I implore you to wait, for just a little while."

"Why?"

"Because there is a worse crime than bigamy or black-mail. And in that room will be somebody who has com-mitted it."

Waller stared at him. He had been longing to ask the direct question, but pride had prevented him. He took a deep breath, gulped, and swallowed his pride.

"Have you found out who strangled Mrs. Faversham?"

"I believe so."

"Was it . . . was it Sandra?"

"It was not."

Mr. Green threw away his cigarette. "The story is in three parts," he said. "I shall just have time to finish Part One before we go . . . to join the ladies. If such a term, in the circumstances, is not too ironic."

VI

"Let us begin," he said, "with what you were good enough to describe as the 'sniffing' part of the evidence. I know how irritating this must seem to you. . . ." He held up his hand as the superintendent seemed about to deny this suggestion. "It is no use pretending, my dear Waller; it *does* irritate you. But I really cannot help the fact that I happen to have been born with an exceptionally keen sense of smell. It is one of the few talents with which the public have ever credited me, and as a rule, I prefer not to dwell on it." He pursed his lips firmly. "One is something more, one hopes, than an animated nose. But in the present case, on two occasions, this peculiarity of mine—for it could hardly be described as an accomplishment—was of great value."

"Two occasions?" echoed Waller.

"Yes. I will deal with the second occasion in its place. For the moment let us keep to Miss Wells.

"I may say that I was interested in Miss Wells from the outset—indeed, even before I met her. She seemed to be regarded by so many people as a paragon; and paragons have always had a fascination for me. I can never rid myself of the suspicion that they have feet of clay, like all the rest of God's creatures.

"Apart from that, she was a *mysterious* paragon. It was almost as though she had descended out of the blue, at a moment of crisis. True, we discovered—or rather *you* discovered—that she had a father, who was a quite respectable retired merchant-seaman, living at Teignmouth. And as she seemed to be the only person who could not possibly have been concerned in the death of Mrs. Faversham. . . ."

"*Seemed* to be the only person?" echoed Waller. "A moment ago you agreed that she *was* the only person."

"I prefer the word 'seemed'," retorted Mr. Green. "Even at the risk of appearing to contradict myself. As she *seemed* to be the only person unconcerned, we made no further inquiries. But I was curious. And then, I had a stroke of luck."

Waller grinned. "Not for the first time—if you call it luck. Which I don't."

"That is very kind of you. But it was luck, all the same. I fainted in the conservatory."

"And what was so lucky about fainting in the conservatory."

"Just this. Sandra happened to be there at the time. She gave me first aid, most efficiently. I was brought into very close contact with her, at a temperature of over eighty degrees, and. . . ."

194

Here Mr. Green hesitated. Across his face flitted an expression of prim embarrassment, as though he had stumbled on a subject of indelicacy.

Waller interpreted the expression correctly, and gave a hearty guffaw. "Is this where we come to the sniffing?"

"It is."

"And what did it tell you on this occasion?"

Mr. Green hesitated. Then he conquered his diffidence. "It told me that Sandra Wells was an Anglo-Indian."

Before Waller could intervene, he continued:

"No doubt the whole subject may sound distasteful to some people. To others it may be merely ridiculous—largely because their minds have been conditioned by so many highly coloured advertisements for deodorants. Sensible men, however. . . ."

"Like ourselves?"

"I hope so. Sensible men will find it neither distasteful nor ridiculous; they will regard it as one of the many miracles of nature—the fact that the pigmentary glands of the human body secrete certain odours which have a power to attract or to repel. The most obvious example, of course, is the odour secreted by the glands of the negro. Most white men find it unpleasant, just as the negro is reputed to be deterred by the odour of the white. I myself have no particular inclination either one way or the other; after all, the atmosphere around us is a battle-ground of conflicting odours . . . however, that is neither here nor there. What is relevant is the fact that there is a very faint odour emitted by the Indian races, which is indiscernible to the great majority of people but is clearly discernible to *me*. As I said before, I do not regard this as an accomplishment, merely as a useful peculiarity.

"It was this odour that I detected, for the first time, when Sandra bent over me in the greenhouse. Where I say I 'detected' it, that is perhaps putting it too strongly. For one thing, I had no reason to suspect from her appearance that she had Indian blood; for another, as she was only half Indian, the pigmentary secretions were far less pronounced.

However, the odour was there, and I felt that it was my duty to explain it."

He looked up sharply. "I am not boring you?"

Waller scowled at him. "That's the silliest question you ever asked."

"Good. I will not ask it again." He glanced once more at his watch. "But it is nearly five o'clock. I must hurry. If I do not finish this part of the story before we—join the ladies—you will not understand the true nature of the drama we are about to witness."

VII

"The more I thought about this peculiarity of Sandra Wells," resumed Mr. Green, "the more I felt that I must prove it beyond any shadow of doubt. Not only because it would fit her into her proper place in the general design but because I had a suspicion that it would throw a new light on Kenneth."

"On Kenneth?"

"Come, Waller! It was you yourself who suggested, right at the beginning, that there was something strange in the fact that Kenneth was the only member of the household who persistently addressed Sandra as Miss Wells."

"That wasn't a very subtle piece of deduction."

"So much the better. It was so obvious that I might have overlooked it. Once it was pointed out, it became extremely significant. Here was a very attractive girl on the one hand, and a very susceptible man on the other. One would have suspected, at the least, an atmosphere of—to use an old-fashioned word—flirtatiousness.

"Instead, he was hardly civil to her. The implication was that Sandra meant much more to him than he was prepared to admit, and that when she appeared, so mysteriously, at Candle Court, she was no stranger to him.

"Take the argument a step further; and the ingredients of Anglo-Indian blood; add, again, my discovery that Kenneth had been in hospital in Bombay, where she had been a nurse, that he had been wounded in the Burma Campaign and posted as missing . . . you see the train of thought?"

"I could kick myself for not having checked up on the possibility of something like that; it seems so obvious now."

"There is no reason why you should have done so; after all, this Anglo-Indian business is highly specialized. It was just a stroke of luck that it happened to be a problem that had always interested me. If it were not such a painful subject I might almost say that half-castes were a hobby of mine. And of all the world's half-castes, the Anglo-Indians are in the most unfortunate position. They are despised by the Indians themselves and mistrusted by the Europeans. They are welcomed by neither society and given the worst-paid posts in the most subordinate professions. The case of the women is especially hard. Their one hope of escape is marriage with an Englishman, and to obtain this they practise endless deceits, such as inventing old family homes in England and stealing faded snapshots of white people in order to pass them off as their grandparents.

"But how was I to *prove* that Sandra Wells was an Anglo-Indian? I wanted something much more conclusive than . . . than the evidence of what we have agreed to call 'sniffing'. And there was only one way in which I could get it."

"How?"

"By examining the lines in the palm of her hands. In the Anglo-Indian, those lines are not flesh-coloured, as in our own. They are faintly tinged with blue. The average man would probably not notice any difference. The expert, if he were given a proper chance of examining them, would know at once.

"But how was I to find that chance? I tried on two occasions." He smiled at Waller. "You remember the first morning, when you were doing the finger printing?"

"Of course."

"I faded into the background as far as possible. But when it came to Sandra's turn, I offered you my assistance."

"So that was it! I wondered why you were so keen on dirtying your handkerchief."

"Quite. I used it to help her wipe her hand. But I was not quick enough." Mr. Green shook his head in self-reproach. "I should have been by her side *before* she pressed her hands on to the pad. That ink is very tenacious, and though I obtained some evidence it was not conclusive.

"The next occasion *was* conclusive, not from what I discovered but from what I failed to discover. The episode occurred at dinner on—I think—the Tuesday. I was sitting next to Sandra. I upset the salt-cellar, in order to steer the conversation to the subject of superstition, and from there, to the wide subject of the occult—which included astrology, palmistry, and the like. I flatter myself that it was quite neatly done, in a few casual sentences. But Sandra saw the trap. When I asked her to let me read her palm, she smiled, and said 'of course' and stretched out her arm, and as she did so she upset her wine-glass. By the time the commotion had passed, the subject was forgotten—or she pretended that it was—and she had turned to talk to her neighbour. I have not the shadow of a doubt that her action was deliberate and that from that moment onwards she saw me as a potential enemy."

VIII

"Only one question remained to be answered—how far had this relationship gone? Well—after your investigations at the bank, we both knew that it had gone pretty far—far enough, at any rate, to involve Kenneth in considerable financial loss. But had there been a marriage?"

He paused for a moment. Then he spoke very deliberately. "I decided that there had been a marriage."

"Wasn't that taking rather a leap in the dark?"

"Yes, and no. In any ordinary relationship, it would certainly have been, at best, a very hazy assumption. But the fact that Sandra was an Anglo-Indian changed the entire complexion of the case. As I said before, the one hope of an Anglo-Indian woman to escape from her environment lies in *marriage*. Anything less is useless—worse than

198

useless. If you have ever been to Bombay, as I have, and explored the fringes of the society where these unhappy people are admitted, you soon realize that the womenfolk have a chastity which one might almost call ferocious. True, they make themselves as alluring as possible; there is no step they will not take to lead a man on; but in the end. . . ."

Waller helped Mr. Green out of his embarrassment. "Nothing doing?" he suggested.

"You put it very precisely," murmured Mr. Green. "In the end . . . ahem! . . . as you said."

"And how often do they get their man?"

"Very seldom indeed. And for a very simple reason. Because in the vast majority of cases the children born of such marriages inherit the female characteristics. They are coloured.

"I have only five minutes more, and so I will not attempt to fill in the bare framework of the facts, as they suggested themselves to me. It is enough that I was satisfied that there had been a marriage, and that when Kenneth was posted as missing, he had taken the opportunity to escape from it. Nor is it necessary to speculate on how she discovered that he was still alive. Quite frankly, I do not know. There were a hundred ways in which she *might* have discovered it. After all, the wedding was one of the big social events of the season. There were the usual photographs in all the glossy magazines—and the glossy magazines find their way out to India, where, incidentally, they are avidly read by the Anglo-Indians, who regard them as a link with 'home'. The only relevant fact is that she did discover it. And that she made her plans accordingly.

"And now—the last question, and the most important of all. Had there been an issue to this marriage? I had what you might call a 'hunch'—that there was an issue, but I saw no means of proving it. However, there were pointers. You may have noticed that I often found it necessary to visit Candle Court at a very early hour—an hour that happened to coincide with the arrival of the postman, with whom I was on friendly terms. . . ."

"So you've been tampering with Her Majesty's mails, eh?"

"Endeavouring to do so. With very little success, I fear. Miss Wells saw to that. But on two occasions the postman was kind enough to hand me the post before she could get at it, and on each of those occasions there was a letter for Miss Wells, in a childish handwriting, with the postmark Hampstead, N.W.8." Mr. Green shook his head. "Her expression, when she saw me glance at those letters, was not at all amiable."

"Was that your only clue to the existence of the little Indian boy?"

"My dear Waller, I am not a thought-reader! It was not a 'clue' at all. It was a pointer—and a very clumsy one. But it was enough to encourage me to continue. And at last I found something that *was* a clue, something significant enough to permit me to regard all these assumptions as a certainty.

"It was on the day that you had gone to London. By a happy combination of circumstances, I had the house almost to myself. I decided to prowl around with my little camera, and in the course of my prowling I found myself in Sandra's room."

"I've been in there myself," grunted Waller. "It was pretty bleak."

"The very word I should have chosen. It was bleak. And strangely anonymous—with one exception. On the table by her bedside was a copy of *Knitting Weekly*. I opened it and turned the pages. At the end of the magazine was a section which she had evidently been reading with special attention. And the pattern—against which she had made a number of pencil notes—was for a jumper suitable for a boy of nine."

Waller gave a low whistle.

"Precisely. That was how I felt myself. Sandra had never been seen knitting. I took the trouble to inquire of Ackworth if there was anybody in the house who knitted, and he assured me that there was not. And yet, women who knit are normally the most gregarious of creatures; they all carry their knitting wherever they go; they use it as an aid to conversation; they leave it lying about in the most inconvenient places. . . ."

"You're telling me!" interrupted Waller, who had painful experience of these matters from his wife.

"I am glad we see eye to eye. It was only a little matter, but I felt one could hardly over-rate its importance. Here was a woman with, as far as we knew, no kith or kin in the world except for her old father—a woman who was obviously bent on endearing herself to the mistress of the house. Why should she conceal this harmless social accomplishment? Why should she regard it as though it were a secret vice?"

Mr. Green stared into the fire. He seemed to be speaking to himself. "I stood there in that room," he said, "and I conjured up a picture of her, late at night, knitting away, with the door locked and everybody asleep, and no sound except the distant roar of the falls." He shivered, ever so slightly. "It was not a pretty picture. None of the pictures in this case are pretty. But they all fitted into a general design."

For the last time he glanced at his watch. "And now," he said, "I think we had better go."

Waller held out his hand. "Wait a minute. There's one thing about all this that I don't understand. You've drawn a very convincing picture. A half-caste . . . a woman wronged . . . worming her way into a family to avenge herself. All very fine and large. But Sandra isn't a fool. She knew perfectly well that it was useless trying to blackmail Kenneth, for the simple reason that he hadn't any money. She also knew that if she spilled the beans the old lady would simply turn him out of the house."

Mr. Green nodded. He spoke slowly and precisely. "It is quite true," he said, "that Kenneth had no money while his mother was alive. But on his mother's death he would be a very rich man. Ripe for the plucking."

"You mean. . . ."

The eyes of the two men met—the puzzled deep-set eyes of the superintendent, the mild, candid eyes of Mr. Green, blinking behind his glasses.

"But it doesn't make sense!" cried Waller in exasperation. "You're laying the trail to Sandra all the time. You're branding her as a murderess with every word you say. And yet you've told me, time and again, that she did not kill Mrs. Faversham."

"Forgive me, Waller," said Mr. Green. "But I have never told you anything of the sort."

He rose to his feet. "And now, I think, it is time to join the ladies."

16

HALF PAST five. A strained silence in the great library. They were all waiting for Sandra to appear.

Beryl and Kenneth sat on the settee which was at right-angles to the fireplace. Mr. Green had a curious impression that this latest family disaster had in some way brought them more closely together. They were no longer man and wife, but they had a common bond of sorrow and of danger. From time to time they exchanged glances which, though they might not be affectionate, were at least understanding. They spoke—at last—the same language.

Crouched in an arm-chair by the fireplace sat Hilary. His eyes were half-closed, as though he were drugged. He was evidently a very sick man indeed, a pale, tired ghost. And yet Mr. Green's eyes brightened when he looked at him. He was the one member in the case for whom he felt any affection.

Pusey sat at a table in the alcove, turning over a sheaf of papers. Now and again he stared up at the ceiling, and then bent down and made a note on the pad in front of him. Mr. Green suspected that these notes were merely scribble, and were only made with the object of impressing his own importance on the rest of the company. He was quite right. Mr. Pusey was feeling bewildered and deflated. He had no reasons of his own for dreading the forthcoming conference.

Nobody appeared to notice the absence of the superintendent, who was safely ensconced in the retreat which Mr. Green had prepared for him.

As for Mr. Green, he was in his favourite position on a stool set in front of the great Beauvais tapestry, which enabled him to exercise his chameleon talent of fading into the background.

At last the door flung open and Sandra entered. She had changed her travelling dress and wore a simple frock of deep black. She paused for a moment in the doorway, a smile of challenge on her face.

"Good evening, everybody!"

None of them replied. She shrugged her shoulders, and walked swiftly to a small desk by the window where, in the old days, she had been accustomed to deal with Mrs. Faversham's letters and accounts.

She dominated the situation.

Mr. Green, as he studied Sandra from his stool in the background, could not withhold a reluctant admiration for the poise and assurance of her bearing. She gave the impression of a woman who had not the smallest reproach to lay against her conscience. So completely self-confident, indeed, did she appear, that for a moment his own conviction seemed to falter. Was it possible that there had been some flaw in his argument? Could he conceivably have made a mistake?

His small pink cheeks grew even pinker as this dreadful thought occurred to him. If at this stage of the game he should be proved wrong. . . .

He had no time for more speculation. Sandra had begun to speak.

"Before I go any further," she said, "I would like to warn you that this little matter of my marriage, and its consequences, is only one reason why I have insisted upon this meeting. There is another and very much graver business which concerns only myself.

"Yesterday, Mr. Green came to see me at my lodgings in London. He asked for an interview which I was delighted to give him. In the course of it, he accused me of being concerned in the murder of the late Mrs. Faversham."

They all stared at Mr. Green.

"Sandra?" murmured Kenneth. If his bewilderment was assumed, it was none the less convincing.

"Sandra?" repeated Beryl, who did not attempt to disguise her note of exultation.

204

From Pusey came only confused sounds of expostulation. From Hilary none at all. From all the sign he made, he might have been fast asleep.

These reactions were not lost on Mr. Green.

She went on: "His story is so completely fantastic that at first I thought he was playing a rather poor sort of practical joke. But as he apparently wishes it to be considered seriously, I decided to come here and face the music, though I'm afraid it will not play the sort of tune he expected. After you have heard it, and rejected it, as you will be bound to do, I shall be glad of the services of Mr. Pusey. The damages for slander should be considerable."

Mr. Green, had he been at a play, would certainly have cried "hear! hear!" It was incredible, her sang-froid. If only it were in a worthier cause, it would be positively heroic.

"But first," she continued, "I should like to congratulate Mr. Green on his discovery of the fact that I am Mrs. Kenneth Faversham. . . . That at least was very astute of him. Or should the credit go to Mr. Waller?" She looked around her. "By the way, where *is* our celebrated superintendent?"

Mr. Green spoke for the first time. "I believe he went out to the stables to interview Wilburfoss."

Beryl turned on him. "How much does Waller know?"

"About what?"

"About this . . . so-called marriage."

Mr. Green blinked at her with the most innocent expression. "Have we any reason to suppose that he knows anything at all?"

Pusey intervened. "If he *is* unaware of the situation," he said, "and if Mr. Green does not find it necessary to inform him. . . ."

"What the devil's it got to do with Mr. Green?" snapped Kenneth. "Why should he be interested in it?"

Pusey held up his hand in deprecation. But before he could speak, Mr. Green had intervened. "I quite agree," he murmured. "I am very little interested in it. There is another matter which seems to me somewhat more important."

"In that case," suggested Pusey, "although it is all extremely irregular, and not at all the kind of business with which I care to be associated. . . ."

He paused to shoot a reproving glance at Sandra, who had interrupted him with a harsh laugh. "Associated," he repeated. "It might still be possible to arrive at some sort of understanding, without . . . er . . . without setting in motion the processes of the law."

"Hell!" barked Kenneth. "Isn't that what we're all here for? Can't we get down to business?" He turned to Sandra. "How much do you want?"

"What does it matter what she wants?" cried Beryl. "If she is a murderess. . . ."

Sandra spoke very softly. "I should advise you to watch your tongue."

Pusey tapped a nervous finger on his desk. "Really, ladies! We shall get nowhere if we have this constant bickering. Unless I am allowed to conduct this matter in my own way. . . ." He made a petulant movement as though he were preparing to shuffle up his papers.

"Pusey's right," said Kenneth. "And you might as well realize that without Pusey we're sunk. We aren't going to get any outsider to take the sort of risks he's taking." He turned on Sandra. "And that goes for you too. It isn't every lawyer who'll act for a blackmailer."

Pusey made a gesture of protest. "My dear Mr. Faversham! Need we use such words? It is merely a question of mutual convenience. And for the last time, I really must insist. . . ."

Kenneth said no more.

II

Pusey addressed Sandra. "I gather that you have agreed, on certain conditions, to take no action in regard to the matter of bigamy?"

"That is so."

"You realize, of course, that you will be condoning a crime?"

"So will you. But we shall both be well paid for it."

He flushed angrily. "You oblige me, Miss Wells, to remind you that your position is not quite so invulnerable as you appear to imagine. You have been living in this house for six months, under the same roof as your husband. During the whole of that time, you have made no protest, no sign, even, of recognition. This behaviour on your part would certainly prejudice your case very gravely if you ever obliged us to go to law." He stared at her coldly from behind his horn-rimmed glasses. "But no doubt that had already occurred to you."

Sandra made no reply. It had occurred to her, but she saw no reason to admit it.

Pusey's confidence began to rise. "We may therefore take it that you have no desire to resume your relationship with Mr. Faversham?"

"None."

"Nor to claim the name of Faversham for your son?"

"It *is* his name, as I have already reminded Mrs. Faversham. But it is the last name on earth that I should allow him to adopt. When he returns to India, he will assume the name of his mother."

"So you are prepared to return to India?"

Beryl leant forward towards Pusey. "Can we have that condition made absolutely binding?"

Sandra turned, her eyes flashing. "You need have no fear of that!" she retorted. "Do you think I want to stay here, in this fog and this damp—surrounded by people like you and men like *him*? Have you forgotten that there's the sun in my veins—which is the reason why you regard me as an outcast? And even if it were not for myself . . . there would be Krishna!"

As she spoke his name her face softened, and her voice grew tender. But only for a moment. There was nothing tender in her accent as she went on. . . .

"Do you think I would have endured the humiliation

that he would have had to suffer? It is bad enough in India, God knows. But here! What would his life have been? What school would have taken him? What society would have accepted him? What woman would have had him for a husband?"

She turned on Kenneth. "It was a charming legacy you left me, that night in Bombay!"

Pusey ignored the outburst. "Then we may take it that as far as the personal side of the question is concerned the parties are agreed?"

Silence gave consent to this suggestion.

"I need hardly say," continued Pusey, with a hint of sanctimoniousness, "that the whole situation is extremely delicate . . . and that I myself would be very reluctant to deal with it if it were not for the fact that the late Mrs. Faversham. . . ."

"You did very well out of the late Mrs. Faversham," observed Beryl sharply. "So perhaps you will try to do as well for the present one."

"If you are referring to yourself," retorted Sandra, "you might remember that I am the present Mrs. Faversham."

"I have no intention of entering into any argument. . . ."

"Nor any power to do so. . . ."

"Ladies, please!" Pusey held up his hand. "Now that we have settled the personal side of the matter—though settled is hardly the word I should use for it—only one point remains. . . ."

"Quite," interrupted Beryl. "How much does she want?"

She addressed her remark straight to Sandra, who replied immediately:

"I want half the estate."

Kenneth jumped up. "Half the estate?"

"That's what I said."

Beryl seemed about to choke. "But that is outrageous."

"You think so? It seems to me quite reasonable."

Pusey intervened. "Perhaps you are not aware of the terms of Mrs. Faversham's will. This request could only be granted if Candle Court were sold."

"So much the better. I have no affection for Candle Court. On the contrary."

Beryl stepped towards her. "This is worse than blackmail."

"You think so? I should have called it generosity. . . ."

Beryl appealed to Pusey. "Tell her it can't be done," she demanded.

Pusey wriggled in his seat. Mr. Green felt some sympathy for him. He had never seen a man more uncomfortable. "In a matter of law," he began.

Sandra took the words out of his mouth. "Quite. By all means let us stick to law. What is the legal situation? It would be interesting to know. Mr. Pusey tried to frighten me, a moment ago, with a lot of nonsense about endangering my situation because I had been living here for six months. But supposing I had done so under protest?" Her voice rose shrill as she went on: "Supposing I had only yielded to the pleading of my beloved husband? Supposing I had sacrificed all my natural instincts merely out of Christian charity?"

She checked her momentary outburst. In her normal voice she resumed:

"I am the legal wife of Kenneth Faversham. My son, whatever the colour of his skin, is his legitimate son, born in wedlock. I should be perfectly justified in demanding to assume my natural position as mistress of Candle Court, and in exposing Beryl as a woman living in sin. . . ."

Beryl turned to Kenneth. "How long are you going to put up with this?"

Sandra merely smiled at her. "Living in sin," she repeated. "You had better listen to me now, or you may find yourself compelled to listen in front of a jury. As it is, in order to avoid breaking up this happy home, and because of the extraordinary sweetness of my nature, I am prepared to step out of the picture, to sacrifice the man I love, to leave this country, which will of course break my heart . . . on condition that my child should have at least some of the advantages in life which should be his by birth."

This little speech was delivered in cool, measured tones. In spite of its irony, it carried an extraordinary conviction.

"That is my argument now," she concluded, "and it will be my argument in a court of law, if you are ever so unwise as to take me to one. I have no intention either of compromising or of waiting. You can settle it in the next ten minutes, between yourselves, one way or the other. If not, I shall settle it for you."

She faced Mr. Green. She seemed to brace herself for a great effort. It was as though, having defeated one enemy, she were picking up her sword to defeat another.

"And after that," she said, "we will deal with Mr. Green's insane suggestions. It seems as though, whatever happens in the next hour, there will be a good deal of work for Mr. Pusey."

She walked to the window, as though washing her hands of the matter. Then she sat down, and stared out on to the garden.

Pusey beckoned to Kenneth and Beryl, and took them over to a far corner, where they began an urgent, hurried conversation. Mr. Green did not attempt to listen to it, he was too intent on watching the figure of the woman with whom he was about to do battle.

The darkness was gathering swiftly, and against the glimmering panes the silhouette of her figure looked frail and insubstantial; it seemed incredible that this little creature could assume so bold a face to him, that with the facts as they were, she could dare to face him at all.

But *were* the facts as they were?

Even as he asked the question, he had his answer in a stifled scream from the window.

"No!" cried Sandra. "No!"

III

For a second she stayed there rigid, staring at something outside the window that they could not see. Then she turned and ran from the room. As she ran, she made little low cries like a frightened animal. They heard her heels clattering on the flagged floor of the hall and the sound of the front door opening.

It all happened in the space of a few seconds. Mr. Green was the first to move. He hurried to the window, and pressed his nose close to the pane. The light was fading fast and for the moment he could see nothing. Then he caught his breath and turned. Behind him stood Waller, who had emerged from his retreat.

"You here?" he murmured distractedly. "Quickly! Follow me!"

He was out of the room in a flash, followed by the bewildered superintendent.

"What the devil's happening?" demanded Kenneth. He too strode to the window, followed by Hilary, who was still dazed from the drugged sleep in which he had been dozing. Beryl did not even turn round, but remained looking into the fire. She heard a shout from Kenneth.

"Good God! She'll kill herself . . . madness to go on those rocks. . . ."

"But the kid's there," breathed Hilary. "Can't you see. . . ."

"No, it's too dark . . . yes I can . . . way out on a branch. . . ."

"Hell . . . they'll both be for it. . . ."

"Wait a minute . . . Waller's just got there."

But he spoke to empty air. Kenneth had gone. They heard him running across the hall and flinging open the great door. He was in too much of a hurry to shut it again. A chill draught blew into the room.

Beryl spoke. "Would you mind shutting the door. Whatever may be happening I don't see any reason why *we* should freeze to death."

Without a word Hilary crossed the room and shut it. Then he returned to his post at the window.

Beryl spoke again. Her voice sounded flat and bored. "I gather that Sandra is in some sort of predicament."

211

"It was the boy. She went after him. He was climbing a tree over the falls."

"And has he tumbled in, or something?"

"I can't see. My eyes are still blurred with these damned drugs. Besides, it's so dark and there are so many figures about."

Was it his fancy, or was the sound of the falls growing louder and more clamorous?

"It might save a great many problems if they both broke their necks," she observed with brutal candour.

"It might."

"But I expect that black creature can climb like a monkey. And in any case, nothing unpleasant ever happens to Sandra, does it?"

He did not reply.

"You're not very sociable," she repeated. "I said—nothing ever happens to Sandra, does it?"

There was a long pause. Suddenly the figure by the window became rigid. He stared into the gathering darkness.

"I think that something has happened to Sandra," he said at last. "Something that can never happen again."

IV

It was almost dark when the tragic little procession made its way back to the house. First came Kenneth, walking like an automaton, looking neither to right nor to left, holding his dead wife in his arms. Her neck was broken. Her body felt light and limp. The wind blew away the handkerchief which they had laid over her eyes; it fluttered into the darkness, unheeded. Her face in the half light, framed in its circlet of dark, damp hair, looked very peaceful.

Waller walked by his side, the prey to a great many emotions. Though he had seen so much of death, he never grew accustomed to it . . . it never failed to pull him up with a jerk, which affected him not only mentally but physically. At this very moment there were warning signs inside him, telling him that he was in for an hour of acute indigestion.

212

He found himself wondering if there was any bicarbonate in the house, and promptly reproached himself for sentiments so unworthy of the solemnity of the occasion. However, a chap could not help the way he was made.

Lastly came Mr. Green, holding by his hand Krishna, who was weeping softly to himself. It was a strange sound that came from his throat, a long monotonous plaint that held all the melancholy of Eastern music. Mr. Green found himself almost wishing that he might cry more loudly; there was something unnatural in this slow, whispering lamentation.

Hilary opened the door for them. Beryl stood behind him. Neither of them spoke. The Ackworths were in the background. A startled cry broke from Mrs. Ackworth. Her husband hurried forward. "Oh, sir!" he murmured in a broken voice, holding out his hands in a hopeless gesture.

Kenneth ignored him; he did not even appear to hear him. He walked straight ahead, holding his burden more tightly to him, and passed up the staircase out of sight. The water from Sandra's clothes dripped on to the stone stairs, leaving a little trail behind him.

Beryl began to speak. "Is she. . . ."

Waller cut her short. "Yes, she is. But you'd better send for the doctor."

"I'll telephone now." She turned, flicking her cigarette. She still seemed quite unaffected.

All the time, the little boy was weeping. Mrs. Ackworth came forward, dabbing her eyes with her handkerchief.

"Shall I take him, sir?" she asked.

Mr. Green felt the small hand tighten round his own. "You are very kind, Mrs. Ackworth, but perhaps for the moment. . . ."

Krishna finished the sentence for him. "Please stay with me, sir," he whispered.

"Very well," said Mr. Green. "Perhaps Mrs. Ackworth would bring us a glass of hot milk?"

"I'll get it right away, sir." She bustled off, thankful to have something useful to do.

213

Mr. Green led his charge up the stairs, and turned into the chintz room, a small bedroom on the right which he knew was unoccupied. A log fire was already laid, and in a moment he had put a match to it.

"And now," he said, "we must take off those wet clothes and put you in a nice hot bath."

"Yes, sir," murmured Krishna. But he made no effort to move; he merely stood there shivering.

"Would you like me to help you?"

The boy shook his head. He put his hand to his throat to undo the button of his shirt. Then he paused and looked at Mr. Green with wide, tragic eyes. His lips moved, but he spoke too softly to be heard.

Mr. Green bent closer to him. "What is it, Krishna?"

Then the words came. "Never no more," he said. It was not a question, it was a plaint. It was spoken in a sad lilting treble that put Mr. Green, once again, in mind of the thin reedy instruments that echo through the hot night air of an Indian village.

"You must try not to think of that just now," he murmured.

"Never no more," he whispered again. His hands were still raised to his shirt, but his eyes wandered slowly round the room, as though searching for something.

There was a knock on the door. It was Mrs. Ackworth with the milk. As he handed it to him, Mr. Green took a small green tablet from his pocket. It was a mild sedative, which he always carried with him.

The boy swallowed it obediently. Then he walked slowly to the bathroom.

"I've brought up an old night-shirt of Ackworth's," said Mrs. Ackworth. "It'll be too big, but there's nothing else in the house."

She went out. When Krishna was out of the bath, Mr. Green helped him into the night-shirt, which fell in folds around his feet. Mr. Green was shocked to see how thin he was. There were deep shadows between his ribs and his legs were like sticks. Thinness always caused Mr. Green

214

inordinate distress—thin puppies, thin kittens, thin ponies, thin children; they went to his heart.

"We must fatten you up," he murmured, patting his frail shoulders. He was thankful to see that at last he had stopped weeping.

And so to bed.

What Mr. Green said to Krishna, that night, as he knelt by the bed, holding his hand, need not here concern us. But it must have been kindly and comforting. When at last his long lashes faltered and fell, his dreams brought a faint smile to the lips which had been drooping so pitifully. For in those dreams his mother seemed to speak to him . . . and though he knew that it would be long before he saw her, and that in some way she had made some terrible mistake, for which they would both have to pay . . . he felt that some day, somewhere, they would meet again.

He turned and sighed and sank deeper into sleep. And the figure faded, and he seemed to be drifting back still further into his youth, back to the hot red earth, and the scarlet flame trees, and the parrots chattering in the branches. At last, even the screams of the parrots died away, and there was no sound save the distant uproar of the falls.

17

THE FOLLOWING day. The same time and the same scene—
the great library, with the lamps lit, and the fire glowing.

But the tension was more acute. All through the night
there had been torrential rains, and the voices of the swollen
falls were more exultant than ever, as though they were
rejoicing over the victim they had claimed. In spite of the
heavy velvet curtains, their distant uproar would not be
ignored. Sometimes, when the wind veered and buffeted the
ancient walls, they seemed to be sweeping towards the
house itself, stinging the window-panes with their icy spray.

And the cast was different. Waller was there. And on the
stool by the tapestry sat Dr. Rudyard, staring at the floor in
front of him. On a table by his side—grotesque item!—was
a large box of chocolates. From time to time he dipped his
fingers into them. The sound of the tinfoil, as he unwrapped
it, was a tinkling triviality against the triumphant chorus of
the waters.

The desk where Sandra had sat the night before was
empty. This time, they were waiting for Mr. Green.

Mr. Green, as we have observed before, had his little
vanities. One of them was that he liked, on occasions, to
play the role of the great detective. After all, he was con-
stantly being informed that he *was* a great detective, and he
felt that it would be an excess of modesty to deny it.

One of the privileges of the great detective is to keep
people waiting, while he prepares the *dénouement*. This is
precisely what Mr. Green was doing at this moment.

He was in the main conservatory, staring at the moonflower.

A sad, shoddy remnant of its former glory, just now.
Flowers there were none. The leaves were jaundiced, and
brown at the edges. About the whole plant there was an

aura of despair; it seemed to be making a final protest against the fate which had dragged it from its natural environment, across the cold seas, to its grave.

Yet it was the moonflower that had led him to the heart of this greatest mystery.

He blinked, and stretched out a podgy finger. Very gently he touched one of the dying leaves. His lips murmured "Thank you."

Then he turned, and went inside. A few minutes later, he plunged into the heart of his story.

II

"When, if ever, this story takes its place in the annals of crime," began Mr. Green, "it is more than probable that it will be known as the Mystery of the Moonflower. For it was the moonflower that told me the truth at last. Sometimes I am tempted to think that it was trying to tell me the truth from the very beginning, if I had not been too blind to see it.

"This is a long and intricate tale, with many twists and turns, and in order to make it comprehensible, I shall have to deal with one phase at a time. The first phase, concerning the moonflower, is the key to all the others. I would therefore ask Mr. Scole to listen to it with particular attention, and to correct me if at any time I appear to be making false assumptions."

He spoke directly to Hilary. "I suggested that I was blind in my failure to interpret the message of the moonflower. That criticism, I think, must also apply to you."

"To me? How was I blind?" Hilary asked the question in a whisper, as though the tide of his strength were at its final ebb.

"I will tell you. You remember when you took me into the conservatory to see the moonflower, on the day of my arrival—the last day of Mrs. Faversham's life? Yes? Then you will also remember that you told me that of the thirteen original seeds which you had brought back, only six had germinated."

217

Hilary nodded.

"You could give no explanation of this. The seeds were identical in age, in size, in condition of health. Moreover, according to Wilburfoss, they had all been given precisely the same treatment—the same compost, the same degree of light and moisture, the same temperature. Yet seven of those seeds had come to nothing."

"Yes. I remember saying that it was one of the unsolved mysteries of botany."

"Quite. But there was an even more curious mystery about those seeds. *And that was the behaviour of Wilburfoss.* According to him, when the seven seeds showed no sign of germination, he threw them away, chucked them on the rubbish heap. You were naturally very angry. But you should have been more than angry."

"I could hardly have been angrier," protested Scole, with more heat in his voice. "I gave him the dressing-down of his life. There were a dozen things I might have learnt from them . . . disease in the seeds themselves, bacteria in the compost. . . ."

"So you told me at the time. What I meant when I said that you should have been *more* than angry was that you should also have been suspicious."

"Of whom?"

"Of Wilburfoss."

"You aren't surely making any suggestion that . . . ."

"I am making no suggestion, I am making a plain statement. It was quite impossible for Wilburfoss to have done a thing like that. It was no more in his nature than it would have been for . . . for Waller to have written *Lycidas*."

"Why pick on me?" growled the superintendent from his corner.

"I beg your pardon. It was the first illustration that occurred to me. It was not intended as a reflection on your intelligence. Let us say, rather, that Wilburfoss could no more have done what he said he did than . . . than I could have composed the overture of Tristan."

"Then were the seeds not destroyed at all?"

218

"Oh, they were destroyed. But not by Wilburfoss."

"By whom, then, for heaven's sake?"

"Naturally, by Mrs. Wilburfoss."

A ripple of excitement ran round the room. Even if, among those present, there were some whose consciences were none too clear, it was quite evident that the name of Mrs. Wilburfoss was the very last that they had expected to hear, as even remotely connected with the crime.

III

Waller was the first to speak. "How did you work *that* one out?"

"I will tell you in good time. But first, let me tell you what actually happened—and even more important, why the destruction of those seeds was such a vital factor in leading me to the person who was responsible for the death of Mrs. Faversham."

He turned to Kenneth. "You will forgive me if I speak frankly? The relationship between your mother and Wilburfoss was. . . ."

"Oh—don't mind *me*," retorted Kenneth with a brutal laugh. "*De mortuis* or no *de mortuis*. She was his mistress. At least, she had been, in the days gone by."

"Thank you." There was ice in Mr. Green's voice. "You have saved me from an unpleasant duty." (To himself he thought, "You have made it even more unpleasant by your vulgarity.")

"As you say," he continued, "it was in the days gone by. But it was fairly widely guessed at in what is known as 'society', and there had been a good deal of gossip in the village. The relevant fact is that Mrs. Wilburfoss herself hated Mrs. Faversham to an extent that bordered on fanaticism. She would have gone to any lengths to hurt her. But the opportunity never presented itself, till the arrival of the moonflower seeds. She was shrewd enough to realize that the moonflower meant more to Mrs. Faversham than any jewel, indeed, than any human being."

"That is literally true," commented Hilary.

"So she set out to destroy the moonflower. I discovered this partly by deduction—(beginning with the assumption that Wilburfoss's behaviour was inexplicable)—partly by elimination—(for there was no other person either with the motive or the opportunity)—and partly by luck. Mrs. Wilburfoss, as you are aware, is a heavy drinker. I was fortunate enough to chance upon her during one of her outbursts, where she shouted a few words which I was able to interpret correctly. The date—roughly ten days after the sowing—seemed fairly obvious. It corresponds with a period of forty-eight hours during which Wilburfoss was laid up in bed, for the first time in twenty years. And it preceded by one day the arrival of the estate carpenter, who set new locks on the outer doors, and new fasteners on the windows.

"It was then that Wilburfoss sowed the six remaining seeds, which some instinct had prompted him to keep back."

"But I don't understand!" It was Hilary who interrupted. He was leaning forward, and there was a flush of excitement on his cheeks. "I don't understand!" he repeated. "The germination period. . . ."

"Exactly," murmured Mr. Green.

"If the six remaining seeds were really sown ten days late, and given the treatment I laid down for them with a mean temperature of seventy-three, they couldn't possibly have been coming into flower at the time of Mrs. Faversham's death."

"Quite."

"Then what does it mean?"

"It means that the seeds were *not* given the treatment you prescribed."

"I still don't understand."

"Even now, when the moonflower is trying to tell you so plainly? You said yourself that at *a temperature of seventy-three* they could not possibly have germinated so soon. But if the temperature in the conservatory had been raised, night after night, to eighty-three? If there had been times when it touched ninety. . . ."

"Good God!" Waller had sprung to his feet. "I believe I get it!"

Mr. Green held up his finger. "Just one moment, Waller. I think you are a leap ahead of the rest of us."

He turned back to Hilary. "It is a question of heat," he said. "It has always been a question of heat."

Hilary's face was a study in bewilderment. "What do you mean by heat?"

"Precisely what I say. The temperature of the atmosphere surrounding us. After all, the first sentences in the whole tragedy were written in a heat-wave." He faced Beryl. "Do you remember the date of your fête last year?"

"Yes, it was 18th July."

"Quite. That was the hottest day recorded since the war. I went to the trouble of examining the records. At three o'clock in the afternoon, in most parts of the West of England, it was well over eighty-two in the shade. It was on that afternoon that Sandra made her first appearance at Candle Court . . . to all intents and purposes a harmless young tourist, studying the stately homes of England. It was also on that afternoon that Mrs. Faversham had her stroke, falling practically into Sandra's arms. . . ."

Beryl gave a short laugh. "Are you suggesting that our wonderful Sandra had some control over the weather?"

"No. I am not. But I am suggesting that the weather gave her an idea."

A strange silence began to fall over the room.

He turned to Dr. Rudyard. "It is true, is it not, that Mrs. Faversham's stroke was induced by the heat?"

"Directly induced, yes."

"And that Sandra was well aware of this?"

"Certainly. Whenever I saw Mrs. Faversham, she was always there. Mrs. Faversham insisted on it."

"And that she must have heard you warn her against excessive heat?"

"On many occasions. With her blood-pressure, she was going about with a bomb in her pocket. For instance, I insisted on her keeping a thermometer in her bath-room. I warned her against staying more than a few minutes in the hot-house, particularly after a meal, and suggested that she should never shut the door from the outer house. . . ."

His voice trailed off, and his mouth stayed open. The full horror of the revelation dawned upon him.

"Good God!" he muttered. "Murder by heat stroke!"

"Of course," Mr. Green spoke again to Hilary. "That was what the moonflower was trying to tell us."

Hilary shuddered and covered his face with his hands. The others merely stared, as though hypnotized, at Mr. Green.

IV

"However, even without the evidence of the moonflower, there were certain peculiarities about Sandra's behaviour which puzzled me, at the very outset. The first of them was her immediate reaction to the news of the murder."

He turned to Waller. "You will remember that we were breakfasting together at the hotel when Ackworth telephoned to her from Candle Court. She was, of course, expecting that telephone call, for she knew that Mrs. Faversham was dead. What she was *not* expecting was the news that Mrs. Faversham had been strangled. Needless to say, it was very good news, as it happened, for it gave her an apparently unbreakable alibi. But at the moment she did not realize this, she was merely overwhelmed by surprise. She repeated the word 'strangled' twice into the telephone, as though she could not believe her ears. She repeated it to me again when she put down the receiver. It would have been more natural to use the word 'murdered', which is horrible enough in itself. She never used it once. It was only a detail, but it remained in my memory, and later on I appreciated its significance.

"But it was of course the moonflower that told most of the tale. As soon as one had grasped this salient fact, the other pieces in the puzzle fitted together with surprising speed. For instance, there was the complaint, by Wilburfoss, that the furnace heating the conservatory seemed to be

222

using more fuel than was warranted. I took the liberty, from time to time, of making myself thoroughly acquainted with the workings of the furnace. . . ."

"So that was where you were always hiding yourself," grunted Waller.

"It is an extremely efficient structure of American design. It is housed, as you are aware, in the annexe to the conservatory itself, and the oil is contained in a large storage tank at a higher level. There are two means of access to it. One is by a door giving on to the stable yard, which was the entrance normally used by Wilburfoss. The other was by a door in the corridor leading from the drawing-room to the conservatory. Why Mrs. Faversham troubled to have this extra entrance into the house I never quite understood. . . ."

"She liked to have her eye on things," said Pusey.

"That probably explains it. In any case, the entrance was there. It was merely a question of opening the door, walking down three steps, and turning a few handles. It could not have been simpler. I myself am totally without any mechanical inclinations, but I was able to grasp the principle of it after one reading of the instructions. And so, no doubt, was Sandra.

"It seems fairly obvious that she must have had a number of rehearsals, in the period between the time the seeds were sown and time of their flowering. Although the seeds were very delicate and volatile it would need a great deal more than a single night of excessive stimulation to bring them to maturity." He turned to Scole. "How many would you suggest?"

"I should say that at least six would be needed."

"So that for at least six nights in the month before the murder was actually committed, Mrs. Faversham sat within a few feet of death. You would probably find, if you cared to go back over your various engagement books, that those nights you were all out of the house. Presumably something happened on each of them to prevent her from carrying out her plan. By the time that the murder was actually committed she must have felt that time was running short. She knew the purpose of Mr. Pusey's visit, and it was actually against her interest to be a beneficiary under the will—it would have deprived her of one of her principal safeguards, the fact that she had no motive——"

In dry passionless tones, he summed up:

"On the night of her death, between the hours of nine and ten, Mrs. Faversham was lured to the hot-house by Sandra on the excuse—almost certainly—that the moonflower was in bloom. She was locked inside, at a temperature that must have been over ninety degrees, judging by certain obvious botanical reactions which I observed shortly afterwards. Once inside, she was powerless; if she had cried out, nobody would have heard her over the uproar of the falls; there was no possibility of escape, for the windows were barred; she was in total darkness, panic-stricken, gasping for breath, with her heart pounding . . . the heart which Dr. Rudyard had so aptly compared to a bomb in her pocket. Five minutes of such an ordeal would probably have been fatal; it lasted for three-quarters of an hour. The result, as Sandra well knew, was quite inevitable."

"And then?" It was Kenneth who spoke, and at last his voice had a note of awe and grief.

"And then," continued Mr. Green, "she was carried to her room and laid in her bed."

"But later?" cried the doctor. "When she was strangled? Who. . . ."

"I shall come to that in good time. For the moment it is enough to say that when—somebody—climbed through her window, and put his hands round her throat, in one quick convulsive gesture, she had already been dead for several hours."

Silence. He glanced round the room. They were all staring at him with expressions which mirrored, very clearly, the nature of their respective reactions.

All except Hilary, who kept his hands over his eyes.

"And now," said Mr. Green, with a sigh, "I think that we should all feel better for a little glass of sherry."

18

WHATEVER MAY be said, in defence or abuse of alcohol, there can be no doubt that in some natures it enlarges the mental horizon. Whether it also blurs it, is a matter of opinion. In Mr. Green's case, alcohol—(in the shape of a small glass of sherry, sipped very slowly, with rather nervous lips, as though it might prove to have explosive qualities)—tended to make him verge from the particular to the general; it was as though it caused him to lift his nose from the track of the bloodhound, and to gaze about him at the surrounding landscape, trying to see himself, and those whom he was pursuing, in their right proportions—as figures in a scene whose background was infinity.

So it was on this occasion. When they had all replenished themselves in their various ways, and were grouped once more, rather more closely, around him, he permitted himself a moment's philosophical reflection.

"One has often heard reports of the perfect murder," he said, staring up at the ceiling. "Sometimes in fiction, sometimes in life itself. As soon as one investigates those reports one discovers that the phrase is unjustified. There is always some elemental flaw, some inherent weakness of construction." He frowned, and shook his head. "It is almost as though the Almighty were saying 'so far, but no further'. It is almost as though He had so ordained things that Death —which is His final punishment, and His final blessing. . . ."

Mr. Green suddenly stopped, and cleared his throat, his little round cheeks blushed a rosy pink. He really should not have allowed himself the glass of sherry. It always made him say more than he had intended. It made him talk about the soul, as opposed to the body, and whenever he began to talk about the soul, it ended in embarrassment. Particularly, in company such as this. But ought he to be deterred by embarrassment? Ought he not to take this opportunity. . . ?

He caught Waller's eye. He saw in it a gleam of deep affection, but also a gleam of warning. Waller might almost have been saying to him: "It's no good, old boy, you're not going to convert *this* lot. Stick to the point. It's bodies we're after, not souls." Absent-mindedly, he shook his head, in mute contradiction. He was tired of bodies . . . the pain of bodies, the uncleanliness of bodies, the sheer bother of bodies. Bodies were always getting in the way. Bodies stumbled and lurched and went to the wrong addresses in life. Bodies fell down . . . bodies bled. Whereas souls. . . .

He pulled himself together, and cleared his throat.

"As I was saying," he continued, "the perfect crime does not exist, for the simple reason that it is, in itself, a contradiction in terms. But this one came as near to perfection as any that I remember, not only in my own career, but in the whole body of criminal literature which has come my way.

"Consider three things about it.

"Firstly, there was a complete absence of motive—of apparent motive, that is to say. It was, of course, a crime of blackmail, on a gigantic scale. But before Sandra could blackmail Kenneth, she had to put the money into his hands. She had to eliminate his mother. In short, she had to commit a physical murder in order to commit a moral murder. It was a thousand to one against so complex a motive being suspected, let alone proved. For all that anybody knew, Sandra would not benefit by Mrs. Faversham's death, she would lose by it. She had no reason to suppose that Mrs. Faversham had left her anything in her will. . . ."

"That would have been altered if Mrs. Faversham had lived," interrupted Pusey. "It was one of the reasons for my coming down to see her."

"That may be so. But at the time of her death, she did *not* benefit . . . moreover, she did not expect to benefit, directly that is to say. It was on Kenneth that her eye was fixed. And that was a secret which she was quite justified in thinking would remain undiscovered for all time.

"Secondly, consider the method. There was no violence. There were no particularly elaborate preparations. There was nothing to be done except to turn the handle of a furnace, and the key of the door. As far as the first was concerned, there was no eye to see her, and nothing to connect her with it. Even if she had been seen, it would have been difficult to give to such an act any criminal interpretation. As for the second . . . nothing could be easier than for her to say that she had no idea that Mrs. Faversham was in the conservatory at all. She could quite easily have said that she was under the impression that she had gone to bed."

"Supposing that Ackworth had come out by chance—to see to the fire, or for some excuse?" asked Waller.

"It was highly improbable that he would so do. He had already said good-night. But even if he had done so . . . what then? Even if he had met Sandra on the staircase, carrying the dead body in her arms, how would that have altered the situation? All that she would have had to do would have been to tell the truth. She would merely have said that Mrs. Faversham had gone into the conservatory, that she must have stayed there too long, and that she had fainted from the heat. All these things were strictly true. In the confusion which would inevitably have ensued, she would have had plenty of opportunity to return to the furnace and to switch back the handle.

"The third extraordinary feature of this murder, which gives it an exceptional brilliance, is more the concern of Doctor Rudyard than of myself, but perhaps he will forgive me if I indicate it. It is the first time in the history of crime —to my knowledge at least—*that the rules of* rigor mortis *have been made to work in the murderer's favour.*"

A long, low whistle escaped from the doctor.

"Am I right in my assumption?" asked Mr. Green.

"Of course—if I interpret your assumption correctly."

"Would you care to explain it to the company?"

"Certainly, if you wish, though I have no doubt that you would do it better."

Rudyard addressed his remarks directly to Waller. "You may remember that at our first interview I had some rather disparaging remarks to make about *rigor mortis*?"

"About the abuse of *rigor mortis*, I think it was, sir."

"Thank you. That was what I meant. I suggested that within its limits it was nearly infallible, but that one must know those limits. I do know them. In this case, I examined the body at eight-thirty in the morning . . . forgive me while I refer to my notebook." He took a little blue book from his pocket and flicked the pages. "Ah, yes . . . here it is. At eight-thirty I examined the body. And I estimated that Mrs. Faversham had certainly been dead for three hours, and conceivably dead for eight, or at the utmost eight and a half."

"And are you inclined to revise that estimate?"

"But of course. The whole thing is changed. The very nature of the murder changes it. A body that had been subjected to such intense heat would take considerably longer to develop the physiological changes which occur in *rigor*, particularly if it was immediately covered after death."

"How much longer, would you say?"

"It's difficult to give a precise estimate. But it might be as long as a couple of hours."

Mr. Green leant forward and again addressed the general company. "You all appreciate the significance, of course? I must confess that for some little while this question of *rigor* gave me a lot of trouble. I had no reason to mistrust the doctor's judgment—on the contrary. And his calculation of eight and a half hours, as the absolute limit, only brought us back to midnight as the hour at which the murder was committed. At that time, Sandra had already been at the inn for over an hour. But now, as we see, the discrepancy is explained."

"Do you think that Sandra had considered this question of *rigor* when she planned the crime?" asked Waller.

"It is possible. She thought of nearly everything. Indeed she thought of just one thing too many. And it was that one thing that proves my theory that there never has been, and never will be, a perfect crime. May I tell you about it?"

The eager faces of his listeners gave him the answer to his question.

"It was my first clue," he continued, "though perhaps I am hardly justified in calling it a clue, for at the time I had no idea what it signified, if indeed it signified anything at all. It was merely a matter of a speck of white powder on the carpet by Mrs. Faversham's bed."

Waller sat up abruptly. "Powder?" he demanded. "On the carpet? I was in there before you. I never saw any."

Mr. Green made a deprecatory gesture. "There was no reason for you to do so, my friend," he consoled him. "It was only the most minute speck, and at first I did not see it myself. I smelt it."

"That damned nose of yours. . . ."

"I was waiting for you to say that. I know that it must seem to you a most irritating organ. It often seems so to myself. But you must admit that it has its uses. So it proved on this occasion. The powder was a white talcum powder, made by the admirable house of Floris in Jermyn Street, and keenly and most accurately scented with rose geranium. It has always been one of my favourite perfumes, and when I suddenly detected a breath of it, in that room, I was very much on the alert."

Mr. Green's small and delicate nostrils seemed to quiver as he went on. "But what was it doing there, on the carpet in her bedroom? That was the question I asked myself, as I bent down, and saw the tiny speck, half-hidden by the curtain. The few cosmetics which Mrs. Faversham was in the habit of using were kept on a table in the dressing-room next door. And in any case, this was not a powder which she would have used on her face—her face powders were a delicate shade of pink, whereas this was pure white. . . ."

He paused, and glanced across at the doctor. "Have you appreciated my train of reasoning?"

The doctor's voice was very grim. "If my interpretation is correct, it is not a pretty one."

"No, it is not at all pretty. But perhaps you would not mind saying it for me? I should like to be assured that I had been on the right lines."

"I imagine that you are suggesting that the powder was used to cover up any traces of suffusion."

"Precisely."

The doctor shuddered. "My God! There was a devil in that woman." He turned to Waller. "It's very simple," he said, "and very horrible. A woman who has died, as Mrs. Faversham died, from heat stroke, would show very obvious traces of it on the skin of her face for some hours after her death. There would be a marked distension of all the small veins that make up what is known as a woman's 'complexion'. In Mrs. Faversham's case, with her constitution, the colour of her skin would have been. . . ." He broke off abruptly. Instinct had caused him to glance towards Kenneth.

But Kenneth did not seem to share his embarrassment. "Go on, old chap," he murmured, apparently unmoved. "It's all most interesting."

The doctor checked the retort which rose to his lips. "I would prefer Mr. Green to finish the story," he said shortly.

"It is already finished," observed Mr. Green. And in his voice, too, there was a chill which Kenneth might have done well to notice. "It was as the doctor has told us. The powder was used to cover up the traces of the suffusion on the face of Mrs. Faversham, in case her death, by some mischance, had been discovered before the morning. Perhaps it would have done so, perhaps it would not. What, in fact, it did, was to uncover the face of the murderess herself."

He stretched out his hand, and reached for a cigarette from the silver box behind him. When Mr. Green permitted himself a cigarette, it was a sign that he was deeply moved . . . either by affection, or by interest, or by anger.

Waller, watching him, had little doubt of the motive which caused Mr. Green to smoke at this moment. Though "smoke" was hardly the word. It was a question of puffing and pressing and shutting the eyes and generally waving the thing about as if it were some sort of infernal machine.

"As Mr. Faversham has observed," said Mr. Green, in choking accents, "it is very interesting.

"And now," he said, "perhaps you would like to tell us precisely why you killed your mother's dog?"

19

"IT WAS only a shot in the dark," said Mr. Green.

Waller nodded. "But it hit the target."

"I am afraid I must have seemed somewhat brusque."

"Does that worry you?"

"Frankly, no." He shuddered. "The cold-blooded beastliness of the man!"

It was after dinner on the same night. The two men had the little inn parlour to themselves.

When they had left Candle Court, a few hours before, the situation had not been a pretty one. More than ever Mr. Green had been oppressed by the sense of a great house in dissolution.

Kenneth had reeled under the shock of his question . . . "Why did you kill your mother's dog?" . . . delivered, as it was, in those biting tones, with a stare of naked contempt. But only for a moment. His native truculence had quickly asserted itself; and from truculence he had gone to fury, to an exhibition of hatred and bitterness which Mr. Green hoped never to witness again.

Waller interjected his thoughts. "The old lady may have been a bit of a so-and-so," he said, "but no woman, dead or alive, deserves to be spoken of like that. And his wife was almost as bad."

"There was murder in both their hearts."

"You knew that all along."

"So did you."

"Maybe." The superintendent knocked out his pipe on the chimney-piece. "I suppose you'll think me a fool, but somehow it seems to make it worse, taking it out on a dog like that."

"I don't think you a fool at all. I feel the same way myself." And indeed, he did. The pain of animals always seemed to afflict Mr. Green more than the pain of human beings. On two occasions in his life he had been involved in motor accidents; one involved a stockbroker, who had sustained concussion, the other involved a spaniel puppy, who had a broken leg. Mr. Green had risen above the stockbroker with little difficulty, but the puppy haunted him to this day.

However, this was not the moment to think of such things. The time for the showdown had arrived. In a very little while the case would be out of his hands, and Waller would be in charge.

He stole a glance at the superintendent, and he must have gained comfort from what he saw, for the shadow lifted from his face. And indeed, Waller, solid and relaxed by the fire, with his pipe in one hand and his pint of ale in the other, was a soothing spectacle. In spite of the tough life that he was bound to lead, he exuded human kindness. There would be need for plenty of that, very soon.

"And now," said Mr. Green, "I suppose you want me to tell you who really . . . strangled . . . Mrs. Faversham."

Waller looked up with a twinkle. "With the accent on the word 'strangled'?"

"Quite. I am afraid that the word has been the cause of some misunderstanding in the past."

"It has. And I am afraid you deliberately fostered that misunderstanding."

Mr. Green made a gesture of dissent. "Deliberately? My dear Waller, what a suggestion! How could you imagine that I would ever mislead anybody—particularly an old friend like yourself?"

"Come off it!"

"I refuse to be bullied. I did *not* deliberately foster the misunderstanding. It merely happened that on various occasions you used the word 'strangled' where you should have used the word 'killed'. I did not correct you at the time because you would merely have been confused."

"What you really mean, of course, is that you'd have let the cat out of the bag."

"Perhaps I do. But that is neither here nor there. The point is, do you want to hear my story?"

Waller stared into the fire. "Of course, I always want to hear any story of yours. Even if I know how it ends."

"You know?"

"Yes." He spoke almost casually. "I have his confession here."

There was a long pause. "Hilary's?"

"Yes. He gave it me as we came away."

Mr. Green gave a long, deep sigh. It was a sigh of profound gratitude, like the sigh of a man who has been relieved from some intolerable pain.

"You want to read it?"

"By and by," said Mr. Green.

Waller drew an envelope from his pocket and tossed it into Mr. Green's lap. He let it fall there, unheeded. Then Waller rose, walked over to the sideboard and filled his glass.

"It's not a pleasant situation," he said.

"It is certainly a strange one."

"Strange! You're telling me! The deputy commissioner might find another word for it. When I think of my own conduct, leaving him up there scot-free, a self-confessed murderer. . . ."

He turned and faced Mr. Green with an expression of bewilderment. "But there are some things in that confession that don't make sense."

"I can well believe it."

"That's why I wanted to talk to you before taking any action."

"I am glad you did. And I think that, when the time comes, we shall be able to appease the deputy commissioner."

"I sincerely hope so. All the same, if Hilary *were* to give us the slip. . . ."

"I do not think there is much danger of that."

Mr. Green leant forward, and picked up the envelope

containing the confession. "As for this," he said, "it is, needless to say, quite worthless."

"Worthless?"

"From the point of view of evidence, yes." A little frown creased Mr. Green's forehead. "In the scale of eternal values, it might be differently assessed."

"For the Lord's sake, stop talking in riddles," cried Waller. "Are you trying to tell me that it wasn't Hilary after all?"

"Of course."

"Then who. . . ?"

Mr. Green allowed himself a last moment of flippancy. He surrendered, for a fleeting instant, to the little imp that was always dancing in and out of his kindly heart. His lips formed the single word . . . "Whodunnit?"

Then his face grew grave.

"It was Meadows."

Waller merely stared at him.

"That is how your story ends," said Mr. Green. "If you will sit down, I will tell you how it begins."

II

"In every case in which I have ever been concerned," he began, "I have always had to confess, at the end of it, that there was a moment when I had a blind spot. And nearly always, it has been over a matter of psychology. One has been so busy with material things, with dates and time-tables and fingerprints and all the rest of it; one forgets that every murder begins in the human soul, and that it is to the human soul that one must look for its solution.

"So it was in this case. I had my nose bent over seed boxes, and my eyes fixed on thermometers. I was muddled up with charts of *rigor mortis*. And when it came to motives, I was almost exclusively concerned—and so, my friend, were you—with material motives. We were so obsessed with the idea that the murder had been committed for money that we never entertained the idea that it might have been com-

235

mitted for love; for the highest form of love, indeed—the love of a man for his friend.

"There was some excuse for me, perhaps, while I was still engaged in working out the details of the first murder—though why I should call it the 'first' murder I do not really know; it was really the *only* murder; one cannot murder a corpse. . . ."

"By the way," interrupted Waller, "that's going to be a very pretty little legal problem, when the time comes."

Mr. Green wrinkled his nose. "Pretty" was hardly the word he would have chosen. Ever since he had discovered the grim truth, his nights had been haunted by the thought of the macabre scene in the bedroom—the window lifting, the sound of the falls flooding the room, the figure climbing in, the powerful hands swooping round the frail neck, closing in a grip of death—a grip that somehow seemed all the more horrible, because of its very futility.

"When the time comes," he commented drily, "the legal profession will doubtless make the most of their opportunity. However, as I was saying, I had some excuse while I was still working on the first problem. Once that was cleared up, I had no excuse at all.

"Look back right to the beginning of this case, to the evening when Sandra told us Hilary's secret. The more I consider the way she told that story, the more I am impressed by her diabolical ingenuity. The timing of it—the appeal to our emotions—the artful way in which she aroused our indignation by stressing the cruelty of Mrs. Faversham—it was all perfect. She pointed her finger directly at Hilary, as a potential murderer, and for a little while we allowed ourselves to be hypnotized by that finger. As I said before, we both had some excuse. You were engaged at Princetown, and the little time you had to devote to the case was principally devoted to Kenneth. As for me . . . well I was trying to read the riddle of the moonflower.

"But the other riddle—the riddle of Hilary—should not really have been a riddle at all. If we had not been so obsessed by material motives, above all by the money

236

motive, we should have realized this at the outset, and we should have wiped Hilary off the slate. We should have admitted the elementary fact that a man does not commit a murder unless he has a very strong desire to live to enjoy the fruits of it, and Hilary had no such desire, and no such hope. He knew that he was a dying man. What could he gain by the recovery of the letter which Mrs. Faversham was holding over him, the letter with which she proposed to send him to his death? A few months' respite, at the most. That was where we were both so incredibly blind. As soon as we had seen the colour of his eyes and the texture of his skin, we should have got our medical report. It would have saved a great deal of useless speculation."

III

Mr. Green filled his glass. That is to say, he very gingerly poured himself out a tablespoonful of sherry to replace the amount which he had already drunk. He did so with a slightly rakish air, as though he were plunging down the slopes of dissipation.

Then he resumed: "And yet, it was a very material thing which first made me realize that Sandra's finger had pointed us in the wrong direction."

"And what was that?"

"It was a little piece of string. The string which had been used to tie up the package in which the jewels were returned to me."

Waller stirred uneasily. If Mr. Green were about to tell him that he had sniffed the string, and blinked, and immediately reconstructed the entire fantastic jig-saw puzzle . . . it would really be too much to bear.

However, for once, Mr. Green was not so irritating. He went on: "Apart from the string . . . to which I shall revert in a moment . . . the mere fact of the return of the jewels seemed to narrow the field considerably. I say *seemed* because the whole case was of such bewildering complications that I hesitated to commit myself. But it *seemed* to exclude

237

Kenneth, once and for all. It was unthinkable that he should go to the trouble of returning the jewels—with all the risk of detection. He would have gained nothing by doing so; indeed, he would have been the loser, for the jewels as it happens were considerably over-insured. The same applies, in varying degrees, to all the other previous suspects. The fact that the jewels were returned at all was a certain proof that the second murderer—to use a convenient expression —was somebody who was animated by no thought of personal gain whatsoever. This would exclude even Wilburfoss, who inherited what was, for him, a considerable fortune. But it proved more than that. It proved that the second murderer was a person of—shall I say—not very exceptional intelligence.

"Which brings me back to the little piece of string round the package in which the jewels were returned."

He saw a flicker of irritation pass over the superintendent's face. He interpreted it correctly.

"No, Waller, I did *not* sniff it. I merely noticed that it was a treble strand tied in two separate sailor's knots. That is precisely how the boxes are tied when they leave Candle Court. And those boxes are tied by Meadows."

"Phew! That was a gift."

Mr. Green bridled. "I do not deny that it was a gift. I hope I am not in the habit of claiming credit where. . . ."

"O.K.! Come off it. I was pulling your leg."

Mr. Green gave a sharp sniff. He was only partially mollified. "And even gifts," he observed, "have to be correctly interpreted."

"How did you interpret this one?"

"I did not immediately leap to the conclusion that Meadows had strangled Mrs. Faversham . . . if that was what you were imagining. I merely noticed that somebody of Meadows' professional experience had tied the parcel. I put the fact at the back of my mind. And I put the paper and string at the back of the drawer."

"And then you went straight up to the house?"

"At once. I did not stop to finish my breakfast. I wanted

to catch them unawares. But as I hurried up the hill, I did some very rapid thinking. That little piece of string had touched off a train of thought. It had made me think of Meadows, and thinking of Meadows had made me remember his depths of character, which we had all forgotten. To our eternal reproach."

"Why are you glaring at me like that?" demanded Waller. And indeed there was a very fierce light in the little man's eyes.

"I apologize. I was not aware that I was doing so. I would be better employed in glaring at myself." He shook his head. "To our eternal reproach," he repeated.

"But why?"

"For two reasons. Firstly, because Meadows' character, as it now transpires, was among the most important single elements in the entire case, and we both ignored it. Secondly, and far more importantly, because our doing so throws an appalling light on our own selves. Why? For a very simple reason; that it proves we are so depraved, so blind to virtue, that we cannot see it even when it is under our very noses."

"Virtue—in murder?"

"In the motive for murder—yes."

"That might be hard to explain in a court of law."

"A number of things that might be hard to explain in a court of law might be extremely easy to explain in the courts of heaven."

"More psychology?"

"Why not? If we do not perceive the psychology of Meadows we are in the dark. If we do perceive it, it lights up the whole scene. He was a man who carried hero-worship to the level of fanaticism. Apart from his mother, there was only one person in his life . . . Hilary Scole. He quite literally adored him. He was more than father, more than brother, more than friend. You may call it morbid, if you like. . . ."

"I don't."

"No, and I thank you for that. There are some who would. All that matters is that Meadows' hero-worship was a fact to be reckoned with. He had already given proof of it once.

239

by risking his life for him when they escaped from Uruguay. He was quite prepared to prove it again, if the occasion should arise. And when the occasion did arise, he proved it."

Mr. Green took out his handkerchief, and blew his nose with some violence. He was well aware that he had just given an exhibition of very incoherent reasoning. The trouble about him was that when he felt very deeply he was inclined to mix his moral metaphors.

Abruptly he said: "Let's return to the scene in the breakfast-room. I need not trouble you with the various reactions of the people at the table, when I produced the jewels. They were what one would have expected. We are both old enough hands to be able to interpret nervous reactions, and in each case the reaction was one of genuine amazement. But with Hilary there was something more."

Waller grunted. "You seem to be attaching a great deal of importance to nervous reactions."

"This was not only a nervous reaction. It was something he said."

"What?"

"He leant forward . . . it was when I had emptied the last of the jewel cases from the box . . . and he said, 'Is that all?' "

Waller sat up abruptly. "Meaning—was there a letter as well?"

"Of course."

"Implying that he would not have taken the safe himself."

"Quite. And also betraying his fear that whoever had taken the safe would now be in possession of the letter."

"What did you answer when he asked, 'Is that all?' "

"I had no time to answer. Hilary left the room. When I was able to get away to follow him, it was too late. He had disappeared. And so had Meadows."

"That was a pity."

"On the contrary, it made no difference at all, as I realized after a few moments' reflection. It was not necessary for me to see those two men, to spy on them or to attempt to eavesdrop on them. I knew what would happen at that interview, as precisely as if I had been there."

"You knew?"

"Yes, Waller, I knew."

IV

Seeing his friend's bewildered expression, Mr. Green gave him a gentle smile, and went on:

"You would have come to precisely the same conclusion if you had been in my place. with my information."

"Trying to let me down lightly, are you?"

"Not at all. What *must* happen at that interview? What is the psychological situation?"

"Pretty damned confused, if you ask me."

"When Hilary went out of that room, he went with a great fear in his heart. He had to unburden himself to somebody. And the only person to whom he could unburden himself was Meadows who—as far as he knew —was the only one who knew of the existence of the letter."

"Do you think he suspected Meadows at that moment?"

"I do not. There is no shadow of reason why he should have done so. Meadows would have died rather than give him a moment's anxiety, or involve him in the smallest degree."

"That's true enough."

"Now let us look at it from Meadows' point of view. We must remember that he was a very simple person, naïve and ingenuous, who could see one step ahead but no further. When he opened the safe and destroyed the letter, that, to him, was an end of the matter. An evil thing, which might have done harm to his friend, was no longer in existence. Therefore, no harm could now come to his friend. It did not occur to him that by sending back the jewels without the letter, he would put Hilary, once again, on the rack. But as soon as he saw Hilary, he realized that was, in fact, what had happened."

"So what did he do?"

"Your guess is as good as mine."

"He told him?"

"I think so. And I think he made his confession then and there. He certainly made it at some time during the day, because it was early on the following morning that Hilary went to London, with results that we all know. But I *think* he made it at once."

"Why?"

"You will laugh at me, if I tell you, because once again it is a question of 'psychology' and 'nervous reaction'."

"I never laugh at anything which works."

"Very well. I think he made it at once because, when I next saw Hilary—it was an hour later—he had obviously been weeping." He paused. "Does that make sense to you?"

"I'd give a lot to say it didn't," growled the superintendent. "But I'm afraid it does."

V

Mr. Green was near the end of his story. He indulged himself in a moment's reflection.

Leaning back, and staring at the ceiling, he said: "One day, Waller, I think that I must write a sequel to *First Principles in Detection*."

"Haven't you caused enough trouble already?"

He ignored this sally. "And in it," he continued, "I shall stress the importance of explaining everything—yes, *everything*—which is in the faintest degree abnormal, when a crime has been committed, I shall emphasize the fact that nothing—that *nothing*—is irrelevant. I think one might almost compare it to looking at a landscape." He waved a podgy hand in the air. "When a murder has been committed, the landscape alters, ever so slightly. There are shadows that are deeper than they should be. There are branches that take a strange twist. There are birds that have flown into the branches, birds that should not be there. If there is a river, there is a ripple, from the wrong way . . . and there is a false note in the sound of the water. . . ."

Suddenly, inconsequently, he broke off and began to chuckle. His pink cheeks swelled and his eyes twinkled and his little fat tummy heaved.

"Forgive me," he murmured to the bewildered Waller, "but I had suddenly thought of something."

"What?"

"Somebody, I should say."

"Who?"

"Mr. Pusey. Oh, dear me!" And off he was again, a plump bundle of jocundity.

"And about time, too," growled Waller, leaning forward, with his hands on his elbows. "What about those damned butterflies?"

"What about them indeed!" echoed Mr. Green, taking out his handkerchief and wiping his eyes. "It was really shameless of me. I owe you an apology."

"You mean to say you invented the damned things?"

Mr. Green sat up sharply. "Certainly not. I am not in the habit of inventing things." He sniffed, with some force. "I am an investigator—not a—not a romancer."

"Then what?"

"I investigated Mr. Pusey." He sniffed again. "And I found that he collected butterflies. I also investigated Kenneth, through Beryl. And I found that he too collected butterflies—or rather, that he had done so at school. It had been quite a passion with him, but like most schoolboy passions it had faded. However, with Pusey it remained. When I was prowling around, taking snapshots, I happened to stroll into the lumber-room which—according to Mrs. Wilburfoss had not been entered for months. I found that it *had* been entered very recently and that something had been removed from it. There was a blank space in the centre of a row of cases of specimen butterflies. The pattern in the dust suggested that the case had been about the size of the suitcase which Pusey carried to the station. And then I began to think. I remembered the character of the two men—Kenneth a dog-in-the-manger, Pusey fussy and acquisitive. I remembered also that Meadows had testified to seeing Pusey hanging round the stables in the early morning. The whole thing fitted. It was typical of Pusey that at a time of murder and sudden death he should think of butterflies. . . ."

"That's enough of that," said Waller. "There's only one other thing I want to know."

"How did Meadows get the safe away?"

"Of course."

"I shall be very happy to tell you. Because it is a perfect example of what I said a moment ago of investigating every *detail*—however trivial—on the landscape of murder."

VI

It was growing late, and he spoke with speed and concentration.

"At first sight it might seem strange that Meadows should go through the elaborate procedure of disguising it among the rest of the packages, addressing it to Paddington, and all the rest of it. But when you come to think of it, what else could he have done? He certainly could not have hidden it on the premises, which might well be searched. And even if he had hidden it, what use was it to him as long as it was unopened? I suppose it is conceivable that he might have bided his time, and chosen some day when he could have taken it out on to the moors, and attacked it with some sort of implement or other, but it needs very little reflection to realize that this was quite impracticable. You cannot open a safe on Dartmoor as though you were cracking an egg in your bedroom. No—he had to get it out of the way; that was the first essential. He had to send it to an anonymous address; that was the second essential. And he had to arrange that it should be called for, not by himself—which would of course have been the height of folly—but by some person whom he could trust with his life.

"Once he had thought of this, the procedure was quite

244

simple. You will remember that when he set out for the station in the van there were—according to Wilburfoss—twenty-eight packages. In fact, of course, there were twenty-nine, for the safe was among them. One of those packages—the one, which was addressed to the lady in Exeter—he disposed of, either on the way there or on the way home. I do not know, and it is of no consequence. It would have been a very easy matter, merely a question of jumping down into a hedge, breaking the box, and trampling the contents into the undergrowth. All that matters is that he delivered twenty-eight packages.

"The only remaining problem was the list of addresses, which had been made out by Wilburfoss. It was essential that he should destroy it, for, naturally, it made no mention of the package containing the safe, the package addressed to Paddington. There fate was kind to him. The list, as he knew from previous experience, was always put on a spike just inside the office door, to be copied into the ledger, later on, by the booking-clerk. In a little station, like that, where he was well-known, where he could wander about at will, and where there was only one porter, nothing could be easier than to stretch his hand through the door and remove the list. Its disappearance, naturally, was a mystery to the booking clerk, but he thought very little of it. He merely carried his ledger out to the platform and copied the addresses from the packages themselves. And it was not till the lady in Exeter wrote to complain of the non-delivery of her own package that anybody thought any more about it."

"And who was it who eventually collected the safe?"

"As I said before—somebody he could trust with his life."

"Who was that?"

Mr. Green gave him a gentle smile. "Who is the one person a man can trust with his life? Who—apart from Mrs. Waller, of course—could you trust with *your* life?"

Waller stirred uneasily. He detected the approach of a sentimental interlude, which always embarrassed him. "Mum, I suppose," he grunted.

"Quite. Mum. Your mother." He sighed, and murmured, "If I were hanged on the highest hill, Mother o' mine". . . . He nodded to himself. "A good son, he was, in spite of everything. But not a very good criminal. It was foolish of him to keep her photograph on his mantelpiece."

"So that was where you got your photograph of the old lady?"

"Yes, Waller. Another of your 'gifts'."

After a pause Waller said : "Where is he now?"

Mr. Green glanced at his watch. "Allowing for the difference in time, I think he should be making his first trek towards the jungle."

"How long have you known this?"

"Since he booked his ticket for Rio."

"So now you've taken to abetting criminals who escape from justice?"

"That is one way of putting it, I suppose."

Waller glared at his old friend with all the ferocity he could muster. But it was not a very convincing glare. After a few seconds it turned to a slow grin. "If I had a pair of handcuffs," he growled, "I'd know where to put 'em. It'd do you good to realize the feel of them."

"Perhaps it is because I realize the feel of them all too well that I try to see that they are never put on the wrong man. All the same—I am at your disposal." And he held out his hands.

"Stow it." Waller got up and poured out a final drink. Then he turned. "You've landed me into a pretty kettle of fish."

"I'm afraid I have."

Waller counted his problems on his fingers. "One, a dead murderess, and a story so fantastic that it'll take weeks to convince the higher-ups. Two, a bigamist—or should I say an ex-bigamist? That's going to be a dainty little problem. Three, a confession of a second murder which A is false and B is a confession of something which isn't murder at all. Four, a young man in a jungle, flying from a crime which may or may not be extraditable—search me. It'd be interest-

246

ing to know how you extradite a murderer for trying to kill a dead woman—or for that matter, a thief who promptly returns all that he has stolen."

"Very interesting," agreed Mr. Green.

"So where do we go from here?"

Mr. Green got up and peered through the curtains. "It is a fine night," he said, "but the wind is rising."

"What's that got to do with it?"

"It must have been a night like this when the whole story began."

"Stop prevaricating. I said 'where do we go from here'?"

Mr. Green turned and faced him. He spoke very deliberately. "It is interesting to reflect, my dear Waller, that apart from myself, you are the only person in the whole world who knows how the story ended. The only person in the whole world."

There was silence in the little room. Mr. Green crossed to the wardrobe and took out his overcoat. "As for where we go from here," he said, "I myself have a fancy to take a last look at the falls. Would you care to come too?"

Waller shook his head. Mr. Green left him staring into the fire. He went outside, and climbed the hill, and skirted the wall of the estate till he came to the wood that led to the higher reaches of the river.

And there we will leave him too—a tubby little figure, silhouetted in the moonlight against the black and silver turmoil of the hurrying river.

"Men may come and men may go," he murmured, "but you go on for ever."

He had always had a penchant for familiar quotations.